The Tan Lady

By

Bertrand Brown

Chapter 1

A hundred dollars? Are you serious? A hundred dollars for what? You have got to be joking. You can't possibly think I'm gonna lay a yard on some ol' tired beat up bitch like you!"

"Bitch?!? I know you didn't just call me a bitch! Nigga if your mama had been half the woman that I am now she would have had the good sense to abort you. Hell, I think the best part of you dripped down your daddy's leg." Mattie said as she stepped into the cold, crisp New York air. It was starting to drizzle now a cold, chilling rain.

By this time their voices had grown loud enough for a few of the other women to hear and suddenly a small crowd began to emerge. One rather distinguished figure arose from the fray. He was a tall gentleman, who stood head and shoulders above the rest of the crowd. He had a cold, no-nonsense demeanor with a piercing steely-eyed glance that sent shivers through the most hardened of men nearly twice his size and now he stood by the woman's side glancing into the car she'd just gotten out of. Never raising his voice above a whisper he inquired.

"You okay Mattie?"

"Yeah, Kane. I'm okay. Just another joker trying to get into King Tut's treasure for a dime and a dub."

"And you let my man here know that we're all out here just tryna make a few ends?"

"I certainly did but he had a hard time accepting that and chose to be disrespectful instead."

"Is that right?" Kane said as he reached inside the car and grabbed a handful of the man's lapel.

Mattie didn't know or like the man who drove the brand new, two door, navy blue, Lincoln Escalade but she'd seen him around and it was always the same. Still, she and everyone else knew that worked the corner of 145th and 8th that a bad word from her would have led to a beat down and no matter what this fool had said an insult wasn't worth that on her conscious. Lord knows she had enough on her plate without having to worry if this poor, stupid, degenerate was going to live or die because he had had too much to drink and too little respect. Sure, this was her profession and even though she was damn good at sending a john home feeling as though he'd died and gone to heaven there were still some who wanted something for nothing.

Mattie had a reputation as being good if not the best out there at her profession and professional to boot but it still wasn't anything she took any real pride in. Now after

2

twenty years of walking the streets she'd grown cold and aloof. This john was anything but typical. He was no different than any other except he had a little too much mouth and had made the fatal mistake of being a little too loud and attracting the attention of Kane, the unofficial enforcer for the ho patrol.

"Motherfucker, I don't know who raised you but that's not how we treat ladies where I'm from." Kane said, all smiles forever gone from the six foot eight mountain of a man who now stood before him gun palmed and pressed to the man's temple.

"I got no second thoughts about beating you down and then capping your little yalla ass but the lady here that you disrespected doesn't seem to want that. But if I had my druthers I wouldn't hesitate to stomp a mud hole in your ass. I will tell you this though home piss. I may just have a flashback and beat your ass just because. Now get the fuck up outta my face and find your way back to Yonkers or Jersey or whatever rock you slid from under."

And with that said Kane released the shaken man's lapel and disappeared back into the blackness of the shadows.

145th and 8th had always been notorious with a homicide rate unparalleled in all the five boroughs but since Mike G. and Kanes's arrival that was now a thing of the past and the police and the under covers didn't even bother patrolling the five block strip while the hookers and dope boys that were granted access roamed freely.

"You okay, Ms. Mattie?"

"I'm fine Kane," she replied flirting openly.

"One day you're going to have to let me repay you for all your kindness."

"I'm paid in full every time I see you walk that fine brown frame down the avenue Miss Mattie."

"And don't you ever wonder. Aren't you just a little curious about what this fine brown frame can do for you?"

Kane smiled. The two had been flirting like this for years never once crossing the line.

"Sure, I am but as long as I have my fantasies I'm good. I can never be disappointed or let down. To me you're the classiest woman I know. And I don't want anything to disturb that groove young lady."

"Ever think that I could enhance your current perceptions?"

"To tell you the truth I never really thought about it but I'm sure there is that possibility *if* somehow you can improve on heaven."

"Never saw it like that. Perhaps we can talk about it over lunch."

"Perhaps but right now your flirtatiousness is distracting me from the task at hand. Can we talk about this later?"

"Lunch it is then. But let's do Soulfully Yours out in Queens. I just need to get out of the city and breathe for a minute."

"Sounds good. I'll pick you up at about three if that's good for you?"

"Let's play it by ear. I have a client coming by at two and as soon as I get rid of him I'll stop by."

"Looking forward to it Mattie."

Mattie's heart skipped a beat. She'd known Kane from the time she'd hit the streets when she was only fifteen. It was Kane who changed her from being a bitter teen who hated men and life in general to a warm, caring, woman. 'Hope' he would tell her was the key to life. And as long as she had hope then she could strive for what it was that she desired and make her world what she wanted it to be.

After her father had died her mother remarried. And whereas her father had been all that a girl could ask for her stepfather was a cantankerous alcoholic who hated the idea of being saddled with another man's kids. At the age of twelve he'd raped her for the first time. After that it seemed that anytime he'd have a drink she could expect a visit from him.

By the time she was thirteen it had become almost ritual for her to go down to the corner bodega to grab him a fifth, bring it home to him before going to her room and disrobe and wait for him to come to her room and avail himself of her until spent when he'd return to her mother's bed to pass out. It just seemed so fruitless and there were many a night when she'd clutch her stuffed animals and cry herself to sleep.

At other times she'd consider stabbing him and maiming him for life while he was in one of his drunken stupors yet as much as she reviled him she could never bring herself to do it and repeatedly succumbed to the abuse. There was no one for her to talk to, no one she could tell, no one but Eva her best friend who was two years older and who Mattie's mom was always saying was 'fifteen going on thirty'. Mattie's mom, Mrs. Mendes had no clue what was happening when she was at work. Trying to raise three girls and maintain a home in Harlem was no easy task. Mrs. Mendes seemed to work all the time leaving Mattie with her two younger sisters.

"You should be glad Jennifer and Deidra are only three and four. That motherfucker, crazy as he is ain't gonna fuck with them babies."

"So you say. Chaz would stick his dick in a keyhole if he could get it to fit."

"And I would kill that Puerto Rican bastard if he messed with one of my babies. 'Sides he ain't gonna fuck with his own kids. He just fucks with you 'cause you ain't no kin to him. Besides how he gonna live in that house and not see that big ass of yours and not be attracted? Shit. Sometimes I look at it and wonder myself. You lucky you my girl and I'm strictly dickly or I might have to jump on that ass soon as he get off," Eva said grinning madly as she hit the Swisher Sweet.

"I don't know why I even bother to talk to you."

"Cause I'm the best friend you got. Matter-of-fact, I'm o the only friend you got," she said laughing at her own crack. "Here hit this. It'll make you feel better."

"No, what would make me feel better was if I could get the fuck up outta there."

"And why can't you?"

"Come on Eva. I'm fourteen. Where the fuck is a fourteen year old gonna make enough scratch to get her own crib?"

"What?!?! Are you stupid? You got more going for you than most of the girls twice your age. You're cute. Got a nice ass and got them 38 double D's. Don't sell yourself short shorty. That nigga Chaz is stealin' your shit everyday but truth is you should be getting paid for your shit."

"Something's wrong with you Eva. That's only making a bad thing worse. Do you hear what you're saying?"

"Oh stop being so naïve Mattie. Ain't like there's a lotta opportunities up here for a nigga. And here you is mixed. You got the best of spic and nigga. You betta use what you got to get what you want. There's men out here that would pay good money for you to do 'em and you lettin' this pervert do you damn near every night for nothin'. You crazy as fuck."

"It ain't like I want that shit to happen Eva," Mattie said the tears flowing freely now.

"I know that baby girl. But that's my point. Since it's already happening you might as well make the shit work to your advantage. If the motherfuckers want it that bad where they riskin' everything for it you should know you got something valuable. Make that nigga and all those like him pay. You can't tell me you don't notice the way all these niggas out here be staring you down. I mean I ain't no bad lookin' sista and I get my fair share of ups and downs but it ain't nothin' compared to the way these niggas be breakin' they necks when you walk by. Like right now.

Anytime you walk up here to Renaissance to pick me up from school these fools lose their minds. All I'm saying is make that shit work for you. A couple of weeks out on the strip doing damn near the same thing that that low-life bastard has you doing for free and you'll be able to get your own crib and tell that motherfucker to kiss your ass."

"Eva, I can't go out there."

"And why not. If Jennifer and Deidra were hungry I bet you'd be out there tryna feed them. It ain't like you born in Scarsdale with a silver spoon in your mouth. We in Harlem and the rules are different down here. We got a shitload of nothin' and gotta use what we go to get what we want. But that ain't to say there ain't no opportunity to get out of this foul shit. It's just harder is all."

"So, you mean to tell me that if you were in my situation that's what you'd do?"

"What I'm telling you is that I'm not in your situation and that's what I do now.""Stop play.""Listen. Mama gets paid every week and very week on the way home she stops on the corner where the dope boys are and gets a couple of twenties and picks up a few groceries for me and her for the week. Then she comes home and we talk while we put away the groceries. Then she goes in the bedroom with her forty and closes the door. As soon as she closes the door I head out and hit the strip and turn a couple of tricks. When I hita hundred I stop by the dope boys and grab a couple of dubs and take them home 'cause I know in a while mama gonna start whining and crying and throwing dishes 'cause she ain't got no money and no more dope to smoke. So just to alleviate her pain and mine I just get the shit. Then I break her off a crumb every now and then 'til she pass out and go to sleep. It ain't that bad and Lord knows I shut down all that whinin' and cryin'."

"You do that?"

"Girl you ain't never seen a crackhead when they fresh out."

"That's so sad."

"Not as sad as when she ain't got her shit. I'm telling you Mattie it ain't so bad though. And with Kane out there motherfuckers know not to come up here startin' no shit. Last week Juan asked me out and with mama really startin' to smoke alot I ain't never got no new gear so I went out just to get me enough for some fly new gear. And within like an hour I had made a little over a hundred. Went right on down to Macy's clearance and picked me up a whole new outfit. I ain't sayin' it's for everybody but just think about it. If you want me to go with you just let me know. I think I'd be out there on the regular but I get tired of them old washed up, dried up bitches out there thinkin' they yo mother and always telling me what I should or shouldn't do. But you come out there with me and it'll be fun and we can get paid too."

Two weeks later everything came to a boil. Mama came home early and found the twins unattended in the front room and when she came to find out why she found Chaz a forty ounce in one hand a hand full of my hair in his other and me on my knees choking on his dick. Mama asked no questions and twenty minutes later I was out on Seventh Ave. homeless for trying to steal her man.

Eva had kept her word and was by my side all the way and I wondered after all her bold talk if I wasn't the one she was leading on instead of the other way around. She was constantly in the middle of something. And I watched her get her ass beat on more than one occasion for trying to hustle a john. Eva made it bad for everyone out there and was soon banned from the strip. No one had a pimp in those days. We just sort of free-lanced and would come together when anything went down out of the ordinary but gunshots and police raids were as commonplace as an umbrella on a rainy day.

Not long after, somewhere downtown in a small café in the East Village two rather smartly dressed Black gentlemen sat sipping espressos while a portly white gentleman sat across from them with a regular coffee and a buttered roll.

"145th and 8th to the Dunbar is yours and Mike I promise you there will be no interference from me or the 28th Precinct. I'm giving you a month for you to assure me that there won't be any shenanigans up there. There are a lot good honest, hardworking folks up there and I don't want them disturbed or in fear. I want them kept safe and unharmed. No robberies, chain snatching, nothing. You want the chance to control your own people's destinies then I'm all for it. Drugs and prostitution will be around for as long as people want it but I want it cordoned off from those God fearing people that don't want it. And I must admit that we haven't had much success at keeping the bottom feeders from leaching off the good citizens of our fair city so if you think you can do a better job I'm all in Mike. You know where to reach me and maybe just maybe I can get these bums to concentrate on some of the other high crime areas now that you've freed up this area. I'll be keeping

tabs on you and you know how to get in touch if you run into some hard heads that don't want to comply"

"Thanks captain but for us it's all about taking our community back. And in the end it's a win win situation. The only losers are those that aren't with the new Harlem Renaissance. The only thing we're promoting is a new community spirit where the hardworking and the seniors can go and come freely and without fear from street punks. Right now we're all about building strong character amongst our residents and promoting community pride."

"Sounds good Mike. I pray all goes well for you. You need anything you just let me know. I wish you gentlemen the best of luck."

And it was with that Mike G. and Kane went about taking back the Harlem of Langston Hughes and Marcus Garvey. Now that wasn't to say that their motives were purely for the cultural upliftment and betterment of Harlem or its citizens. Quite to the contrary. Mike G. had long been known for his underworld ties to drugs and prostitution but even he knew that the constant shootings and turmoil on the streets only served to hurt his profits. A police raid on prostitutes and drugs would often shut down business for days and even weeks depending on the severity of the crimes committed. And it was just such an incident that prompted Mike to have a sit down with his boyhood friend Kane a month or two before Eva and Mattie decided to join the ho patrol .

"How long we been down Kane?"

"Been a little over three weeks."

"And all 'cause that little rat bastard Tyreke came through thinking he was Pretty Boy Floyd and spraying up the place."

"That's about it. Killed ninety two year old Mrs. Johnson. That woman was a saint. She practically raised me."

"And me as well. Then they killed that little seven year old girl. And for what? Over a fuckin' eight ball. Two innocent people's lives were sacrificed for a beef that amounted to two hundred and twenty five dollars. This shit is crazy Kane and it's gotta stop."

"You right."

"You know when we got out of the game we agreed to leave it alone and use our talents in other ways."

"We did."

"But I don't know if that's possible Kane."

"I know you're not serious but if you are you're on your own. You know I love you fam but the streets don't love nobody and we was lucky to stay in the game as long as we did and come out unscathed."

"No, no, no. I'm not suggesting we get back into the drug game and I damn sure don't want to have anything to do with prostitution. No. Not at all. What I'm suggesting is that we set up something similar to a demilitarized zone where we're the only one's holding jumps. We say who sells what and where and offer protection to all that inhabit and work within the zone. You know sorta like the U.N. Peacekeeping Committee and then we take a percentage of their profits for their protection."

"So,

what you're really talking is extortion for protection."

"Don't put it like that. These brothers ain't tryna see their business dry up for three weeks. It's all about making paper out there on those streets."

"Could very possibly work. And once those crackers from Jersey, Connecticut, and upstate find out there's an actual safe haven where they can come and buy their drugs and women without getting hit in the head or ripped off business will increase ten-fold."

"Right you are my brother. But not only that we will select the best and the brightest out there. We don't want those with a strong proponent for being thugs and violence. We're only interested in those where the almighty dollar is the motivator."

"So, you're talking Cyrus?"

"Yeah, Cyrus and Marcus pride themselves on the quality of their dope and are only interested in one thing and that's fair play and an even exchange."

"The other fellas ain't gonna like that."

"Well, that's too fucking bad. They can either come in under them or find somewhere else to sell."

"And the women."

"I'm not sure about the women."

"Why aren't you sure about the women?"

"They're sheisty and always fighting amongst themselves. I just don't know if all the effort it takes to corral them is worth it. A good deal of the chaos is them holding out on their pimps. What's to say they wouldn't do the same o us?"

"Let me handle that Mike."

"You sure you want to do that? I'm telling you they're more trouble than they're worth."

"I don't think so. And they can help in the community as well. Let me take care of that little problem. I have just the person to take care of that."

"Who's that?"

"Mattie Cruz."

"You can't be serious. She's just a baby. She can't be more than fifteen or sixteen!"

"And how old were you and I when we got our feet wet?"

"You're right but some of them ho's you're trying to get her to run are damn near twice her age and crazy as hell. They'd eat her alive."

"Not with me backing her every play. Listen the girl is smart as a whip and has been out there for the last couple of months and is the top money earner and has picked up the game better than some of them ho's that have been out there for years. And it's very rarely, if ever that she gets into anything with her tricks or the other women. She's already gained their respect."

"And you think she can do her thing and work as your bottom bitch?"

"No, I want to pull her up offa the streets altogether. The girls got far too much going for her to be out there trickin'. I want her in college or trade school where she can reach her full potential. That old crazy ass Eva talked her into trickin' when she was going through a bit of a rough patch but it ain't no career move. She's got way too much going for her for that."

"You sound rather adamant about this so you go ahead and take care of that but don't you let those crazy ass bitches fuck up this opportunity. This is a chance of a lifetime. It's good for us, good for the ho's and the dope boys and good for Harlem. Like I told the captain it's a win win situation."

"Trust me I got this Mike."

"Never any doubt my brother. I just know how much you value your peace and I think you takin' on these whores is gonna end all that. Tell me though how long do you think it's gonna take to take the streets back?"

"That's kinda hard to put a number on Mike. I know most of the major playas out there and I think most of 'em will fall right into place without too much coercion but there's always that one or two freelancers that's going to buck any type of authority. In fact I know Marcus ain't going for it before I even approach him. We may have to throw him a bone and offer him some other turf but the rest of them should go for it. Might be a dust up here and there but everything should be well in order before this time next month."

"Okay then good brother just tell me what you need and let's make it happen."

"No doubt. Matter-of-fact I'm going to make a few calls and call a sorta impromptu meeting up in Sugar Hill and see how Marcus and a few of the dope boys take it."

"You do that and hit me up when it's over and let me know how they take it."

"Will do and I'm going to put Black and Supreme and his crew out in the streets to provide the law until everything falls into place."

"Black and Supreme from South Jamaica?"

"The very same. That way I don't show any favoritism to any of the crews from uptown and once the law is established and if they have to bump heads there won't be any repercussions or retaliation when it's all over."

"Good thinking."

"Alright my brother. Don't forget to call me when it's over."

"I'll do that."

"And Kane?"

"Yeah Mike."

"You be safe man. You're all the family I got."

"Always."

Kane stepped into the dark, brisk autumn air and made his way down 8th Avenue towards the strip. The street grew more and more crowded and was fully alive by the time he arrived at 148th.

Kane shook hands all along the way and stopped briefly to share a greeting here and there until he saw Eva who he approached cautiously. He knew her and knew her to be trouble. When he set up this new commission he knew that she was one of the ones that would not make the cut and would have to go but he was getting ahead of himself. Right now she if anybody would know where to find Mattie and Mattie was as integral a part as anybody and when he made his proposition he would need her by his side to legitimize her claim to the throne. Sure she was young, only fifteen at the time but he could see even then that she had what it took.

"What's up Eva?"

"Ain't nothin' Kane."

"Why you all the way up here sweetheart?"

"You know them niggas up on 145th is shootin' over some dumb shit and I didn't want to get caught up in it so I just came down here. Ain't as much traffic or dollars up here but it's less chance of me catchin' a stray."

Kane dropped his head and let a slight smile emerge. Maybe there was a chance she could come under his wing. She was certainly attractive enough to make the cut.

"That's using your head."

"If you're going up there to post up then I'll walk you up there."

"Not tonight Eva. You're doing the right thing by being up here. By the way I'm looking for Mattie. Have you seen her?"

"Yeah she was up there parlayin' with some ofay the last time I saw her. She left right before the fireworks started. She should be back by now. Tell her where I am if you see her."

"No problem."

"See you Kane."

"Later Miss Eva."

Eva smiled. She liked Kane. Always had. He was only a couple of years older than her but he was an old soul. He was dignified, spoke little and had an easy smile but no one messed with him. He didn't play and those that did mess with often came up missing.

"Say Kane," she yelled at the figure fading into the darkness.

Startled Kane turned only to see Eva running his way.

"Yeah Eva?"

"I just had a quick question. You can tell me to mind my business if you feel it's too personal."

Kane stared deep into the young girl's eyes.

"Yes Eva."

18

"Do you have a woman?"

Kane smiled.

"No, Eva. Why do you ask?"

"Was just wondering? Tell me something then? Are you feeling my girl Mattie?"

"I don't know what you mean am I? Am I feeling her?"

"You know exactly what I mean Kane. Do you like Mattie? Do you have feelings for her?"

"Why are you asking me this? Sure, I have feelings for Mattie but then I have feelings for you as well. I have feelings for all my ladies."

"Oh, Kane. I can never get a straight answer out of you."

"I gave you a straight answer," he said smiling. "Perhaps it was your question that was vague. Think about it. I'll be back in a bit. Maybe you'll be more specific then."

Turning and walking away Eva stomped her foot and felt the sting of the hard concrete underfoot.

Kane watched the street in front of him. The dope boys were having a good night as cars rolled up routinely. Shoving and bickering they pushed and shoved each other to the side to see who would eventually get the sale.

"Hard white player! Got that hard white!"

"Nigga don't know what hard white is. Don't listen to him playa. I got that killa. Got that Whitney Houston!"

Kane smiled. If half of these kids had half an education they'd be down on Fifth Avenue at some high end marketing firm writing ads for TV. But without that education they were just so many tragedies in the making a few dollars here and there selling the other man's product and biding time until their number came up and they became just another statistic written off the American landscape. Kane knew he couldn't change that but he could insulate them from becoming statistics at least for now anyway.

He'd left word with all the drug boys that he wanted a scheduled parlay with their bosses and now all he needed was Mattie but there had been no word and he began to grow worried. Sending a runner back up to 148th he summoned Eva who was there in a matter of minutes.

"Eva Mattie's not back and I've been out here more than an hour. Do you have any idea where she might be?"

"No clue but I think I have the answer to my question."

"Don't go jumping to any conclusions Eva. I've simply got a business proposition for her."

Quickly realizing that any business proposition for Mattie could have a profound impact on her as well Eva began to think in earnest. Let me run back to the crib and see if she's home. I'll call you if she's there. You call me if she shows up."

Before she got home she received the call from Kane. He'd found her.

"Hey Miss Mattie. I've been looking for you for damn near half the night. Where've you been?"

"My daddy died when I was two Kane."

"I was just worried is all. I didn't mean to come off like that."

"Why you worried Kane?"

"You were gone more than an hour and it just doesn't take that long."

"Eva called me and told me there had been a shooting so I didn't rush back. Why what's up?"

"Nothin' really. Somethin' came up and I nominated you and just wanted to run it by you and see what you thought. How long you been out here tonight?"

"About two hours. Why?"

"And how much you make so far?"

Mattie went into her boot first and then her bra before going into the lining of her coat.

"I've got a little over four hundred."

Kane was shocked.

"You do pretty well out here don't you Mattie?"

"I survive."

"From what I hear you run circles around these girls that have been out here for years. And there's never a problem between you and the johns or the other girls."

"I do okay and you know me Kane. I keep pretty much to myself."

"Do you enjoy what you do Mattie?"

"C'mon Kane. What the fuck kind of question is that? What kind of girl wants to be considered a ho? It is what it is. I don't take any pride in this shit."

"So despite the money you're pulling in you wouldn't be opposed to giving up the money?"

"Enough with the twenty questions Kane. What's this really all about?"

Kane broke it down to her and though skeptical Mattie agreed. What Kane hadn't realized is that whatever proposition he would have proposed Mattie would have agreed.

Chapter 2

All that had taken place some twenty years ago and though
a bit apprehensive at first Mattie put her faith in Kane. He
was one of the few men she trusted. And though it hadn't
been easy at first for most of the other girls to accept this
new girl coming in and running the show with Kane's
backing there was far less backlash than anyone would
have imagined.

Mattie still kept her other job just in case and at Kane's
insistence enrolled in City College and soon picked up her
degree in Business Administration. With his continued
insistence she would later pick up her MBA and for this
Mattie was grateful. He also insisted on her putting away
half of everything she made. She wasn't too thrilled about
this but it was hard to say Kane didn't know what he was
talking about. He'd hit a lick back in the 80's when crack
first arrived on the scene, made a bundle and had the smarts
to get up and walk away from it. He went to school and
was now for all intents and purposes ready to retire at the
ripe old age of forty and drove a brand new Beamer and
had a fly apartment and was fresher than any of the fellas
out there working every day. At six foot eight with his

chocolate brown complexion looking like a taller Idris Elba the boy was just plain smooth.

From the first time she met him she admired him and the way he moved. He was like a feline, like a panther, sleek and proud. And my God was he ever handsome with his chiseled features and Roman nose. She had only loved one man in her life and that was daddy but after daddy passed she had no interest in men and came to despise them for the most part. As far as she was concerned they only had one purpose for her and that was to pay her. Even the boys in school who pretended to be her friends eventually propositioned her but with Kane it was different. Never once in their twenty years had he even come close to approaching her.

When she'd hit the streets for the first time and was homeless it was Kane who'd befriended her and taken her home with him and took care of her until she'd been able to get a place of her own. She remembered him asking her then telling her that the streets were no place for her but she'd been hard-headed and had little trust in him and men in general even though he promised her their relationship would never evolve into anything more than his taking care of a younger sibling. After three or four months Mattie found her own place but never forgot the kindness and respect Kane bestowed on her in the time they spent together. And over the years Mattie and Kane's friendship evolved.

When he first put her in charge the other girls resisted her and were jealous of the friendship but in time they came to adjust to the fact that there was a very special bond between the two and accepted it.

24

Mattie climbed to the top step of the stoop, caught her breath and threw the cigarette to the ground below before reaching into her bag and grabbing the bottle of Dolce & Gabanna Light Blue and spraying it liberally. She waited a few seconds for it to air out before knocking. Kane hated the smell of cigarette smoke and she wanted her first impression to be a good one.

"Hey Mattie," Kane said before lowering his head and shoulders and kissing her on the forehead. Mattie immediately felt her libido rise and her inner thighs grow moist. This was in itself an anomaly and seldom if ever happened but sometimes just being in the presence of Kane she would damn near come just from his touch or his glance.

"Damn you!" Mattie muttered to herself.

"You say something?"

"No just thinking out loud."

"Care to share?"

And if I did what the fuck good would it do? Mattie thought to herself.

"Come in Mattie. There's someone I want you to meet. By the way you look very nice. I'm loving the look. You have that school marm look. Worked for Sarah Palin, well it worked for her 'til she opened her mouth," Kane said laughing at his own joke.

"Mattie I'd like you to meet Naomi Sims." Kane said escorting Mattie into the elegantly decorated parlor.

The young woman who now stood before Mattie rendered her breathless. Beautiful women were a dime dozen in New York but this woman was not only beautiful she had some other qualities Mattie had a hard time describing. She was in fact indescribable. There was no doubt there was something clearly African and regal about her with her dark complexion yet her eyes and features gave her a uniquely Asiatic look and the combination along with the closely cropped haircut made her almost exotic. She was young, not much older than Mattie when she started. Eighteen at the most…

"Naomi I'm Mattie."

"It's so very nice to meet you. Kane has told me so many wonderful things about you that I almost didn't want to meet you," she said laughing exhibiting a smile that would have left toothpaste execs cringe. Never had Mattie seen a more perfect woman.

"It was that good, huh?"

"No, no. Don't get me wrong. He had nothing but good things to say but he failed to tell me just how beautiful you were."

"I don't hold a candle to you dear. What you see here is Mary Kay."

"You are far too modest."

"Okay, but before you two drown each other in compliments let me get to the root of the matter. As I told you earlier Mattie is more or less my partner and sees me through most of my dilemmas. She's my confidante and perhaps my dearest friend. And I trust her with my life so don't think I'm throwing this out to a complete stranger Naomi. Not only that but Mattie has been in a similar situation. But let me get some wine and some goodies and while I'm doing that why don't you two get acquainted a little better. In the meantime you can tell Mattie your situation and we'll mull it over over a glass of wine and see if we can't work something else."

Mattie found herself in the antique Queen Anne chair she'd insisted on Kane buying. Crossing her leg she was cognizant of Naomi who watched her every movement admiringly as though she were a Hollywood star or an Egyptian goddess and wondered what Kane had told the impressionable young woman.

"Well, it's like this. Mrs. Cruz."

"Please call me Mattie."

"Alright Ms. Mattie. I guess the best place to start is at the beginning. I'm from the Sudan in Africa and I don't know if you're familiar with the Sudan or not but there is a civil war in the Sudan and all kinds of atrocities are taking place and no one is safe. The rebels took my two brothers who are eleven and twelve to join up with them. If they hadn't they would have been killed. That was two years ago. I haven't seen my brothers since they were abducted. Seven months ago the rebels came to our village again. They raped my mother and my sister. After the raid my father who is not a rich man appealed to some foreigners and they helped to

arrange safe passage for me to the United States. I hated to leave my family but my father insisted that it was a chance for a better life, a new beginning. He said if I did what I was supposed to do, you know do well in school and find a good job that I could send for them.   I've always been at the top of my class and have always wanted to be a pediatrician so I saw everything he said as very feasible. So, I came here to stay with my uncle up here in Harlem in the Dunbar. But my uncle is not so good. He drinks and he smokes crack and when he drinks too much he comes in late at night and…"

The young woman dropped her head and Mattie could see the young girl was overcome with grief as the tears flowed down her face. Mattie got up, feeling the anger growing within, and took he girls head in her hands and pressed it into her shoulder.

"It's going to be alright child. It's going to be alright."

The thoughts of Chaz came flooding back and she wiped her own tear stained cheeks. She'd seen her own mother just twice in the years since and they had yet to speak. From what she understood Chaz had been locked up for something or another was awaiting his parole after having served eighteen years upstate in Elmira or so Kane had informed her in passing. Mattie had made a mental note but for right now she had far more pressing matters to deal with.

Kane stepped into the room and the smile on his face faded.

"Was kinda afraid you were going to have this reaction. I'm sorry for waking up hose skeletons Mattie," he said as he took Mattie into his arms.

"I'm okay Kane. That was a long time ago. I just hate that this child and any one has to suffer through something like that. I am glad you brought it to my attention though. I'll take care of it."

"I told you she would," Kane said turning to Naomi. "But listen I have an important lunch date so make yourself comfortable. There's plenty of food in the fridge and plenty of DVD's in the entertainment center next to the TV. If the phone rings or if anybody knocks just ignore it."

"And I'll get you situated as soon as I get back," Mattie said in hopes of comforting the young woman.

The temperature had dropped in the short time Mattie had been there. Throwing he scarf around her neck she stopped and turned to Kane who was securing both bottom and top lock.

"Where did you find this stray?"

"Her first night out on the strip, scared shitless, standing off to the side trying to work up the courage to get out there with the big girls. She reminded me of you for the world."

"You can't be serious. With the right connects that girl could be America's next top model."

"And you're saying?"

"There's beauty and then there's attractive. That girl's a natural beauty."

"And you still don't see the similarities. Come on lady."

So this is how Kane saw her. Mattie couldn't help but smile inside.

"Do you know her uncle?"

"I don't know him but I know him to see him. You do too. He passes through about once or twice a week."

"Point him out to me the next time you see him."

"And why the hell would I do that Mattie? My job is to keep the peace not to incite a riot. That's the last thing I need is for you to go off half-cocked over this moron. Besides I put Eva on him and then Marcus' crew when she gets finished with him."

"Eva will play that fool for months and take every dime he has."

"Exactly! A beat down will heal in a couple of weeks but there is nothing worse than falling in love with a woman and have her use and take you for everything you've got. That's a hurt you don't just get up and walk away from. That is a hurt that you carry with you the rest of your life."

"That seems be something you seem to know quite a lot about. Are you speaking of something that you've experienced?"

"In a manner of speaking."

"In a manner of speaking? And you just stop! My goodness having a conversation is hard as hell with you Kane. Inquisitive minds want to know. Now tell me."

Kane smiled. He had long ago found out what it was that got her goat and loved to pull her chain just to see her lose it.

"Tell you what?"

"Oh my God! You want me to say fuck it or never mind but I'm not going to do it. No, I'm not going to do it this time. You're going to tell me before either of us gets out of this car what the hell happened to you that makes women a turn off to you. I know you love them to death by the way you treat them and I know you ain't gay so what is it. It's like you're flame retardant when it comes to women and you and I know some of the most beautiful women in the world pass right by you every day."

"Oh, is that what you're asking me?"

"Oh, my God! I feel like I'm back in high school playing truth or dare with the shy guy that's still a virgin. The question is why don't you have a woman Kane? That's it! There! It's out on the table. Now will you please quell my curiosity?"

Kane continued to smile as he pulled up in front of the restaurant.

"No sir. You are not going anywhere until you've answered my questions and take off those sunglasses," Mattie said as she snatched the glasses off of Kane's face.

"Mattie we have reservations and we're already late. Why is it so hard for you to talk to me Kane?"

"It's not hard I just choose not to discuss certain subjects with you."

31

"But why Kane?"

"Because you're a woman."

"And what the hell is that supposed to mean."

"C'mon Mattie. We're just built differently that's all."

"Well, that's obvious but what's that got to do with why you do or don't have a woman."

"Who says I don't have a woman?"

Mattie was stunned. So Kane did have a woman. It made sense now. Probably had her sequestered over in Jersey or out on Long Island away from the filth and garbage of the streets. Probably had a couple of babies too. Why hadn't she ever considered it? After all these years. She was sorry she'd asked now and turning to Kane she tried to compose herself.

"How come you never told me Kane? You must have known that I've always had feelings for you."

"How was I supposed to know?"

"Well they tell me that women have a knack. What's it called?"

"I believe you're referring to women's intuition. And no that doesn't apply to something such as this. I've known you for twenty years Kane and we've shared the same house, talked intimately and I considered you my best friend and confidante and still. You never mentioned another woman. Wow!" Mattie could feel the anger and tears welling up within her. "So, where is she?" She said wiping away the tears.

Kane could not resist the smile.

"Sitting right next to me."

It took a minute for Mattie to digest the fact that Kane was referring to her but when it finally did sink in she exploded with a joy she hadn't seen since daddy was alive. It seemed like the dam had finally burst.

"Oh Kane. And when if ever were you going to tell me?"

"Well I knew from the first time I saw you but think about it Mattie. I was nineteen and you were all of thirteen or fourteen. How would that have looked? I made you go to college and get your degree hoping that would change your mind about the streets. I even created a job so you wouldn't have to deal with the streets and you still chose the streets. I guess what I wanted just wasn't as strong as whatever those streets had to offer but I wanted you as my wife. I didn't want my wife to be a common everyday street walker. I guess your women's intuition just wasn't working."

"So why didn't you just come out and say that Kane. When have you ever asked me something that I didn't comply with?"

"I did ask you in not so many words."

"I guess you did," Mattie said smiling. "But then I'm also sure that you knew how much of a backlash that would have stirred too. Every girl on the streets from Eva to

Kitten has her eyes set on you and they all expect you to sweep them up and be their savior."

"Never thought about it."

"Oh please! You're three thoughts and a half a day in front of everyone out there."

"Ya think? I think you give me more credit than I'm worth. Can we go inside now Ms. Mattie?"

Mattie was elated. It was as if she had had an epiphany and felt her leggings to see if they were wet.

"Table for two?" the maître d questioned.

"Yes sir we have reservations. The name is Cruz. Mattie and Kane Cruz."

"Oh yes. I have your reservations. If you would follow me please."

The tiny Italian restaurant was half full.

"Thought we were going to Soulfully Yours."

"I needed a break Mattie. Don't get me wrong. I love my brothers and sisters but I just didn't want to spend half the time I had to spend with you sharing it with someone I haven't seen you in a minute. Forgive me for being selfish but I do that every night. I just wanted to have this time with you."

"You are forgiven Mr. Kane. Tell me something though. What are your you going to do with Naomi?"

"Nothing."

"Nothing? It wasn't a good look when I came to the house earlier and found her there but after this little revelation outside it's definitely not okay now. Now if you're on some medieval crusade to clean up the world that's fine. I'll do everything to aid you but she can't stay under the same roof with you. That's far too much temptation even if you are a saint. Now I have three bedrooms and she's welcome to stay there even if I am a bit apprehensive about taking in vagrants."

Kane was still smiling.

"Are you ready to order?"

"Mattie?"

"I'll have whatever you're having Kane."

"I'll have two veal ptarmigan dinners and two salads with blue cheese and a nice carafe of your best wine." Kane said to the waiter.

"Kane are you listening to me?"

"I can't help but listen to you. I think the whole restaurant is listening to you," Kane said still smiling.

"Seriously, Kane."

"Perhaps you'd like to hear my plans?"

"*Please. Tell me something.*"

"What do you pay for your place Mattie?"

"About twenty five hundred a month. Why?"

"Well, what if you could live rent free?"

"That's a no-brainer. Who wouldn't want that?"

"Okay then it's agreed. I'll get some of the fellas to move you in with me tomorrow under one condition."

Mattie was too elated to protest.

"What's that?"

"I want you off the streets."

"Not a problem sir. Is that all?"

"No, Mattie that's not all. I want you to establish a program to help get some of these young girls like Naomi off the street. There are a lot of girls out there that are just like you were and have the potential to go to school and make something of themselves. I want you to start with Naomi and a couple of others."

There was a moment of silence.

"You okay Mattie," Kane inquired. "I've never seen you this quiet."

"I'm okay. Just trying to weigh what it is you're asking me to do. You know I've never done anything else so it's not going to be easy or happen right away. All-in-all I'm pretty much in shock. I like what I hear but the transition may take awhile. Just be patient with me sweetheart."

"No rush, no pressure. You take your time. Rome wasn't built in a day."

36

As if somehow on cue, Mattie's phone rang. Seeing Eva's name come up she stated not to answer it but thought better of it.

"Hello. Whoa, whoa, whoa! Slow down Eva. Hold on. I don't know what's wrong. Eva wants to talk to you. She says she's been trying to call you but hasn't been able to get through," Mattie repeated handing Kane the phone.

"Hey sweetheart I hope this is important. I'm in a very important meeting right now."

"Kane he beat me. I didn't do nothing and he beat me. He raped me and then he beat me."

"Whoa! Whoa! Slow down honey. Who are we talking about? Who beat you? Isn't Marcus out there?"

"No. Nobody's out there. It's too early. I went out early to try and pick up a couple of dollars and this guy took me home with home with him. Said it was cheaper than the hotel. He didn't want to go to the hotel. Said it was nasty and he paid up front. I see him around all the time. He's from the neighborhood so I thought he was on the level."

"Okay Eva. How bad are you? Is anything broken?"

"I don't know Kane. I managed to crawl out of the apartment after he passed out and Ms. Murphy—you know ol' lady Murphy—dragged me into her apartment. I can't walk though. He took a broom… Oh, Kane!" She was crying again.

"Okay Eva. I'll have Marcus or one of the other fellas stop by and bring you a little something to ease the pain. Mattie and I are on our way. Just hang in there. Put Ms. Murphy on the phone. I want to know if she thinks I need to send an ambulance."

"No Kane. The hospital will call the police and they'll put me in the Tombs and charge me with prostitution just because."

"Eva do you trust me."

"Yeah Kane but…"

"Then if Ms. Murphy says you need an ambulance I don't want you to give them a hard time and don't worry about 5-0. Trust me I'll take care of all that. You just go with the EMS workers. You hear me?"

"I hear you and thanks Kane."

"By the way Eva, what apartment is he in?"

"18G. He's two doors down from Ms. Murphy."

"One last question Eva."

"Yeah. Oh, Kane it hurts so bad."

"Easy baby. It's goin' to be alright. You just hang in there. Help is on its way but tell me this. Did you happen to notice if he was strapped or not?"

"No, he ain't carrying nothing. The niggas high as hell and drunk off his ass. He just picked up an eight ball from TJ but he didn't even open it. He's got two or three g's in his jacket pocket too."

"Okay, you didn't do anything to bring this down on you did you? You didn't try to rob him or anything did you?"

"No, Kane wasn't even any time for that. As soon as I walked in behind him he turned and backhanded me. I'm telling you this mothefucker's sick."

"Okay, listen did you leave his door open?"

"Yeah. It's wide open."

"Okay tell Ms. Murphy to close it but make sure she doesn't lock it. You hear me. Tell her to close it but make sure she doesn't lock it. When she gets back make sure she calls me. You just sit tight."

Kane hung up the phone as Mattie handed him her cell.

"Got Marcus on hold," Mattie said as she put the contents of what was supposed to be their lunch in the take home cartons.

"Listen Marcus I've got a little situation I need you to take care of for me."

"What's up boss?

"Are you packin'?"

"Always. You already know son."

"Good. Listen. Take this address down. Then I need you to go to this address. Take TJ with you so he can identify this piece of shit. He just bought an eight ball from TJ then talked Eva into going to his place and stomped her. She's two doors down at Ms. Murphy so be careful I'm about to send EMS and so the police may roll up. Wait 'til they leave to do anything. If you can get to her and give her something for the pain and then do what you have to do but don't hurt him too bad. I still have a score to settle with him about something else. I don't want any of those trigger happy niggas going with you packin' though. I don't want no accidents. Eva says he never opened the eight ball so that should be there for you and he's supposed to have two or three grand in his jacket pocket. She says he's high as hell so he shouldn't be a problem. Let him know you've been there and then when you finish drop his ass over in the Jersey swamps."

"Not a problem. But tell me this boss. Do you think Eva's on the up and up? I mean you don't think she did any sheisty shit to bring this on?"

"If I had to go on just Eva's word I wouldn't send you. I'd talk to my man myself and make sure but I have another young lady who just went through the same thing at the hands of this clown."

"I'll call you when it's done."

"Do you have someone reliable on the street to look out while you take care of this piece of work?"

"I'll leave TJ out there as soon as we pick this motherfucker up and he I.D.'s this mope. He's the most levelheaded and most feared."

"Good. Good. And I'll take care of you tomorrow. You be careful. Remember we ain't got no jurisdiction over in Esplanade Gardens and a lot of these old racist cops that don't think there should be a drug free zone would like nothing better than to hang Captain D'Amato. So make sure when you head that way that nobody's riding dirty and that everything's clean. Whatever profits you lose I'll make right tomorrow."

"Ain't no problem Kane. I gotcha."

As soon as Kane hung up from Marcus Mattie handed him his phone back and reclaimed her own.

"Hello. Ah yes. Ms. Murphy how's she doing?"

"Hold on Kane. Someone's at the door." Moments later she returned. "I take it those are two of your boys."

"Yes mam. I asked them to stop by and check on her. How's she doing?"

"Not too good I'm afraid. I think her jaw is broken and she's bleeding from her vaginal area. Did she tell you what that animal did to her?"

"Yes ma'am."

"I tried to call the cops and the ambulance but she won't allow me to although she needs both. That fool needs to be locked under the jail for doing something like this to that girl. Eva ain't no angel but nobody deserves this. You should see this poor child's face. I don't think she'll ever recover from the beating he gave her. It may be a blessing in disguise though. It may just make her rethink her line of work."

"Yes, ma'am. So, you think she definitely needs an ambulance?"

"The way she's bleeding from the genital area. Yes!"

"Okay Ms. Murphy. Are those gentlemen still there?"

"Hold on. Let me check. Yeah they're still here."

"Okay, instead of waiting for an ambulance tell them to get her to the hospital. And Ms. Murphy I don't mean to inconvenience you but could you go with her?"

"I know you didn't just ask me that Kane. I've known this girl since she was a baby. She's like one of my own. Do you think I would just put her out?"

"I'm sorry Ms. Murphy."

"I'll tell you this though. I ain't taking her to Harlem Hospital. I wouldn't take my dog there. I'm going to run her up to St. Lukes. It's a much better facility."

"Okay Ms. Murphy. I'll meet you there. I'm in Queens now so give me a few."

"As long as it takes…"

"And thank you ma'am."

"Hurry son. She ain't lookin' all that good."

"I'm on my way."

Mattie was already at the car.

"I didn't get the full story and not sure that I want to know but…"

"Stop. The bottom line is that same bastard that was abusing Naomi took Eva home and raped her and basically brutalized her. From what Ms. Murphy told me she's got a broken jaw and is bleeding vaginally and Lord knows what else. I need you to run up to St. Lukes and check on Eva while I go and take care of this little problem."

"Kane."

"Yeah Mattie."

"Did you ever think that God has something else for us? You know like we were born into this life but it's only a trial and we don't necessarily have to wallow or remain in this cesspool."

"Everyday baby. Every damn day. But you know God doesn't just put us down here to enjoy the fruit of his labors but he puts us down here to labor on behalf of ourselves and those less fortunate around us. You know Ms. Murphy?"

"Yeah, she's a good woman."

"Well, she found Eva and took her in. She could have just as easily gone back in her apartment and closed her door. When I asked her to go up to the hospital with Eva and wait 'til we got there she jumped on me for insulting her by asking her. You see for a lot of people feel it's their duty to help. Some are doctors, some are teachers. Others are regular folks like you and I. At least I'd like to think that you and I are like that too Mattie. I think there's some goodness in us. And that's why we do what we do but you asked me am I tired of this shit? Hell yeah. I'm ready to get me a house in the country and lean back. Just as soon as I get everything established and running on its own that's exactly what I plan on doing."

"Eva Jones?"

"Room 232. Second floor. Make a right when you get off the elevator. Walk straight ahead. It should be on your left."

"Thank you ma'am."

The two rode the elevator in silence.

Reaching the room Kane squeezed Mattie's shoulder.

"She needs you to be strong so no matter what be strong Mattie."

Mattie reached back and squeezed Kane's hand before pulling the curtain back and entering the room.

Eva was if nothing else heavily sedated and only moaned upon seeing Mattie and Kane. Mattie hugged her and a tear dropped. Eva's face was swollen and disfigured but she still managed a smile. It was obvious her jaw had been broken but she was still determined to lighten the situation.

"The guy's loaded if you want to take him Mattie. I'm pretty sure you can take him. Just remember to duck."

Mattie smiled. "You know you're crazy don'tcha Eva?" Mattie said smiling. "Well, at least you're in good spirits. It would be stupid if I asked how you're feeling wouldn't it?"

"No it wouldn't. This might have been the best thing to happen to me believe it or not."

Mattie glanced over at Kane at this remark.

"Hey Kane. Mattie. I sure am glad to see you two. Just stepped out to get Eva some jello. I feel sorry for these poor folks. She gonna run somebody to death."

Mattie laughed.

"Thanks for looking out for her Ms. Murphy."

"No problem. Kane you think those boys will give me a lift back home?"

"I don't see why not," Kane replied said escorting the woman from the room and sliding a hundred dollar bill into her hand.

"No sir," the old woman said in protest. "How would that be to take money for taking care of one of God's children in need?"

"Thank you Ms. Murphy," Eva managed to whisper.

"No problem child. You just stay offa them streets. Same thing I been telling you for years. Stay the hell offa them streets."

"I will Ms. Murphy."

"Move over cow," Mattie said easing onto the hospital bed. "Now what were you saying

about it not hurting so bad?"

"Oh, it hurts. I ain't never say that. But you know the whole time I was lying up there at that old woman's apartment all I could think about was what my mama used to say God rest her soul."

"What's that Eva?"

"Mama used to tell me that you never learned nothing being on the mountaintop but only when you're down in the valley. I never knew what she meant until tonight."

"And?"

"And as long as I was flying high I never thought about nothing but getting high, partying, looking fly and stacking mad papers. Matter-of-fact when old boy bought the eight ball I knew then that he was two sheets to the wind. His ass was so drunk he gave TJ three hundred instead of two and TJ gave it back to him. I knew right then. I was gonna go and smoke a little then slip him a Mickey and take him for everything he had and go home and chill. I guess someone was looking out for him."

"So what did you come up with?"

"I learned Mattie that I can't keep going on this same path. I'm already looking fifty and there just ain't no future in it. If I keep going like this I'm gonna wind up in a plot right next to mama. Dead."

"You're right Eva."

"The same goes for you Mattie. Kane told you that when he sent your ass to college and made you his right hand man and your dumbass is still out there hustlin' like your ass depends on it."

46

"You right. I can't argue with you Eva. Funny thing is Kane and I were just talking about that when you called. And I'm out baby. I'm moving in with him and gonna try that and see how that works. May even get a j-o-b if my record doesn't get in the way. In the meantime, we're going to start a wayward home for girls and try to give them options other than the street."

"Oh my God. That's wonderful. I just hope you include me Mattie."

"I'm sure there's something for my favorite girl. Let me get outta here. The nurse said you had a broken pelvic bone, a fractured jaw and some internal bleeding but you should be up and around in a few weeks. Give me the key to your apartment so I can grab a few things and don't worry about anything. I'm thinking you should give up the place and move in with us until you decide what you want to do."

"Do what you think is best Mattie."

"Okay. I'll be back in the morning. Call me if you need anything."

"Love you Mattie."

"Love you more."

Chapter 3

"What's up Marcus?" Kane said giving his second lieutenant some dap. "Sorry I'm late. I had to drop Mattie off."

"No problem. Everything's cool. Niggas upstairs passed out. I don't know what he's into but I think you might want to go slow with him. We found a couple of grand just where you said it would be and close to twenty grand in a suitcase under his bed. I don't know what he's doing but ain't a lot of niggas sittin' on that kind of cheddar."

"You'd be surprised. Africans ain't like us son. They save and send it back home. Do you know what a dollar can do in Africa?"

"I hear you. But there's something else that bothers me too Kane."

"What's that?"

"This kid is sitting on two bricks of damn near pure."

"Stop playin'"

"I kid you not. And it's obviously not his or why else would he be buying an eight ball from TJ?"

"You right. Damn this makes the shit a lot more complicated than I first thought. Did you touch it?"

"Not until I got the word from you. I wasn't doing shit until I got the word. We're in a good spot. This could start a war. We don't even know who we're fuckin' with."

"Smart Marcus. Real smart. Good man. I'm thinking though if this fool is as fucked up as you say he is and left the front door open with that much cash and yayo then anybody passing could have gone in and robbed the place. Whoever he's holding for ain't gonna hold nobody responsible but him. And the ass whoopin' we was gonna bestow on his ass will pale in comparison. Who's up there with him now?"

"Dre and TJ."

"They won't mess with the shit?"

"No. They my most loyal workers. Both of them is good boys."

"They got phones on 'em?"

"Yeah."

"I don't want to alert him. You want to run up."

"No, they got they phones on vibrate. Give us some credit Kane. We be holdin' it down. All a us been doing this for more than a minute. Believe it or not we put in work before. We ain't no newbies son."

"My bad. I just want to make sure there ain't no slip ups or anything that's gonna trace it back to us."

"I feel ya. So you just gonna let my man off the hook? You know the first thing he's gonna think is that Eva got him. He gonna go after her for real then."

"Good point. I need to get her moved with the quickness. You know he broke her jaw, fractured her pelvis and she's got some internal bleeding."

"Not saying what he done was right but you know if it hadn't been him it would have been somebody else. Somebody's gonna kill her if she doesn't get her shit together."

"Hate to say it but this may be the best thing that could have happened to her. Might be just the wakeup call she needed."

"If it wasn't for Mattie she'd be nothing more a memory now. Here they come now."

"Okay Marcus this is how we're going to do this. I want the twenty g's. Give the two grand to TJ and Dre. You keep the two keys. My gift to you. That's forty grand in your pocket with no luxury tax but don't flood the streets with this shit and arouse any unnecessary suspicion. If this motherfucker comes around asking any questions tell your boys to either say they haven't seen her or she's in jail."

51

"Thanks for showing me that love Kane."

"Everything that looks good ain't always good for you. Remember that boy. And hold it down for me tonight. I'm heading in. It's been a rough one. Call me if anything pops off tonight. If not shut it down around five so the old people ain't gotta encounter them fiends and ho's on their way to work in the morning."

"Call me when you get up in the morning. We need to talk. I've got some serious shit to lay on you man."

"I know you got some shit with you Kane but why you always got to make a big deal outta shit and make it so formal."

Kane smiled and wiped his forehead.

"You ever done any time Marcus?"

"Been in and out of Rikers mores time than I'd like to remember."

"Me. I ain't never done a day. And let me tell you why young brother. It's because I plan out everything before I even consider doing it. I think son. That's the key."

"And what's that got to do with why we can't talk right here instead of having a meeting in the morning. I get off at five in the morning and my girl's already sleepin' but when I wake up around eleven or twelve and she wraps one of those thick, chocolate thighs around me and my Johnson starts to rise the last thing I want to be thinking about is meeting your Black ass out here in the morning."

Kane laughed and slapped Marcus some dap.

"So, then you feel me then son?"

"Yeah, I feel you. But with two kilos sitting on the passenger seat of your Beamer in plain view I'm gonna have to insist on meeting you tomorrow my brother. You see two kilos is a whole lotta time and I ain't got no time to give away."

Five minutes later Kane was at home. Mattie met him at the door.

"How did it go?"

Kane brought her up-to-date on the night's activities much to Mattie's relief.

"I believe in letting the Lord exact His revenge. I know you're known out here as the peacemaker but the Lord will take care of it all in the end Kane."

"That may be all well and true but in Harlem a lot of these niggas ain't never heard of God but they come around 145th and 8th they heard a Kane. But in this case this nigga got a pass for what he did to Eva but the way I figure it he owes somebody sixty g's and I can tell you he ain't gonna get a pass on sixty g's."

"It's crazy. I'm so glad you gave me a way out."

"It is. And I'm right behind you. I haven't told Mike yet but after I meet with Marcus tomorrow I'm turnin' over the reigns I'm done."

"Oh, baby I'm so happy for you. I'm so happy for us. Now we can look at all our options and to the future without ever having to look back."

Kane went on to update Mattie on the night's activities. Afterwards, Mattie sat there for quite some time without speaking. When she did Kane was surprised to find her attitude on the whole thing was pretty much in concurrence with his own with one small difference.

"You know when you left Eva in as bad a shape as she's in looked she looked at it as a blessing and I have to concur. And you know as well as I do that if she'd found the money we would have been visiting her at the morgue and not the ER."

"How do you think she's gonna react to being relocated?"

"To Queens? That's like putting her out in the desert somewhere. I think she'll be okay as long as she's broken up but as soon as they release her she'll be yearning to get back to Harlem."

"That's kinda what I figured so all we can do is hope and pray that this whole thing blows over and they think she skipped town before she returns. I have TJ and Dre admitting her into Jamaica hospital tomorrow morning under an assumed name and I'd like for you to talk to her in person if you can. Just try to get her to understand the magnitude of the situation and let her know that I and no one else can protect her if these people really want her."

"I'll do my best."

"How's our other young lady doing?"

"You mean Naomi?"

"Yeah," Kane grunted more fatigued than usual.

"I'm not sure. She was asleep when I got home then she came downstairs and I asked her if she wanted some tea and she declined. I tried to talk to her but she seemed distant almost like she was in another world. When I mentioned her family she broke down altogether."

"Yeah she's been traumatized here and at home. It's gonna take some time to get her back on her feet but I know if anybody can do it you can."

"I'm glad you have so much faith."

"I've been watching you for years handle the hardest of cases andwatched you make 'em melt right before my eyes. That's a gift. You should have been a therapist or a social worker."

Mattie smiled.

"I guess have been in an unofficial capacity at best. Each one's different and believe me things aren't always what they seem. You take Eva for example. She's easy. Everything you want to know is right before your eyes. She's transparent whereas it could take years to peel away the layers of hurt and pain and distrust to finally get to the source in Naomi's case. And then there's no sure way to know how scarred she is and if there's any chance of recovery. But I'll be patient with her."

"What more can you do? Listen. I got a big day ahead of me tomorrow so I'm heading to bed. Care to join me?"

How long had Mattie waited for Kane to say those words and immediately felt the sweat gather on the bridge of her nose and between her thighs. She would make this night, their first night together special. Mattie checked on Naomi and entered the bedroom only to find Kane in the shower and a deep mist hovering inside. She considered undressing and joining him but didn't want to seem too hungry, or too forward. But most of all she didn't want to seem like a sex craved whore. No she would do it right and went through her belongings until she found her long flannel gown and toiletry bag and proceeded to sit in the recliner and channel surf until he was finished. Hearing the showering stop Mattie grabbed her belongings and proceeded to the bathroom when Kane opened the door and stepped into the bedroom.

For twenty years Mattie had made the bedroom the room she most frequented, the room she felt most comfortable in, the room she spent most of her time in with all shapes and hues of men and after some time it had all become second nature. But tonight she was in awe, speechless and found herself forced to sit back down as she watched the water glisten and bead up on the tall, bronze figure before her.

Composing herself as best she could Mattie stood and made her way to the bathroom brushing against Kane as she did. Showering quickly she wondered why this man had such an effect on her where no other had come close to making an inroad although many had tried. Was this love? After all this time is this what she'd blotted out?

Again she the felt warmth between her legs and the thought of finally having this man in her clutches riding her slowly as he whispered in her ear made her nipples erect. She wondered if after all this time and thousands of men if she could still give him what he needed, if she could satisfy him? The time for those thoughts were over as she rinsed her hair one final time and stepped out of the shower onto the cold bathroom tiles. Dressing quickly she sprayed just a nuance of perfume on her. Mattie eased the bathroom door open to make love for the very first time only to find Kane fast asleep and snoring softly.

"Morning Naomi."

"Morning Kane."

"Listen there's plenty of food in the fridge. Help yourself but I want you to stay here until Mattie or I get back and keep the doors locked. I'm running late for work and have a very important meeting this morning. Don't answer the phone. Think about what you're going to need and write a list. Mattie's going to take you shopping when she gets back so be ready," Kane said hugging the young woman.

"I am?"

"Yes, and thank you love, "Kane said smiling before pulling Mattie to him and kissing her on the forehead. "And please make sure you get Eva to understand what exactly is happening and how imperative it is that she chill for a couple of months. Talk to the doctors at Jamaica Hospital and try to impress on them the importance of extending her stay for as long as they can. Offer them a few dollars to postpone her discharge."

"What's a few dollars?"

"Whatever it takes. Gotta go. Call me baby. I'm running late. We'll talk."

"Love you Kane." "Love you more."

And with that Kane threw Mattie a set of keys and headed for the front door.

"Mr. Kane is a very busy man isn't he?"

"Too busy if you ask me," Mattie said grabbing her cigarettes, cell phone and stuffing them in her Coach bag. "Listen Naomi do you have any clothes with you?"

"I had a pair of jeans and a t-shirt but they had blood on them. I think Mr. Kane threw out so no I guess I don't have any clothes. Miss Mattie can I ask you a question?"

"Sure. Anything you like Naomi. Shoot."

"What does Kane do for a living?"

Mattie had to pause.

"Mr. Kane controls a very important bit of real estate dear. I guess you can say he's responsible for making sure that it runs smoothly and that everyone works and gets along and there's no confusion."

"Confusion?"

"Yes confusion. When you have a lot of different factions and investors all vying for the same money and profits you have to have someone who mediates their differences and makes sure that a greedy faction doesn't step on someone elses toes or take all of everything for themselves."

"Oh he's like Kofi Annon and the UN."

Mattie had to laugh at the analogy but yeah that summed it up better than all of Mattie's liberal attempts.

58

"What size are you? I'm thinking about a six?"

"No actually I'm a two now but I have picked up a little weight so you might go with a four."

"Damn girl. Have you ever thought about modeling?"

It was the first time Mattie had actually seen Naomi smile.

"I think about it all the time."

"Well you certainly have the looks. You're tall and beautiful and with that pretty assed complexion I think you're a natural but we'll leave that for another day. I have to run out and take care of a little business. I'll bring you back a pair of jeans and a sweater and then I'll take you over to the Short Hills Mall in Jersey and we'll have a girl's day out; maybe get a manicure, a pedicure and a massage."

Naomi looked puzzled.

Mattie laughed at the expression on the young girl's face.

"Trust me it'll be fun. Just be ready by one o'clock and like Kane said don't answer the door or the phone. I have my key."

"I'll be ready."

"Okay, see you then."

As Mattie got into the silver and gray Sonata her thoughts again turned to the girl and saw her as the daughter she never had. As many girls as she'd come across in her travels they were all the same. They were all longing for one thing. Love. Maybe with Naomi she could supply that one thing and save her before it was too late and before she turned into another Eva. Maybe she could provide hope for the hopeless. In Eva's case it was far too late.

"What's up girl?"

"Mattie why in the fuck am I out here in Osh Kosh b'Gosh?"

"Whoa! Slow your roll Eva. We put you out here to keep you safe. When that rat bastard wakes up and finds that he's been rolled he's gonna come lookin' for your dumbass."

"Dumbass? Who the fuck are you callin' dumbass bitch? And I didn't roll nobody!"

"I'm callin' you a dumbass. You're always, ever since I've known you getting caught up in some shit and ninety percent of the time you have no one to blame but yourself. Kane set up trap houses with bodyguards just so this sorta shit wouldn't happen but could you go to one? No. Your ass had to go to his house. That's in the fuckin' manual. Streetwalkin' 101. You don't let a trick take you anywhere. You take the trick where you want him to go. And we have people in place so if a trick even thinks about robbing you or beating your ass he's out on the street so fast he won't know what hit him but no you trying to be sheisty and save ten bucks so you go with him so you can rob him. You sheisty dumbass bitch!

And if that's not bad enough you put ten other people in danger because they gotta go rescue your stupid ass. Well, in rescuing your ass the fellas found a couple of kilos and a bunch of cash and the nigga was so bent that he never knew they were there but when he wakes up the last person he's gonna remember is you so we moved you so you wouldn't be killed and your ass is still bitchin' and complainin'. Damn Eva! I honestly thought that last night you finally came to see the light. A broken jaw and pelvis Eva. That's what you did. Nobody but you. What we did dumbass; what your friends did was keep you out of some fuckin' jail's infirmary and catchin' a charge. We put you into a hospital where you could do two things. One your body has a chance to mend and the other thing you should be doing is reflecting on what a fucked up life you have and where you're going when you get outta here. Now I just talked to the doctor's and they got the healing process underway. Now what you're gonna do, and I mean right fuckin' now is start reflectin' and get to healing your mind so the next time we have to come get you you're not in the fuckin' morgue."

Nurse Betty knocked lightly before pushing the door open.

"Ma'am we're going to need you to keep the noise down. We have other patients who need their rest."

"My fault. I'm just tryna get my friend to sit back and relax. She's been through a terrible ordeal. I do so apologize. Think about what I said Eva," Mattie said smiling at the nurse before walking out.

She wondered why Kane had sent her on this mission. Out of all the girl's out on the strip Eva was the worst. She had no morals and would rob her mother as quickly as anybody else. She lied, cheated. You name it. Eva had done it and now she was too old to change her ways. Kane knew it and yet he'd sent her to try to make order out of Eva's chaos. On the way back Mattie knew there was little she could do to make Eva change her ways. She'd been trying for years. What Eva didn't realize however was if she didn't listen this time she'd soon be dead.

The drive back into the city despite the midday traffic gave her a chance to clear her head. Next was Naomi and she didn't know why she'd promised the girl the Short Hills Mall. By the time she'd pick her up and do a little shopping and try to get in a manicure and massage it would be damn near midnight by the time they got back and she hadn't seen Kane all day.

The thought immediately occurred her that she hadn't talked to him since this morning and picking up her Samsung Galaxy she simply said Kane and it began dialing.

'You have reached Kane. Leave a message at the tone.'

Damn she couldn't wait 'til their lives slowed down to a crawl when she could stare across the fron't lawn and see him with his straw hat, beads of sweat glistening and dripping chocolate brown from his cheeks as he toiled with the azaleas under the midday sun. Damn how she wished for those days.

Meanwhile at a small coffee shop uptown now frequented by preppy young Columbia University students who thought it was chic to live in Langston Hughes's Harlem sat Kane. If it was one thing Kane hated was tardiness. He'd met Mike at noon and commenced to working out an agreement where Mike would bankroll the cost of him setting up a non-profit women's center in exchange and a retainer of a hundred large for Kane to train and be a consultant to the enforcement council about to be put in place. Mike figured it would take a good six months for the transition to take place and although Kane argued stringently it was Mike who ultimately won out. Kane awaited his successor. Kane already angry grabbed his jacket and Kangol off the chair when Marcus walked in. Always upbeat he looked worn.

"What's up Kane?" he said grabbing the older man's hand and bumping chests.

"Nothing Marcus. But if I say meet me at one that's what I mean. Not a quarter after one. Not one thirty. You so busy trying to lay up in some pussy you forgetting the scrilla. It's money over bitches nigga. A true playa knows that."

"Yo chill Kane. I ain't about no dumb shit today. I was out there 'til close to nine o'clock this morning dealin' with that silly ass nigga."

"Who you talkin' about?"

"That nigga we rolled for mad stacks and that yayo."

"What happened?"

"Well, I had to wait until Jasmine came back from her final run which took damn near three hours. She had this old White dude from Jersey. Some politician. And he's got mad stacks and flashing rolls of money and steady spending. He buying both grams and eight balls. And so she's conducting business and everybody's just chillin' by this time or gone in. Like I said it's a round six in the morning when this other monkey ass comes staggering down the street waving his gat talkin' bout how he's gonna shoot the bitch that robbed him and all the old people are coming out on their way to work like Ms. Murphy and so I called J. And so J posts up on one side and when he sees J he confronts him and asks him where Eva is and J tells him he ain't seen the bitch. So this nigga points the freeze at J. Kane I'm telling you this nigga woulda capped J. and thought nothin' of it. The boy's sick. So I approach him and ask him what's up. And he tells me that this bitch robbed him of his money and his dope with J's help so I acts ignorant and tells him that that's real fucked up in an attempt try to win him over. Then I explains to him how he gonna make it real bad for him and everybody else out there by waving that piece and bring the heat but I promised to ask around and find out about Eva's whereabouts. Then I tells him she ain't gonna be around if she did rob him and told him to go get some sleep and I'd give him a call if I heard anything. An hour later he's back but this time without the freeze but still rantin' and ravin' about his money and shit. That shit went on 'til damn near now. I posted J. up in Chandra's apartment so he could watch the street and he just called me to tell me the motherfucker's still pacing."

"Well, let the motherfucker pace," Kane said smiling. "I remember when I was just a young cat over in Irvington. One night me and my crew went with Mike G. to this little set down in Newark to parlay and cop some blow. And on the way we was getting' cheebad up and passin' the Richards and just wilin'. We was all high as hell when we got there. And clean. Everybody had on some new Forces. You know we was young cats just getting' a taste of the good life. But before we went in Mike gave us some of his words of wisdom. You know how Mike is. Anyway, the brother says 'I ain't gonna lie to you and say I know these niggas cause I don't. But one thing I do know. Niggas in

64

Newark go hard so let's go in there and handle our business, do this transaction and break the fuck out.' But what happened was we went in and it was this older crowd with some fine ass older bitches and they was real friendly like. They offered us a taste of this and a taste of that and a couple of my boys was trying to go hard too so they went into the room with these older bitches and shot up some of that fire with 'em and went into a nod and woke up with no clothes, no jewelry, no shoes. They were assed out. Came to me and Mike wantin' us to shoot up the place. But Mike packed up our shit and shook the hosts hand and we left. When we got outside Mike said, 'I told you motherfuckers before you went in don't sleep. You sleep. You donate.' I never forgot that shit and I ain't feelin' nobody that can't hold their liquor or their dope. Ya feel me?"

"I feel ya."

"Now the way I see it, we basically have two choices as far as this nigga goes. We can put him to sleep and not worry about him anymore or we can suggest that he relocate and chalk up his losses."

"You know me. Sing him a lullaby and be done with him."

"Well, Marcus from here on out these are your choices to make."

"I'm not understanding."

"It's not hard. I'm out. I'm moving on. It's all yours. I just met with Mike and I named you as my successor. Out of everyone out there I think you're the most level headed and conservative. Out of everyone out there you're the only one that understands that the only motivating factor is making that cheddar. All the other bullshit has to subside in order to make that money. So, in your new capacity you'll be expected to maintain the peace and as long as there is peace you'll take a fraction of everything that goes on out there and you're gonna be amazed at what a mere fraction of everything is," Kane said smiling.

"You serious man?"

"Dead. Mike wants me to stick around as a sort of consultant in case you need advice or something comes up that throws you for a loop. In that case, you can give me a call. I love you man. You made my job that much easier but don't you call me. Whatever the fuck it is you work it out. I'm retired. Now I'm gonna give you Mike's number and if you think you can't handle it you let him know."

"What do you think?"

"About what?"

"Do you think I can handle it? You know what your opinion means to me."

"I wouldn't have nominated you for the position if I hadn't been impressed with your management skills," Kane said looking at Marcus who was clean as always in his tan warm-up suit, and fresh white Forces.

"Okay. If you think I can do it then I'll accept the position. What advice can you give me to take me forward?"

Kane leaned forward and sipped the remainder of his espresso.

"Well, Marcus if I had to give you some advice I'd tell you this and I know you're looking for something specific but there is nothing that covers every encounter on the street. Each one of them is distinct and has its own individual qualities so those you'll just have to encounter and figure out but what I will tell you is that my best asset on the street was not my gat. And in thirty years out there I can only remember having to show it less than a handful of times and I still had fingers left over.

My best and most important assets were you and Mattie. And by the way Mattie's out as well. Those were my two best assets. You have to learn to delegate to others and be comfortable leaving them in charge to carry out your orders. The other thing I'd recommend you learn to do is to seek out every possible avenue to alleviate a situation other than violence. Violence begets violence. Last night you came up with the idea of taking ol' boys shit and keep it moving. Today you want to off the motherfucker because he pestered you. But you and I both know that ain't that boys shit which means you off him then whoever the shit belongs to is gonna come lookin' for you thinkin' you robbed him that's why you were so quick to kill him. So, before you make a move think about it from every possible angle and then think about it again but never be hasty. Outside of that you have to basically pick it up on the fly baby boy."

Marcus was visually shaken with the pronouncement.

"I'm a hold it down Kane," he said getting up and hugging Kane.

"I know you will Marcus. And let Mike take care of your money for you. That way you'll have some money when you walk away." 'If you walk away' Kane thought to himself.

"You need a ride anywhere?"

"Nah son. My whip's outside. Mike's gonna call you and brief you on the police and the rest. You be safe."

"Love you man."

"Love you more."

Kane got into the two door BMW and breathed a sigh of a relief. After twenty five years this chapter of his life was finally coming to a close.

Chapter 4

In the days and weeks that followed Mattie had never been happier. It was the first time in Lord knows how long that she had experienced family and though she nor Kane or Naomi were married each quickly fell into their roles without being assigned.

Mattie wasn't sure of which roommate she adored more and often found herself weighing her options when it came time to take sides.

"The Knicks are at home baby and I got courtside seats. I know you ain't crazy about Spike but Durant and OKC are in town."

Mattie had always been an avid Knick fan and hardly ever turned down a request from Kane but tonight she was bushed. She and Naomi had gotten up early to go and check on Eva and from there had gone down to midtown to do a little shopping and then to NYU to check out the campus and possible housing for Naomi. From there it was off to the East Village for lunch and a little more shopping. By the time they returned home it was after four and no sooner had she gotten in the door than the phone rang. She'd totally forgotten that she'd promised her younger sister Deidra that she'd take her up to Greenwich for the annual wine tasting festival. So, she dropped her bags and was off again. By the time she arrived back home Mattie was so worn out that all she could manage to do was grab a quick shower, throw on that old flannel night gown and climb into bed."

"C'mon Mattie? How you gonna say no to Westbrook and Durant?"

"Ahh baby. If it were any other night… Why don't you give Mike a call and go with him?"

"Why would I call Mike when I could go with the most beautiful girl in NYC?"

Mattie smiled as Kane bent down and kissed her.

"Okay love. I should be back in a couple of hours. You get some rest."

"You can best believe that. Did you talk to Naomi?"

"I peaked in on her but she was already asleep."

"I guess so. She ran me to death today but she wanted to tell you her good news. They offered her a four year academic scholarship to NYU but she hasn't decided on whether she wants to go there or Columbia. I think she's leaning towards Columbia just so she can stay here. I took her down and rode around NYU and the East Village but after her last fiasco I don't think she's too inclined on stepping out on her own just yet."

"Well don't push her. We have enough room here and she's really no bother. I kind of like having her around. And she'll make that move when she's comfortable."

Mattie smiled. Kane was a good man.

"See you in a few."

"Love you Kane."

"Love you more."

It seemed like only minutes later that she heard the bedroom door open and Kane climb into bed next to her. But tonight was different. She'd grown accustomed to him wrapping his arms around her and just holding her. They had yet to have sex and her thoughts were mixed when it came to that. She'd had enough sex to last her this lifetime and the next so the lack of it didn't bother her in the least. If he wanted her she was there for him and if there ever was a man that she wanted it was Kane Close. But he would have to make the first move and in the three and a half weeks she'd been there the most he'd done was a hug and a kiss on her forehead. Mattie was in no rush but after twenty years she wondered why he hadn't at least tried. How many times had he commented on her being attractive and yet still he'd made no move. Well, that was until tonight. As he slid in she awoke to find his hand on her breast. She immediately became aroused and turned to face him. Taking her face into his hand he kissed her softly, passionately before thrusting his tongue into her awaiting mouth. She sucked hungrily as he lifted her gown and parted her thighs. She was moist and hungry for him. Feeling her need he entered her slowly but firmly. Mattie gasped. An hour later she rolled into his loving arms, satisfied and closed her eyes.

The morning came with a spray of sunshine and Mattie wondered how things could get much better. She was a little sore in her genital area and thought of the Frankie Beverly tune Joy and Pain. A warm bath with Epsom salts and she would be back to normal. This had long ago become a regular routine after a particular rough night and she figured after close to a month of non-activity this was to be expected. But the increasing fatigue she felt was all new to her.

"Have to meet with the lawyer's today sweetie. I made fresh coffee. I'm out. There's some onion bagels on the top of the fridge. And by the way you were better than the fantasy. Gotta run." Kane said grinning from ear-to-ear as he pulled the door behind him and headed for the BMW at the curb. Getting in he opened the glove and pulled out the cell. It had now become common to leave the phone in the car at night. That way he could relax with his new found family without drama and interruption. And for the first time he was beginning to come to know inner peace and tranquility.

Turning on the Samsung Galaxy, Kane glanced the messages. There were a dozen or more texts most of which were from Mike and Marcus which he knew couldn't be good. Now he wished he hadn't taken the retainer. Whatever it was he didn't want to be bothered. Still, all he had to do was listen, troubleshoot and offer a viable solution to whatever it was. But with Mike calling it had to be serious.

"Mike just got your text. What's good?"

"I wish I could say. But listen, that kid Marcus has been blowing my phone up. I guess he couldn't get in touch with you. Anyway give him a call. I think he's in trouble."

"Okay Mike I'm on it."

"Peace."

Kane was a firm believer that most trouble that people incurred they brought upon themselves and in the case of Marcus with his rash and impulsive nature he was almost sure that this was the case.

"Marcus my brother, what's good?"

"Wish I could call it Kane. I tried to hold off on calling you know. Didn't want to bother you my brother but this shit is getting crazy down here. Can we meet?"

"Yeah, I have a meeting right through here. Give me—oh say an hour—and hour and a half and I'll meet you in the Men's department at Macy's 34th Street."

"Cool. See you then."

Kane got out in front of the attorneys office and walked quickly, briskly into the office.

"Good morning Mr. Close," the shapely young secretary said smiling broadly. Kane had taken her to lunch and was not impressed.

"Morning Ally."

"I owe you a lunch date," she said attempting to flirt.

"You know I've been so busy trying to open this women's center I haven't had a chance to breathe but the first opening I get I'll give you a call. Your number's still the same."

The dejection apparent she shook her head.

"Mr. Harrison is in his office."

"Thanks Ally. Let's say tentatively the early part of next week shall we?"

"I look forward to hearing from you Mr. Close."

Kane smiled and headed down the long hallway and through the glass doors until he reached the attorney's office.

"Hey Harry," he said shaking his boyhood friend's hand.

"Kane I'd like you to meet Mr. Ivan Rothstein. Mr. Rothstein is the owner of the building you are trying to purchase on Lenox. He's agreed to your offer of nine hundred and seventy five thousand for the building. I've read over the terms and everything seems to be in order. He's waived the closing costs and all that's needed now is for you to read over the contract and sign on the dotted line."

"Did you read it over Harry?"

"Yes, I did."

"Then there's no need for me to."

"Then if you're in complete agreement and everything is within compliance then all that's required is your signature."

"How long will it take to have it up and running?"

"Building inspectors will be in there today and tomorrow. Construction workers start the remodeling on Friday."

"Good. Mr. Rothstein it was nice meeting you. Hope we can do business again. Gotta run Harry. Give me a call tonight."

"Oh. I almost forgot," the attorney said handing Kane a large manila envelope.

And with that said Kane made his way to the car winking at Ally on the way out.

He had ten minutes to get to Macy's and midday traffic was at a standstill. He hated to be late even if it was just Marcus and especially after he'd been on him about his own punctuality. Kane arrived at Macy's a few minutes late but Marcus who was busy shopping hardly noticed.

"What up Kane?"

"Not a whole hell of a lot. Just chillin'. Trying to enjoy the good life is all."

"I hear you. I can't wait 'til its bitches and barbeques for me?"

"Tired already."

"Not just tired but stressed like you wouldn't believe."

"Oh I know. You forget I put my time in."

"I know that's right but I tried to follow your advice and keep everything on the down low."

"And?"

"And instead of eliminating the situation it's only escalated."

"Okay go back to square one."

"Man we're still dealing with that motherfucker that beat Eva and you weren't wrong about him either. He's connected with some outfit from Brooklyn. Seems he was holding for them and he must be a pretty stand-up guy 'cause they ain't done nothing to him. Instead they started posting up on the strip and every day they post two or three dudes out there and they're always different. I don't know how big their crew is but like I said up to this point they look to be at least fifty deep. At first they were just asking about Eva but now they're trying to sling. And the product they're pumping is not only damn near pure but their undercutting us. Our business is off by damn near fifty per cent."

"Who's running the outfit?"

"Like I said every day it's another crew. Every evening around six a van pulls up and four or five soldiers get out and a couple of young cats that be slinging hit the corner pumpin' hard."

"Have you tried to have a face-to-face and explain how things work."

"Yeah but they ain't tryna hear nothin'."

"Did you approach them personally?"

"Yeah. Went up to this one cat who looked like he was running things and tried to rap to him and this nigga told me to get the fuck out of his face before he capped my ass so I took your advice and backed the fuck off. And that's basically where we are now. Losing real estate and face at the same time."

"That's about the size of it."

"Hmmm… That's interesting. Okay Marcus I don't want you to do anything. Let me go home and sleep on this for a while. Your initial play though it seemed hasty may have been the right one. Maybe it would have been better to off this guy. Do you have a name?"

"Yeah, his name is Abdul Muhammad. I believe he's from the Sudan."

"Good. Good. I'll talk to Mike and put some feelers out and see what I can find out and then I'll get back to you. Just chill for now."

"Okay. Will do."

Kane called Mike from the car and was surprised to find that Mike was already fully aware of the situation and had already come up with a plan of action.

"Tell Marcus off the streets for the next couple of weeks. I've already contacted the captain and he's gonna conduct a series of sweeps for the next two weeks. They come back but we can get a better feel with who and what we're dealing after they hit central booking a couple of times. That way there's no bloodshed and no collateral damage."

"I'll give Marcus a call now and tell him to shut it down and keep his people away."

"You be good Kane and if you can't be good then be safe."

"Always."

Kane made a couple of more stops then shot over to 8th to see if the building

inspectors had arrived. Pleasantly surprised he found both building inspectors and painters there. The building was in relatively good shape and needed little in the way of work. And after speaking with building inspectors, construction workers and the painters he was assured that it would take no more than two weeks for most of the work to be completed.

Aside from the Marcus situation his life was really starting to take form and with Mike's business acumen he would not only be able to rescue some young girls but would stand to profit too and maintain his lifestyle without a drop-off or he having to worry about the dangers of the streets. He only hoped Mattie was home so he could share the news with her.

Pulling up he saw the silver and black Sonata and his heart jumped.

"Hey baby. You here?"

"In the bedroom." Mattie shouted.

Kane headed up the stairs two at a time.

"You sure have been spending a lot of time in the bedroom lately."

"I was hoping you'd get the hint," Mattie said pulling him down and kissing him passionately.

"They tell me it's better in the Bahamas," Kane said handing her the manila envelope. Inside Mattie found two first class tickets to Freeport.

"*Oh my God!* I've always wanted to go to the islands. Oh baby. Bring yourself here and let me love my baby the way you should be loved."

"Save it. We have two weeks to do nothing but that. This is the honeymoon before the wedding. By the way how did Naomi's interview go?"

"She got in. They offered her a partial scholarship and a nice little package but nowhere as good as NYU so she's disappointed. She doesn't want the burden to be on you for the rest of her tuition so she's out now looking for a job but other than that she's fine."

"Well, let her look. It'll be a good experience for her to beat the streets trying to find a job. I have something set up for her when we get back though. In the meantime, is there anything you need to grab, a bathing suit, or anything else that you might need. Our flight leaves at ten a.m."

"If I don't have it I'll get it there."

"I hear ya."

"You know I've been fortunate. I should say blessed enough to make a few dollars and put away a few dollars but I have never had a chance to take a vacation or leave New York. And here you are talking about going to the islands. *Kane Close where have you been all my life?"*

Mattie was up the next morning at the crack of dawn.

"Kane you up?"

Kane stirred and turned to the small clock radio. It was six fifteen. Goodness. Kane thought about the wisdom of bringing a woman into his otherwise peaceful abode. She'd certainly shaken things up.

"Yeah sweetheart."

"C'mon. Breakfast is ready and wake Naomi up. Tell her breakfast is ready and she's going to be late for class if she doesn't get a move on."

Kane groaned before grabbing his robe and heading downstairs. Knocking on Naomi's door he repeated Mattie's orders. "C'mon girl. The drill instructor has summoned us."

"Huh? What time is it?"

Kane entered the kitchen and kissed Mattie.

"Morning sweetiepie." Mattie was always chipper in the morning but was oddly enough more than her usual exuberant self this morning.

"Goodness, Mattie I think you beat God up this morning."

"We have a plane to catch in less than three hours and with rush hour we'll be hard pressed to make it and you're not even dressed yet. You know they say you're supposed to be there an hour before boarding?"

Kane dropped his head and smiled. He'd never seen Mattie so excited.

"Eat baby. From what I hear they've really cut back on the airlines and you don't know when the next time you're gonna get a good meal."

"Yes ma'am," Kane said still smiling.

The flight out of LaGuardia was less than spectacular though Mattie squeezed Kane's arm so on takeoff that he still had her fingerprints when they landed.

Mattie was speechless upon arrival and the weather at somewhere around seventy-five degrees and sunny was a welcome relief after an unusually y cool fall in the city. The hotel which faced the beach was a four star and though the casino was directly across the street Mattie spent most of her time between the sandy beach and the crystal clear blue waters of the ocean when she wasn't snuggled up close to Kane. Every day was the same and Mattie wondered how life could possibly get any better. Here she was. Twenty years of enduring pure hell only to finally wind up on a beach with the love of her life, a man who loved her for more than the way she looked. What more could she possibly ask for?

Kane handed her a pina colada and for a moment Mattie thought of the girls on the strip. If they could only see her now.

"You hungry love?"

"Not especially but I could eat if you're ready?"

"I made reservations for us. I think we have just about enough time to grab a quick shower," Kane said holding out his hand to help her up.

"Why can't we just order room service? You know I'd much rather get undressed than dressed. You've got me hooked baby," Mattie said kissing him gently, seductively.

"I'm glad you think so and I'm in total agreement but there's something a little different I want you to see tonight love. So, will you humor me tonight Ms. Cruz?"

"For you Mr. Close, I would do anything."

Mattie was adorned in a plain black knit dress that gripped every curve and did nothing but accentuate her fine figure. And some simple silver hoops was all she needed to have every head in the restaurant turn in her direction.

"Mattie."

"Yes love."

"You know I had you come here tonight because I have a confession to make."

"Yes Kane?"

"Well, you know I've never made it a point to get close to anyone because of the nature of the work we're in and growing up on the streets I've seen too many people I've grown close to over the years get snuffed out before their time."

"I hear ya."

"But Mattie I've always despite my efforts let you get closer than most."

"I sure couldn't tell," she laughed, "I spent twenty years trying to seduce your ass and you wouldn't give me the time of day."

"You'd be surprised," he said leaving his seat and dropping to one knee. Heads turned. "And today this is to your persistence overcoming my resistance and after twenty years as my best and closest friend I'd like to take our relationship one step further and ask you to be my wife."

Kane then went in his blazer pocket and pulled out the largest most beautiful diamond Mattie had ever laid her eyes on as the whole room broke into applause and Mattie broke into tears.

"Well," Kane said nervously.

"After twenty one years of chasing you… Of course I do."

The next day Kane grabbed the houseboy and maid to be witnesses and they were married on the beach.

The two weeks were coming to a close and to Kane's surprise Mattie's mood became more and more somber.

"Everything okay sweetie?"

"It's just that everything is so peaceful and calm here. It's like paradise and just the thought of returning home has me a little depressed."

"Ahh baby. There a ton of little islands like this where the quality of life is just like this and they're affordable so anytime you want to take a month or two and just come down and relax and get out of the hustle and bustle of the city you can."

"Why do we even have to leave? I know it's cheaper to live here and we're basically retired so what's the rush and need to go back?"

Mattie was dead serious. It was obvious she was tired.

"My work isn't done yet Mattie. You know I'm under contract to Mike for the next six months and what happened to the women's facility you were so adamant about and all the young women you wanted to help?"

"You're right. I apologize for being so selfish."

Kane grinned.

"No need to apologize sweetheart. The islands will do that to you. I was the same way the first time I came here. Enjoy it though. We still have a couple of days left. I'm going down and lie on the beach and read you want to come?"

Mattie laughed.

"The last time you went down to read you had your sunglasses on and the book was upside down."

Kane laughed. He had to chuckle again as he got on the elevator but only to have his thoughts interrupted by his cell.

"Hey Mike what's up?"

"Did you do the damn thing?"

"Yeah man. We got married the day before yesterday."

"Congratulations my brother. I think marriage is right for you. You enjoying your stay?"

"Lovin' it and Mattie's having a ball. She doesn't want to go home."

"I'm sorry to have to put a damper on that but things haven't gone exactly as we expected and Marcus is a good kid but I think he's in over his head."

"Why what's up Mike. I thought we agreed to let the police do the dirty work this time around."

"They did. Did three or four raids and rounded up thirty-seven different people all a part of this African cartel working out of Brooklyn and Queens. I guess they didn't realize there was any money to be made uptown until they started looking for Eva but when they discovered that we were out there getting paid they saw another way to recoup their monies. But they're smart. Thirty six of the thirty seven arrests made were minors and almost all were first offenses so there's nothing really to keep them off the streets and the bail posted is more or less just an occupational hazard and pales in comparison to what they're bringing in so the police raids have done little."

"So what are our options?"

"Well, we're trying to get in touch with the man running the outfit. Once we do that we need to parlay with him—you know—sit down and have a face-to-face and either lay down the law and take back our blocks or work out an agreement so we can wholesale from him and sell his product at his costs."

"And if he doesn't agree? After all, he's holding all the cards right now."

"If they don't agree to either one then we go to war."

"Do we really want to do that Mike?"

"Hell no but we will if we have to but on their turf. From what I understand they are looked upon as stellar members of the community and like us don't want nothin' to disturb the groove but we gonna rain all over their parade. We're gonna make war on their turf not ours."

"Okay Mike we'll be on the next flight."

"Thanks and I am sorry Kane. Apologize to Mattie for me."

Kane hadn't even thought about Mattie. She was the best thing that had come his way in a long time and he truly hated to disappoint her but it would only be for a few more months and then he'd have a chance to make it up to her. He only hoped that she had the patience and could understand.

"Baby. Mike just called. We have to leave."

Mattie did not say a word. Kane took her in his arms and held her tightly.

"Six months baby. It's only six months."

"You do what you have to do Kane. I'll support whatever decision you make,"

Kane knew that if Mattie could have had her way she wouldn't have gone back tomorrow or ever but it wasn't her way to go against her man who she knew was in some ways even more tired than she was.

The flight arrived at Kennedy at a little after ten a.m. the following morning and as much as Mattie tried to stay upbeat she was nevertheless somewhat dejected by not only having to return but having to come back early. Still, she was coming back a newlywed with a loving husband who catered to her every need and after twenty years of having to fend for herself on the cold streets of New York City she was happy to at least have a man who not only had gotten her off the streets but promised to love, protect and provide for her until death do they part. So, despite the fact that their paradise had been forced to come to an early close she was adamant about putting on her best game face and being supportive.

Standing waiting for their baggage Kane's cell erupted.

"Kane here."

"Are you back in the city?"

"At the airport. Soon as we claim our bags we're on our way into the city."

"Good the meeting's scheduled for one o'clock at the Ritz Carlton."

"I'll see you there."

"Thanks again Kane."

"Not a problem."

As bad as Mattie felt about her forced return stepping into the warmth of her new home helped to relieve much of her anger and anxiety. But nobody seemed as happy as Naomi who came bounding down the stairs.

"Mattie. You're home. I am so glad to see you. I was so lonely," the girl said hugging Mattie.

"Glad to see you too," Kane said teasing Naomi who had ignored him completely.

"Oh, Kane you know I missed you too," Naomi said hugging Kane.

"I could tell," Kane said feigning anger.

"Stop being mean," Mattie said to a smiling Kane.

"Listen I gotta run. I need both of you to be ready by three o'clock. I have someplace I want to show you."

"Baby, I'm bushed."

"I've been hearing that a lot from you lately. You get a chance make a doctor's appointment Mattie."

"Oh Kane I'm alright. I'm just adjusting to a new lifestyle and believe it or not between you and Naomi I didn't run this much when I was in the streets. You two have just about run me to death."

"Just make the appointment."

"Yes sir." "And I'll see you at three. Be ready," Kane said slipping out the door.

"So how was your trip."

"Couldn't have been better," Mattie said holding out her hand to show off the carat and a half. "But I'll tell you about it when I wake up. Maybe Kane is right. Maybe I should make an appointment."

Chapter 5

Kane pulled around to the front of the Ritz Carlton to valet parking

where he was promptly given a ticket as he strode into the front of the plush hotel and was greeted by the maître d.

"I'm supposed to meet me a Mr. Michael Grayson here at one."

"Yes sir and you are?"

"Kane Close."

"Ah yes Mr. Close," the maître d said glancing his watch. "I believe they are awaiting you. Please follow me."

Kane who was always meticulously dressed sported a charcoal gray Brooks Brother's suit, white shirt with a gray and black paisley tie. From all outward appearances he looked as if he were ready for the weekly board meeting at A&G and no one would have guessed he was the primary muscle for one the largest and most feared crime syndicates in Manhattan.

Entering the bar all heads turned.

"Gentleman I'd like to introduce Mr. Close."

The group of men nodded accordingly and Kane chose the seat next to his good friend Mike.

"I was just informing the gentleman that the areas between 135th and 150th Streets and 8th Avenue have for some time now been real estate held and operated by The New Harlem Renaissance Conglomerate. And that their current presence is commensurate to our owning a home for some twenty years and one day Amtrak running a rain through our living without asking our permission or paying the tolls for the use of our land."

The middle aged man who sat opposite Mike smiled at the analogy. Graying at the temples he looked at Mike appreciatively. It was obvious he was no novice to these face-to-face meetings and moved gingerly through these proceedings but he was not one to be coerced and his mind seemingly made up long before meeting the likes of Michael Grayson. To him deliberations such as these had now simply become a matter of protocol. His objective and the objective of the cartel was to expand into as many different areas of the tri-state area as possible and bring as many of the independent crews under his wing as possible all for the growth and profit of the cartel. He saw Michael Grayson's operation as just another one to come into the fold.

"I'm impressed by both your colorful analogy and your delivery Mr. Grayson. And I really do appreciate your meeting with us on such short notice. Where I believe our current differences lie are not in motive but in ideology."

"Sir?"

"Give me a minute and I will explain although I am sure not quite so eloquently as you. You see Mr. Grayson my organization is made up primarily of immigrants trying to set foot in a foreign country which holds a fair amount of opportunity. And in our quest for this new opportunity we sometimes had to ask and at other times take. But in the process we were informed that some things were public and private and we took our liberties with that which was public and availed itself to everyone. The streets are public domain and like your organization we have taken them and run a very lucrative business. And like your organization we also abhor violence. Violence is bad for business so we try all costs to minimize it. Still, all too often it is the only means of establishing peace. I hope this isn't the case for us but I'm sure we have a superior product and because of the volume or quantity we sell we can undercut our competitors drastically thus eliminating little local crews and taking them under our wing and making it where we all stand to profit. I hope this is the case with your organization. We are however primarily a drug cartel and do not engage in prostitution or too many other illegal activities. And because we are concentrated in this one area we are the best at it. We would be happy to have you join us and in unison we can not only monopolize the drug trade in the five boroughs but become very rich in the process."

"You speak eloquently my friend and much of what you say is true you're right. Our ideologies are somewhat different. We set up this drug free zone not entirely with the idea of becoming wealthy but because we had a vision. This place known as Harlem is our home and the home of too many great Blacks that had a profound impact on

93

shaping this great nation of ours. But somehow in the turmoil of the times we lost our

community and all its richness to the drugs and violence that plagued our streets. Mr. Close and I sort to restore the community where good hard-working people weren't in constant fear. We weren't so naïve as to think we could eliminate the drug trade in Harlem so we simply put parameters on when and where vice will be permitted and that is only after the hard-working people of our neighborhoods have conducted their daily business.

Too many of our young people were dying needlessly in those same streets over petty cash and petty altercations and being jailed at record rates. We eliminated that by policing our own neighborhoods and setting up our own judicial system. It was a hard and painstaking process that has finally come to fruition after close to twenty years establishing this.

My oldest and dearest friend Mr. Close, who is semi-retired, is currently in the process of establishing a women's center to help give some of our young women and alternative to these very streets and prostitution. We are both very rich men so we are attempting to give something back to our community. You, Mr. Chase, on the other hand, are like the White realtors who inhabited and raped Harlem for so long. You don't see Harlem as home or a community but only a source of profit. So, yes I guess it is a difference in ideology but it is something that I am quite adamant about and although I respect your business acumen and your need for profit and monopolization I am sorry to say that we cannot join with you and all I ask is that you be gracious enough to leave Harlem out of your need to monopolize."

Mr. Chase hung his head despondently and sat for a while before attempting to speak.

"I am sorry to hear that Mr. Grayson. I had so hoped that our meeting today could have come to a more fruitful resolve."

And with that he stood and simply said 'gentleman' before turning to his lieutenants and nodded.

Kane, Mike and Marcus stood and looked at each other speechless.

"So, where does that leave us?" Marcus asked.

"War," Mike said seemingly unhinged by the whole transaction.

Not exactly sure of what that meant Marcus stared straight at Kane.

"And?"

"And you do nothing. Stay off the block and keep all your people on lockdown until you hear from me. We don't anyone getting caught up in the mix until we find out what this motherfucker's got in mind."

"Gotcha boss." Marcus said heading for his car.

Mike lit a cigarette and stared next to Kane.

"You know Mattie wanted to stay in the Bahamas," Kane said staring off into space and reflecting.

"Kind of wish you'd listen to her now don't you? No doubt they have better sense than we do."

"No doubt."

"I thought I was all done with this shit years ago."

"Money and power. That's all it basically boils down to. It's all about greed and ego."

"That's all."

"Now how many innocent young boys will have to die before he acquiesces and says enough?"

"Not many if I can help it. I don't think any if this is properly played."

"What do you have in mind," Kane queried.

"Simply going to use a ploy the government employed in the civil rights movement."

"And that is?"

"Kill the head and the body will follow. Ain't no need for all these young boys to die because of Chase's decision. We'll simply limit the war to Mr. Chase."

"So we eliminate Chase and squash the whole charade?"

"Precisely."

"And you think we can get to him?"

"We have to. And we need to knock off all top level management as soon as possible."

"Did Captain Murphy give you the list of names and addresses?"

"Yes but I want to avoid any collateral damage. It would be nice if we could get Chase before he arrives home but wherever we get him we don't want the families involved."

"C'mon Mike we've been down this road before. That's a no-brainer."

"To you but to a lot of these new kids there are no rules. I just want you to make sure that they get the message. Nobody cares if a well-known dope dealer gets offed but let a pregnant mother or child get caught up in the melee and they'll be hell to pay. We'll have not only the authorities searching for us but the local media and we want to keep this as quiet as we can."

"I gotcha. Fax me the names and addresses and I'll get right on it."

"No need for that. This is gonna be like the old days. I'll be riding shotgun."

Kane smiled at the thought. With Mike riding it would be like the old days and he wouldn't have to worry about anything. He wouldn't have to worry about watching anyone's back and even though it had been a minute since Mike had ridden he knew that Mike was one of the best to do it. They'd made quite a pair back in the day with Mike usually taking the initiative and having no qualms about pulling the trigger.

"I'll meet you at the house. How's five sound."

"Not good. I promised the girls I'd meet them at three and take them out."

"It's always been money over bitches Kane. Ain't nothin' changed has there?"

"No. Nothing's changed. I'll see you at five."

"Love you man."

"Love you more."

It seemed that ever since he'd committed to Mattie life had been nothing but one continuous disappointment after another. And the more he tried the harder it seemed. He should have never accepted Mike's proposition.

Long ago he'd accumulated enough money through his investments to make sure that his kid's kids lived comfortably so why was he still out here jeopardizing his life and now that he had a wife why was he jeopardizing his marriage as well. In the beginning it had simply been loyalty between two friends. That loyalty turned into a small empire but now after twenty years why were they still out here fighting these silly turf wars. For Kane there was no reason. Mattie was right. They should have been lying on some beach soaking up the sun and the cool breeze and reminiscing on all the good times that had come and gone and been dreaming of the future. So, why was he going home to strap up like he was some poor ghetto kid going to war?

Arriving home at a little after three Kane found both women fast asleep. Maybe he was finally getting a break at last. At least he wouldn't have to disappoint his girls on this day.

"I'll be there in five minutes. Look for me. You know I hate to blow the horn."

"I'll be out front."

"No. Kane. Stay in until I get there. You never know. They may be planning to hit us too."

Kane, a victim of countless street wars had already considered this and kept a vigilant eye on the street below from the third floor window. Nothing seemed out of place and there was little or no movement on the street below. It would have made sense to hit 'em early and when they least expected but he and Mike weren't novices when it came to the art of war and both new that arrogance and pride were often the downfall of many a competent man. And Chase appeared to be just that way. He was up and coming and basking in his own success. Arrogant to a fault he was just the sort that thought he could march in and just take over without so much as giving the opposition a second thought. And that's what Mike and Kane were hoping on.

Mike circled the block twice as Kane watched awaiting the call on his cell.

"I'm in the gray van."

"I see you. I'm on my way."

Kane tip-toed down the stairs exited the brownstone and put the double lock on before heading for the gray van.

"Haven't felt like this in a long time."

"And's not a feeling I want to know better," Kane said matter-of-factly. "A month ago I would haven't felt one way or another about this but now there's a whole lot more riding on it. The decisions I make not only affect me but could have repercussions for Mattie and Naomi and if anything ever happened to them I don't know what I would do."

"It's a dangerous world we live in my brother and I recognized that a long time ago. That's the main reason I never married or had kids."

"And you don't regret it?"

"Hell yeah. I regret it all the time. I can remember when we first started out, when we first started getting paid. Man those were some good times."

"Damn sure were."

"Remember when I got my first crib up in Sugar Hill."

"Yeah man. That was like my home away from home. I actually think I spent more time there than I did at the rest. I think that first year we had half the girls in Harlem there. Dominicans, Puerto Rican, Jamaican… Man that was like the Olympics. Every country was represented at one time or another."

The two men laughed.

"But you know when the crib was empty I used to think to myself. I'd be like 'man you came into this world alone and I'd say I'll be damn if I go out of this motherfucker

100

alone'. I used to say that all the time but as time went on and the more work we had to put in to hold on to what we had I wondered if bringing a woman and child into this hell was fair"

"So why didn't you get out?"

"Because my twisted sense of ethics really believes we werere doing some good. And I think it would be selfish for me to leave for the sake of myself and abandon the thousands that can now go and come from work without being threatened and harassed and even killed."

"So, you're sacrificing your life for the common good?"

"I'd like to think so but then my life isn't all that bad. There are residuals," Mike smiled.

"I'm sure. You were never a one woman man."

"Too many flavors out there for me to settle on one. My palette keeps changing. One day I have a taste for chocolate; the next day it's mango and banana. I'm too damn fickled and bore too easily to be with one woman. And there are weeks and months where I don't want the constant chatter. There are weeks where all I want to do is read without interruption so I guess I've grown into my reclusive lifestyle and it suits me fine for the most part."

"It always did."

"Okay listen up Kane. The first player is the accountant. A little middle-aged Jewish cat. He takes care of the cartels books. He's not really involved in the day-to-day operations but they're basically at a loss without him. But most importantly it sends a message. A lot of people will be shook up if we can get the books. We'll have a better idea of who's receiving what. We get the books and we'll have the names of all the judges, politicians and all the police that are receiving kickbacks. They'll run scurrying back to their holes and they'll put as much pressure on the cartel as we will in attempts to cover their own tracks. They may very well leave them six feet deep and face up if they feel they can finger them so he's our first stop. He runs the little bakery over on Nostrand. He works out of there and locks the doors at eight every night. On most nights he receives a police escort but tonight there won't be one. We're coming off as common street thugs trying to rob him and when we get him inside and get the books we're gonna lullaby his ass."

Kane said nothing as they sat in the car outside the tiny bakery. How many times had he'd been in similar situations? In the past he never gave it a second thought. Pulling the trigger on a rival that had all intentions of taking both his livelihood and life away only made it that much easier. But now he was second guessing his actions. No longer was killing second nature and as he sat there he wondered if the little Jewish baker had a family and kids. He wondered if he was a good father and would he be leaving them financially stable? The hollow sound of Mike's voice broke his train of thought.

"It's five to eight; time to do the damn thing," Mike said adjusting the gun in his waist band and checking his pockets. "Stand on the other side of the street and let me know when he's coming out."

Kane crossed the empty street, leaned on a parking meter, took out the pint of Wild Irish and sipped slowly. He nodded his head twice. That was the clue. As the man turned to lock the front door Mike was on him. Startled the man swung the door open and tried t retreat into the bakery. Mike was on him and no sooner than the man was in than Mike was raining the butt of his glock down upon the small Jewish baker's head. The man threw his hands up to ward off the blows and it was Kane who finally grabbed Mike's arm.

"It'll all be for nothing if you kill him."

Something must have hit home and Mike grabbed the man to his feet.

"Please don't hurt me. What do you want? I have money. I'll give you money but please don't hurt me anymore," the old man cried.

"Shut up," Mike said and with one swoop backhanded the man with the butt of his gun scattering several of the man's teeth across the floor. "Where do you keep the books."

The man seeing now what the gunmen wanted became hysterical.

"No please. I'll give you money. I have money," but seeing Mike's hand rise again he pointed to the backroom.

"Watch him," Mike said but there was little watching to do now as the man remained still shaking with fright. He looked up at Kane with begging eyes.

"Please don't take the books. They will kill me if anything happens to those books."

"It's a dangerous game you chose to be in," Kane said glancing away purposely not looking at the man.

"Got 'em," said Mike smiling before grabbing the man's arm and dragging him into the kitchen of the bakery and pulling him behind the counter. "You want the honors or should I?" Mike said staring at Kane as he screwed the silencer on and draped an apron over him just in case the blood splattered.

"It's on you," Kane said turning from the pleading little man and walking back into the front of the bakery.

It was a sound he'd heard countless times but one that had never bothered him until now.

At the car Mike Kane turned to Mike.

"Where to?"

"Akeem Akbar, Chase's first lieutenant. Brooklyn Heights."

In a matter of minutes the gray van pulled up in front of the newly renovated red, brick, condos and remained parked at the curb as the busy street bustled with preppy couples.

"How we gonna do this?" Kane asked.

"Old school style. We just gonna blast away with the shoddy's. Might be some collateral damage but that's all part of the plan. Our goal is to let these motherrfucker's know we're coming guns blazing and we ain't playing. We want to shake Chase's ass up. Let's see how he reacts under pressure. We ain't playing. He made his play and

104

now we're coming and we ain't half steppin'. We're comin' guns a blazing for his ass."

"Thought we were about the people and trying to preserve a better way of life. If we go in blazing and innocent people are hurt then we're no better than the thugs we're trying to guard them against. And for what. C'mon Mike. What kind of a statement will we really be making?"

"Don't tell me you're going soft on me Mike?"

"Ain't never been soft but c'mon Mike we ain't kids no more. We don't go in blastin' away. We're better than that. We supposed to take ol'boy out then that's what we do and we keep it nice and tidy. I'm a professional man. You want a drive by then you could have had Marcus and his crew do this shit. That ain't the way I work."

"Alright already. Damn! Don't get your panties all up in a bunch."

"C'mon Mike. I left it up to you. I thought you had a plan. This wild west shit ain't the way we do things."

"Okay, pardner then you make the call."

"What time is he supposed to arrive?"

"Should be here momentarily."

"Alright and where does he live?"

"Right across the street. Driver and bodyguard let him out right across the street in front of the building. He walks up to the gate…"

"Then that's where we drop him. At the gate. By the time he walks up to the gate he's out of pedestrian traffic and by that time his car driver and bodyguard should be rounding the corner or in the parking garage and out of the way. I'll take the target. If his bodyguard gets out with him then you drop him. I'll take the player and drop him at the gate and clearly away from traffic."

"Sounds like a plan."

"Much better than blasting away like some west coast gangbangers," Kane said disgustedly.

"Post up. I'll take the boss. You take the bodyguard."

Kane moved across the street and took up his post in front of the gate to wait. Mike, who up to this point hadn't entered into the day-to-day street activities seemed to be relishing his new found role as tough guy and Kane wondered if he weren't enjoying it all a little too much. He suddenly got the sense that this wasn't the same person that he'd gone to battle with so many times before and on so many occasions to preserve what was rightfully theirs.

Kane pulled the bottle out again and leaned, sipping slowly, keeping his other hand on the gun in his pocket. It was quiet now and there was little traffic. Most people were at home now and tucked away for the evening when Sanchez walked up. He was a happy little Nigerian with a head that seemed to erupt from his shoulders like lava from a volcano. He approached the gate nodded at Kane and walked up to the steps where Mike was standing. Again he nodded before putting his pass code in. Mike approached the man from the back and put the nine millimeter to the back of his head and squeezed. The man fell to the ground as the blood squirted in spurts. Ignoring this Mike bent over and put the gun to his temple and fired twice more before walking briskly down the steps and over to the waiting van.

"Two down, one to go." Mike said nonchalantly. "Over to Fort Greene and that should do it."

Kane was in another world. It had been years since he'd been involved in a hit and he hadn't missed it. He'd never enjoyed it. It was a job requirement. Nothing more but he had never relished it the way Mike seemed to now. Perhaps it was his inactivity. Perhaps it was the fact that Mike had always enjoyed this part of the job. The danger, the excitement, the mere rush he got from putting someone to their final rest. He'd read about it and never shared the profile of killers. No, instead he wrestled with the demons that constantly clouded his thoughts. He was no killer. He was a survivalist. He did what he had to do to live but he had never taken any pleasure in it the way Mike had. And when this was over he was through. It was time to change his life; time to undo some of the wrong he'd done and if God was a forgiving God the way Mattie said he was he was going to work just as hard as he could to once again be in His good graces.

"Now all we have to do is hope and pray that Chase is a s arrogant and egotistical as I believe him to be. If he is he won't have a need for bodyguards or a freeze. As long as he thinks he's invincible then he's susceptible."

"Where's he rest at?"

"The second brownstone from the corner. By my calculations and from everything Captain Murphy said he should be pulling up somewhere in the next fifteen minutes or so. When we lay him down that should be it. Business as usual."

"For you."

"And what's that supposed to mean?"

"That means after tonight I'm out. No more consulting. No more meetings. No more advising Marcus. No more senseless killings over turf that neither you nor I own. We're not preserving the legacies of Malcolm and Langston. Half of these fools out here in these streets don't know who Malcolm or Langston are? Can't you see that? I've had it. I'm done. All we're doing is getting rich off of people's misery."

"Okay. And? I'm feeling to see the problem," Mike said smiling.

"The problem is if we're not killing them with the dope then we're gunning 'em down. It's senseless and I just can't do it anymore and look myself in the mirror."

"Oh, so after twenty years you've suddenly grown a conscious. Or is it now that you're paid you've grown soft. You've made enough. Is that it."

"Give it a name. Call it what you like. After tonight I'm out. You can get someone else to do your dirty work."

"Hold up. Fuckin' with you I lost focus. There he is in the navy blue trench and ain't no way we gonna get to him before he gets inside the building. C'mon Kane we're gonna have to take him from here."

108

Not having time to put the silence on the first bullet exploded ove the fat man's head alerting him. Chase Devinger turned when he heard the shots and with the speed of a thoroughbred went into the pocket of his jacket and what seemed to be one fell swoop pulled out a gat and returned fire. Bullets hit the van causing the two men to dash for cover.

Chase was now seeking cover and moved first to an old garbage can and then to a parked car at the curb where he resumed fire. Firing from both sides resumed for another two to three minutes until there was a blood curdling scream from Mike.

"Kane I'm hit."

And with that all firing ceased and the fat man retreated to his own front door where he turned to scream at Kane and Mike.

"You motherrfuckers want war then I'll show you war."

Kane moved around the car and saw Mike lying there. He'd taken one in the chest. Badly hit he was fading fast. Kane moved quickly now and grabbed Mike under the arms and pulled him to the passenger side of the van and lifted him in but Mike didn't cry out. It was almost as if he hadn't noticed the softball sized hole and the blood spilling from him.

"He wasn't supposed to be armed. Captain Murphy gave me bad intel. We got to get this motherfucker Kane. We worked too hard to build it. We got to get him Kane."

"We'll get him Mike. We'll get him," Kane said peeking out the driver's side window before jumping in, gunning the motor and heading to the closest hospital. St. Mary's in the heart of Bedford Stuyvesant was crowded as usual and the lobby looked more like a mash unit as people layed around at random. There were mothers screaining, infants crying, and men with gunshot wounds moaning all vying for some attention while nurse Ratchet moved at a snail's pace. She had long ago grown accustomed to the pain and suffering that came along with being born poor in the ghetto.

"Nurse my friends been shot in the chest and needs help immediately."

She looked up at him from her paperwork and raised an eyebrow.

"I'm not sure if you had a chance to look around but this is the ER and all of these people before you have serious cases and need help immediately. Unfortunately there is only me and I am doing the best I can under the circumstances."

Kane wondered how many times she'd said those very same words and seeing that his mere presence was having little or no presence decided on another approach. Looking at her name tag he changed his whole tactic. He focused his eyes on her dark brown face and chubby form and did his best to try and locate her best quality. It was difficult.

"Cynthia. May I call you Cynthia."

"Sir, as I told you before…"

Kane cut her off mid-sentence.

"I understand you fully Cynthia. These people were here first and they by all right should go first. I wasn't even thinking about that. I was just admiring your hair do. And I sure would like to get that for my sister. Does it have a name?"

She was smiling now and Kane wondered how long it had been since anyone had paid any attention to the woman.

"They're called cold waves," she said now noticing the man in front of her. She smiled showing the gold tooth in the front of her mouth. Kane wondered why people chose to let everyone know that they were ghetto. "You really like them? You know it's my first time having them put in and I really wondered if I was too old for them."

"You're only as old as you feel. How old are you anyway?"

"How old do you think I am?"

"I'll tell you in a minute. Let me go check on my friend."

"Oh that's right. Your friend. Let me take a quick look."

Mike's head was slumped down on his chest and blood had started to seep from between his lips. Seeing him nurse Cynthia screamed.

"Triage!" Two orderlies rushed out and put Mike on a stretcher and wheeled him through the swinging doors. Mike sat down and Cynthia returned with a clipboard.

"I'm so sorry. I never realized. I hope he makes it."

In days past Kane would have had to sit there alone with his thoughts. But now Kane pulled the cell phone out and called Mattie..

"Hey baby. Did you stop by to pick us up?"

"I did but you were both sleep. I figured you must have been tired from all that shopping you two have been doing the last couple of days."

Mattie laughed.

"I'm exhausted but I think we're finally finished. Naomi will be the best dressed young lady on campus."

"I'm sure she will."

"Where are you?"

"I'm at St. Mary's in Bed Stuy."

"Oh my God. Is everything alright? Are you hurt? Give me a few. I'm on my way."

"No, Mattie. I'm fine. I'm here with Mike. He's been shot."

"Mike?"

It was true. In the last twenty years Mike had been almost completely divorced from any street activities and as a businessman he hardly ever engaged in any types of violence.

Nowadays he had almost made it customary to delegate any action that involved gunplay to Kane or the police. Now here he lay close to death.

"How's he doing?"

"Chest wound and it doesn't look good."

"Okay, I'm on my way."

"Baby you don't have to."

"I'm aware of that. I'll see you in half an hour."

"Baby?" Kane repeated but the phone had already gone dead. Kane smiled. He couldn't count the times he'd been through similar situations and he'd always been the one those around him leaned on for strength. He had to admit that it was good to have Mattie to lean on.

Twenty minutes later Mattie arrived and Kane recounted the night's activities. Mattie hung her head.

"What is it they say in the Godfather?"

Kane had been thinking the same thing ever since he'd gotten the call in the Bahamas.

"Every time we try to get out they pull us back in again.'

"Is that how you really feel Kane?"

"Yes, and before this even happened I told Mike that this was my last night. The senseless violence is all a bit much for me."

"Perhaps he understands your sentiments a little better now," Mattie said almost sorry she'd let the words slip.

Kane shot her a look that confirmed her mistake.

"C'mon Mattie. Let's see if there's any word."

No sooner had he gotten up than the doctor came out.

"Are you Mr. Close?"

"I am."

"Dr. Mohammed. Mr. Grayson is requesting your presence. Please hurry sir. He's fading fast."

"Is he going to make it doc?"

"Mr. Grayson has quite an extensive amount of internal bleeding and I'm afraid there's not much we can do."

"Thank you doctor."

Kane entered the room.

"How you doing old man?"

"Hurts like a motherfucker but listen Kane. The doc said I don't have long but don't let that motherfucker get away with this. My lawyer will take care of everything else. He will give you the keys to the ranch. If anything were to ever happen to me then I left everything to you. I love you man."

"I love you more man."

"Oh and Kane..."

"Yeah Mike."

"You know what we were talking about in the car."

"Yeah Mike."

"I think you were right," Mike's head fell to the side and Kane knew his man and best friend was gone. Bending down he kissed him on the forehead and felt a tear drip before glancing one last time and then turning and leaving his friend forever.

"How's he doing?" Mattie asked seeing the strain on her man's face.

"He's gone," Kane murmured grabbing Mattie's arm and leading her through the sick and infirmed.

"I'm sorry Kane," she said knowing her words were little consolation for Kane's grief.

"You know Mattie… Mike was the only true friend I ever had. If only he could have left the streets alone."

"You're hurt and I understand that but he made it a whole lot better place to live for a lot of us."

"I suppose he did but look at the price he had to pay."

"The greater the deed the greater the price."

"You've become quite the philosopher," Kane said smiling.

"So, where does that leave us?" Mattie said praying that Kane would stay true to his word and Mike's death would not only serve as a warning but as an end to his ties with the devil. In Mattie's eyes he was the only connection Kane had to his past. Men and their chivalrous nature... Loyalty would get him killed. Kane had to see that now and if she meant anything at all to him she was sure he'd walk away now.

"Like I told Mike. After tonight I'm out. His last request was that I meet with his lawyer and settle his affairs and get the man that did this to him. I will meet with his lawyers to make sure his affairs are in order but as far as seeking revenge I am sorry I can't honor his last requests."

"Oh, Kane," Mattie said leaning over and hugging him tightly.

"Careful woman," Kane said swerving into the other lane. "I didn't survive the night for you to kill me," he laughed throwing his arm around her and squeezing her tightly.

They made love that night, Mattie giving herself to him but it wasn't the same and although it was wonderful Mattie sensed something different. Mattie felt the anger, the sadness and his apprehension. She felt his exhaustion but most of all she felt his love. When he'd spent himself she held him tightly in her arms until he was snoring softly. And she prayed that there would be peace in the coming days.

But in the coming day's peace was as far from the realm of possibilities as it had been twenty years ago when they'd started out. And after twenty years it seemed as if he hadn't grown a bit. Two days after Mike had been killed he'd arranged an appointment with Mike's attorney and been sprayed leaving the house. He'd gone unscathed but the police counted twenty eight spent bullet casings in front of his house.

Later that day Kane met with Mike's lawyer.

"I'm sorry about Mr. Grayson and congratulations to you. He told me you were getting married."

"Thank you."

"However, I do believe that Mr. Grayson may have seen this day coming even as far as last week. He changed his will the day you were married and left you as executor. He also left you the home in the Keys as well as the condo which he made the final mortgage payments on last week. The rest of his assets which are worth some eighteen point four million are tied up in stocks and bonds and are kept in three separate off-shore accounts and a Swiss bank account. Mr. Grayson was also involved in several rather lucrative real estate properties in and around the city. Now I don't know but I'm sure you

have your own attorney and you may want him to look over Mr. Grayson's will and holdings but from what he tells me all you're interested in is an early retirement. So, sir if I may give you my advice and it's the same advice I gave Mr. Grayson I would liquidate my real estate holdings in and around the area except for those prime holdings here in Manhattan and simply live on the proceeds of those and enjoy my life and my family but that's my personal feelings. I hope I haven't overstepped my bounds."

"Not at all sir. Tell me something how long were you Mike's attorney?"

"Twenty four years."

"And he trusted you?"

"Like a brother. I was a struggling lawyer when I came out of Columbia Law School and Mike picked me up and forced me to continue my education in all forms of law and under his tutelage made me a very rich man. I owe everything I have to Mr. Grayson."

"And do you know how Mr. Grayson came to acquire his wealth?"

"That was something he never made me privy to. All I know is that you and he were partners and he loved you like a brother."

Kane smiled. Mike had always played things close to the vest and in twenty four years had never given his own lawyer access to his business.

"Okay, Mr. Rosenberg. I appreciate all you've done for Mike over the years and would appreciate if you'd get all the paperwork in order for me to take over his estate."

"I've already had it prepared Mr. Close. All I'm going to need is your signature here to make you executor of his estate. But perhaps you'd like your attorney to look it over first."

"I don't think that will be necessary. Where do I sign?"

The lawyer who was now getting on in years stood up and walked around to where Kane was sitting and handed him the pen and pointed to the line.

"There will be substantial taxes on the inheritance but ask your lawyer to seek out tax shelters and write offs and he should be able to decrease them considerably."

"Okay, Mr. Rosenberg this is the way we're going to do this. I want you to do whatever it is that you do. Seek tax shelters and anything else that will decrease the taxes on that money. And when you get finished I'd like for you to draw up a contract in the same exact manner that you and Mike had."

Rosenberg's face lit up like a Christmas tree.

"You know Mr. Grayson was my only client. He wanted it that way. Said he only wanted me to concentrate on his financial affairs and growing his assets. I'm glad that you have put the same trust in me Mr. Close or I'd be facing unemployment."

"Not a problem. Mike thought the world of you so you come with the highest of recommendations. And if that's all I'll be awaiting your call."

"Give me a day or two and I'll be in touch."

"Oh and before I forget, I'd like you to set up a line of credit for my wife. Say five hundred thousand for my wife Mattie. Here's her number and make her the beneficiary and executor of the estate should something happen to me. And please make that your first priority. Then I'd like for you to give her a call and set up a meeting at the new women's center and make suggestions on how to set it up where it can not only provide the best possible service but become funded through grants and not out of pocket as it is currently."

"Will get right on it."

"Oh and Mr. Rosenberg thanks for everything."

Chapter 6

Everything was so tense these days and everyone was
losing money. A moratorium covered a good deal of
Harlem and no drugs could be found on the street. Fiends
were fiending and the dope dealers cried over their losses
but when Kane said there was a moratorium no one wanted
to test the wrath of the new boss. Everyone that knew him
knew that he was not one to be fucked with. And so the
streets were empty and for the first time since Kane could
remember Harlem was quiet.

On the third day of the moratorium to honor the late
Michael Grayson and old heroin addict known only as
'Willie' decided to test Kane's moratorium and was
brutally beaten then shot and hung from a streetlamp with a
note attached that simply said moratorium. No more
messages were needed. Not even Chase's dope runners
were seen. And the moratorium went on for a week after
the funeral which Rosenberg and aside from Kane and a
few boyhood friend's was rather small and low-key.

And for the first time in his life Kane could walk the streets of Harlem realizing what it must have been like when his grandparents had first come here from the South seeking a better life. This is what it was supposed to be like. This is what they expected when they left the South. A better life, a better quality of life with all the opportunities America had to offer. They like so many others had come seeking the American dream only to watch their dreams become an American nightmare. Now here he was with the chance to transform it back into what they saw; into their vision of what America was supposed to be, the ideal, the American dream.

It had been a pleasant walk. He usually ran from Sugar Hill over to the Polo Grounds and then back home but today he was content just to walk down St. Nicholas and stop into the local groceries and pick up a few items here and there. He was a fixture here and enjoyed mingling with the friendly folks in the neighborhood and despite the fact that there was a war going on he feared nothing and no one. Stepping back into the house he was greeted by the sweet aroma of biscuits baking and bacon frying.

"Hey Sweetie. How was your run?"

"I didn't run. I did a little something different today. I just walked through the neighborhood. It has a different feel to it."

"There's a good reason for that."

"I'm listening."

"People see you differently now. How many times did you try to purchase something this morning and people said 'no that's alright' or 'it's on the house'?"

Kane thought about it and had to admit that she was right but then that wasn't uncommon. They'd always done that here or there.

"You're the new 'King of Harlem'. That's the way they see you now. You're basically 'the mayor'. You don't know how many calls I've gotten since Mike's death asking me what your plans are. All of the girls have called asking me either when you're going to lift the moratorium or to tell me to tell you that they're really starting to feel the pinch."

"And what do you tell them?"

"I tell them the truth. I tell them that I have nothing to do with Kane's business and that they should address you because I am not only tired but retired."

"And how's that working for you?"

"It's not. It got so bad that I just turned my phone off. I actually ordered myself another phone."

"I'm sorry baby. Where's Naomi?"

"She had an eight o'clock class."

"What time does she get out?"

"What's today? Wednesday? She should be home in the next half an hour or so."

"Good. What do you have on tap for today?"

"Actually, I'm free. Wanted to do a little research on women in prison and specifically in The Tombs. I want to know the recidivism rate and what programs are out that lower it and give alternatives to prison and the streets. Then I was going to go out for lunch with the some of the girls tomorrow and brainstorm a little around ways to help and dissuade these young girls from letting the streets govern their lives."

"Okay well I have a little something to show you that might help you in your quest to being Harlem's lil version of Mother Theresa."

"Oh, stop patronizing me silly. It's the least I can do."

"I'm just teasing. Listen, I'm going to close my eyes for a minute. Let me know when Naomi gets here."

"Okay baby. By the way, just out of curiosity, when are you going to lift the moratorium?"

"I'm going to meet with Marcus and a few others when I finish with you and Naomi to let them know just that. Probably tomorrow although I wish I never had to."

"And I hope you're grooming Marcus or somebody to take the reigns so you can fulfill your promise to me about getting out."

"I'm working on it. Trust me Mattie there's nothing better that I'd like to do. Wake me when Naomi gets here."

Kane thought about what Mattie had said and had to admit that it felt good to be the king but he also knew that with the title came a ton of responsibilities that he had always been okay with letting someone else bear. The fact remained that he hadn't bargained for this but with Mike's death he was the natural successor. Still, it was a torch that he would gladly pass on to the first applicant that claimed it.

"Kane honey. Naomi's home and we're ready to go."

Kane awoke from his deep sleep. He hadn't realized just how tired he was but with all that had taken place in the last two or three days between the impending war and Mike's death he'd been overwhelmed and things were only going to get worse the way he saw it.

He'd gotten word to Chase that in respect for his closest and dearest friend he was having a two week moratorium on all activities and Chase had respectfully assented. Today was the last day and he'd sent word again that they should have a face-to-face before any more blood was spilled. That was two days ago and he had yet to receive a reply.

Dressing quickly he was glad fall was turning into winter. With the weather turning colder people were far less inclined to just hangout. that meant fewer casualties should it turn into a full-fledged war. Most of these young cats had never been in a full-fledged war and weren't battle tested. He wasn't sure how they'd react and aside from a few stone cold killers on the payroll Kane knew he had no real soldiers whom he could depend on. There was the crew in South Jamaica. Most of whom had started out with him but had been gotten their own real estate. They were his boys but he hadn't really stayed in touch and most were fat cats now with no more interest in a war or taking to the mattresses than he was but the time for parlaying had come to an end or so it seemed since Chase wasn't willing to have a sit down. And following Mike's orders to assassinate them at their homes not only made him vulnerable every time he stepped foot out of his house but the girl's too.

He'd need to provide them with a few safe houses should things really begin to escalate so they'd at least have a safe haven and they'd be protected. Funny thing was he'd never been a proponent for war and if he'd been a true consultant Mike would have had asked him what he thought and he would have agreed to a partnership with Chase with certain stipulations but there had been no compromise and the little Jewish baker with the wife and kids who had no active role in the whole state of affairs was now just a memory. So, was the African who had nodded on his way home. Gone because of Mike's inability to see anything but his own nearsighted vision. And now here he was stressed on the brink of an upcoming war that would send countless soldier who were only there because the other alternatives were none and non-existent. How many innocents would be caught in a deadly crossfire that they had nothing at all to do with?

"Kane where are you?"

The sound of Mattie's voice brought him back to earth.

"Sorry. I just have a lot on my mind."

"He didn't call you back did he?"

"No."

126

"Just give it to him. Give it all to him. We'll be fine. How much are you worth? C'mon sweetheart. How much is enough? Baby, what's it going to take?"

"I would if he just sit down and talk but I think the time for talking is over as far as he's concerned. He's already felt the loss. He's hurting, angry and if I were him and had lost the people closest to me all I'd want to do is strike out in revenge."

"Oh c'mon Kane you make it sound like two kids in a playground fight at school."

"What do they say? Men are little boys that just got taller."

"Well, break the stereotype and find him and force him to come in and sit down. Explain to him that you're not Mike and all you want is peace. Don't you know that the police won't interfere? That's all they want to see is Black men out there killing each other off. Explain that to him. Make him understand that war is a lose lose situation for everyone involved."

"I wish I could."

"Do you want me to find him and bring him to the table?"

"No, Mattie. You stay out of this!" Kane said adamantly pulling up in front of the building whose face had been recently restored. The awning read '8th Avenue Women's Center'.

Naomi sat listening but as was her way said nothing.

"What's this?' Mattie asked only too glad to change the subject. "This is new. Oh this is splendid Kane. I was considering checking out some of the one's around the city and getting some ideas on how we can best serve our own unique population. You know they have them in almost every place you don't need them but right here in Harlem where we need it most they don't have anything for our young ladies."

"Well, they do now," Kane said smiling.

"I'm just sad we didn't get here first. Still, I'm glad there's someone that appreciates the need for it."

"Oh, but I'm thinking we did get here first."

"What do you mean?'

"Come on."

"Oh my goodness. It's gorgeous."

Kane grabbed Naomi by the hand and sat her at the front desk in the lobby.

"Stay here for a minute beautiful," he said to Naomi before taking Mattie's hand and leading her to the large office in the rear of the building. The large mahogany desk and matching furniture were exquisite.

"See this is what I'm talking about. When I get our center set up I want it to be modeled after this. This is what I'm talking about."

Kane pulled her to the captain's chair behind the large desk and eased her down into the desk.

"Oh, Kane this it. When we get it set up I want it to be just like this."

"You said that already," Kane smiled before pulling out a name plate that read 'Director/Mrs. Mattie Close'.

"Yep. Just like that."

"It's yours Mattie. The women's center is yours. This is your office."

"Oh my God. Kane are you serious?"

"Yes, baby," he said handing Mattie a set of keys. "I don't have time to give you a complete tour but there are four apartments upstairs that are vacant but I don't know what you want to do with them. They're beautiful and when you come back tomorrow take a look and then we'll sit down and weigh the options. C'mon Mattie I want to talk to Naomi real quick before I go and meet with Marcus."

"Kane come here," Mattie said standing and holding her arms open. She hugged Kane tightly and felt the tears rolling down her face.

"What's wrong baby."

"Nothing," Mattie said. "It's funny when I married I thought that there was little more than a woman could want. After working all those years I never had any hopes or dreams when it came to settling down. After all, who would marry a whore? But then you shocked me and asked me to marry you. And when you did I said what more can I ever ask for and now this. I'm just overwhelmed and to think you believe that I can actually do this? I'm just overwhelmed. You keep shocking me. I am truly in awe. You're a good man Kane."

"I try to be," Kane said. "C'mon. Let's go baby. I gotta run."

Kane led her back to the outer lobby where Naomi sat bopping her head and leafing through a Time magazine.

"Naomi Mattie tells me you've been looking for a job."

"Yes. I have been. Every day I go here and there but nobody wants to hire me. Everyone says that I have no experience but how can I get experience if no one will hire me?"

"I understand. So how can we remedy that problem Naomi?"

"I don't know. I guess I'll just keep looking and maybe something will turn up."

"Well, Naomi I think I may have a way for you to get some experience."

The young girl's face lit up as she pulled the ear buds from her ears and slammed the magazine shut.

"How is that Kane?"

"On Monday morning a woman will be in to train you on how to properly answer the phones and the proper procedure to handle prospective clients for Mattie's women's center. This will be your desk while you're in school and will give you some spending change so you won't have to feel like you're relying on Mattie and me."

And like he'd done with Mattie he gave Naomi her very own nameplate. But there were no tears this time as Naomi leaped from behind the desk and leaped up wrapping her legs around Kane.

"Oh, Kane you are the best," Naomi said screaming excitedly.

"C'mon ladies. You can come back tomorrow and rummage through everything but right now I have someplace to be and you two are not going to make me late."

Mattie who was in the midst of exploring found her way to the front door where Kane and Naomi were waiting.

"It is absolutely fabulous. And who picked the colors and décor."

"I just went with brown since that's your favorite color and then all shades of it."

"You are some kind of something special Mr. Close? I just wish I was younger so I'd have more time to spend with you."

"It's not the amount of time. It's what you do with the time you have m'lady."

Pulling up at the house they both kissed him.

"I have got to be the richest man in the world," Kane said. "I should be home in an hour or two at the latest so you can keep telling me how wonderful I am."

Kane drove the few blocks to the Dunbar Apartments
where he found thirty or forty young men in attendance.
Walking through the crowd a loud cheer went up.

"We going to war boss?" Born Ready shouted over the roar
of the crowd.

"I certainly hope not," Kane mumbled on his way in to the
trap house.

Once inside most of the men were anxious to hear what it
was their new boss had in store for them.

"Yo," Marcus said in an attempt to get the young men's
attention. "Listen up!"

The young men quieted almost immediately. "I'm sure
everyone here knows Kane. He's the one most responsible
for keeping the peace and keeping the police away. You
never have to watch your back and we all are getting paid
and can feed our families because of one reason and one
reason only and that's this man right here. Kane Close!"

A cheer went up that was almost deafening. Kane stood up
and raised his hands and again the room fell silent.

"I'm glad to see y'all. That means you're still in business
and still doing well. Twenty years ago my partner and best
friend had our own little crew and thought we were the
hardest niggas out on the block. And I guess we were
'cause twenty years later we were still out on the block.
Two weeks ago a few out-of-towners decided that they
were going to come in and take over the blocks we worked
so hard to call our own. My partner and your boss Mike G.
was killed trying to defend what is ours. We retaliated and

now we are in a full-fledged war. Born Ready asked me if we were at war. He seemed anxious. Well, I can tell you as a soldier and war veteran that you don't want to go to war. You don't want to die and you don't want to see your boys die. I know I would rather be stacking mad paper and lovin' my woman than thinking about dying. Problem is everyone doesn't think that way and so this outfit from Brooklyn has decided that we either join them or die trying to keep what's ours. I sent a peace offering with the hopes that we could have a face-to-face and work something out instead of dying in the streets and interrupting business but they declined. So, for you young cats out there that don't know. Stay in, stay strapped and be ready to go.

We do nothing here where our families are. We take care of what's ours and we didn't ask for war or for there to be unnecessary casualties on our end so we're going to take it to Brooklyn and camp out and post up in the cut and wait for them and pick them off at every chance and every avenue we get until they concede. I hope and pray that it doesn't last more than a couple of weeks but during the entire I want us to take to the mattresses. That is I don't want to show our faces at all. We'll be broken down into units and each unit will have a lieutenant who will receive orders from me and only me. My lieutenants will make sure you will have food and what other necessities are needed and you will not leave the trap house for any reason unless you receive orders from me to engage them. Is that understood? No women, no family members and absolutely no children are to frequent you at any of these trap houses. If there is a family emergency have your lieutenant contact me and I will get word as to how to handle the situation. Say goodbye to your girlfriends, your wives or your boyfriends tonight. Make good love like it's the first and the last time 'cause Lord knows when you'll get to smell the pussy again. Does everyone here understand? Love you fam and good luck."

The young men were not the least bit deterred by Kane's words and most seemed anxious and several could be heard mumbling with zeal that they were going to war. A few of the lieutenants who had been down this road before were not quite so enthused.

"They don't know what's ahead of them," Marcus remarked to Kane.

"Unfortunately they're going to find out soon enough," Kane replied.

"If they could only see the bigger picture. They don't know that while they're out there shooting off their freezes that they can't make any money 'cause everything comes to a halt during war and they'll never be the same after they take a life. They don't get it."

"That's the crime of youth."

"What's that Kane?"

"The crime of youth is the lack of experience. Knowing and experiencing the pain and hardship can only strengthen a person and make a boy a man."

"I don't know if I ever went through that phase."

"Not all of us have to. Just like I knew a couple of months ago when I told you that it was time to get out. I didn't have to encounter a bullet or be dragged off to jail to know that I was lucky to have survived the streets for this long and would be wise to get out while I was still healthy and try a different avenue of life. And that's why I'm telling you that as soon as this war is over with and perhaps even before it's over with I'm turning this too over to you."

Marcus smiled.

"I learned the last time you offered me something to be careful of what I wished for," Marcus said laughing. "I appreciate the love Kane but I think I'll pass on that one at this stage of my life."

Kane was tickled seeing how much the young man had grown in the past few months since he'd been put in his new position.

"Funny thing about this business. Unlike other businesses you can't just turn down a promotion Marcus."

"I'm aware of that but I don't fully have this position down yet."

"You'll be fine Marcus I'll be with you every step of the way."

"That's what I'm afraid of."

That night Kane sat in his favorite recliner in the living room. CNN was on but his thoughts were elsewhere. Kane watched as both Mattie and Naomi bustled around the house. Printers in all three rooms buzzed at the same time. Mattie sat across from Kane poring over books on child abuse, prison reform and recidivism. She'd already amassed a bevy of papers and articles on the high school drop-out rate for teens in the New York City school system and the progressive reform programs that were meeting with success in curbing this trend.

"Kane may I use your phone?"

"Tonight's not a good night babe," Mattie immediately stopped leafing through the papers and looked up. She reminded Kane of a Black Sarah Palin with her keen features, the tight bun and her schoolmarm glasses at the tip of her nose.

"Oh baby, I was so excited and so concerned about the center that I forgot to ask how your meeting went."

"Went alright. Was more like a coronation than a meeting but I guess it went alright. I hope you plan on adding an educational component to the center. These young kids are so lost. It's really sad to see. They're so anxious to go to war as if taking another person's life is really going to make them men. I mean these kids are chomping at the bit and I'm dreading it and hoping for a reprieve. This is Mike's war not mine. I was and still am totally against it but I'm shutting it all down and just going to have to play it out."

"I was wondering why you were so quiet but then I'm over here so wrapped up in my own little thing that I neglected to ask you how you were doing? I do apologize husband. But as far as the war Kane; it might not be as bad as you think and may actually help a lot of them."

"How so?"

"Well, all of those that wanna rush in to this bloodbath only want to do so because they don't know. What they do know is what they've gotten from television. But to actually be on the frontlines and hold their best friend who's dying in their arms will be an eye opener for many of them and make them think. Look at Marcus who was jumping up and down when you promoted him to your position. He's not so quick to jump this time around. For most of our kids coming out of broken homes with no father to guide them and a school system that's goal is to fail them experience is their only teacher and though it pains me to say so this war may be a good thing."

"I hear you. It's a shame it has to be this way. I wish I could set up some youth centers for our young men to go along with your women's center. These kids need strong positive role models to give them direction."

"You're absolutely right and there's no reason you can't do it."

"You're right on both accounts. And I do believe that a war will be food for thought and most will suffer remorse and won't be so quick to want to be soldiers in the future. And as much as I've been applauded the last few days how do you think I'll be received when I knock on someone's door to tell them their son is dead?"

"I don't envy you General Kane," Mattie laughed hoping to make light of the situation. "Let's just hope it's nothing protracted and it all comes to an end in a day or two."

"Been praying for that since Mike's death. You know this was Mike's call. I opposed it from the very beginning."

"You know I know that. But it's too late for hindsight now. Your job now is to save as many lives as you possibly can."

"And how would you propose I do that?"

"That's not my forte but there are several ways I'd approach the whole situation. Obviously you can send a statement and hit 'em hard and disrupt his trade but you and I know most of these mooks running things out here don't give a damn about these kids. All they want to know is where there money is. Half of 'em would snuff a kid themselves if their money is short so you're not really hurting them in a street war. Most of 'em could care less about the lives wasted and there are so many kids lacking and ready to replace them that it doesn't make sense to make war in that way."

Mattie had Kane's interest.

"What you need to do or better yet what I would do if I were in your shoes is make sure all of your assets were secure yet accessible and you had absolutely no paper trail to speak of. Then I would turn to a trusted attorney, maybe Mike's and let him see Chase's books. Ask him how to proceed as far as leaking small bits of incriminating evidence at regular interval unless he gives his word that there will be a truce and there will be no play uptown by he or any other outfit. In other words, not only would he not try to make inroads into your business but would police your business free of charge against any other groups with the same ideas in the future. In time you could probably strengthen the alliance between you two and maybe even do business. Like I said this isn't my forte but that's how I would play it. "

"I may just have to fire Marcus and hire you," Kane said smiling appreciatively. He did have all the paper's from Chase's accountant and hadn't even considered using those but yes that could be much more damaging to Chase's cartel than any street war. Still, he wanted to keep his soldier's on standby.

But Mattie was right. The loss of lives wouldn't bother Chase in the least. He'd just keep on throwing waves and waves of young boys to their deaths without remorse. No, she was right. You had to hit where it hurt and that was in his pocketbook.

Mattie continued her research until the wee hours of the morning with Naomi poring over books in similar fashion. Kane smiled as he watched his new found family before dozing off.

Hours later the sound of the phone awoke Kane.

"They hit the pool parlor at around two in the morning. No one was hurt. Old man Grady said he saw a blue van pull up and four masked men got out and sprayed up the place."

"And no one was hurt?"

"No. He was closing up. Said when he saw them getting out with guns he hid behind the counter."

"Well that's good."

"All he keeps saying is he has no insurance and the pool hall was his life. I feel sorry for the old man."

"Don't feel sorry for him. That's your family now. Replace the front windows and fix the damage. And do it now. And when you do make it better than it was. Might cost you a few grand but you're responsible for every last

person in your jurisdiction. You're the mayor now.
Handle it Marcus."

So this was how Chase was gonna play it. Kane knew he
had to retaliate or it would be a sign of weakness. He'd
met with Captain Murphy and told him of Mike's death and
the good captain had all but assured Kane that he would
support his efforts but also informed him that the police
free zone that Kane and Mike set up was not a big hit
although reports showed that crime was for the most part
non-existent and the area had the lowest crime rates of any
urban area in the city. Always a straight shooter the captain
knew that dirty cops encouraged crime in inner-city
neighborhoods and were the first to benefit from the local
drug trade; lining their pockets and filling their quota when
it came to arrests so no he couldn't expect help from the
other precincts but he could supply important intel on the
locations of the trap houses run by Chase and the names
and   addresses of the important players.

Kane took this info and called Marcus back.

"Call Team One and tell them to get ready. It's two
o'clock now. I want them to meet me at Juniors by the
Alby Square Mall in Brooklyn at six. Have another car
carry the weaponry. I want four cars with three people to a
car and in the fourth I want only the buyer preferably a
white boy transporting the guns. Make sure he's a user but
trustworthy. Promise him cash and a taste if he pulls this
off and keeps his mouth shut." Six o'clock and don't be
late."

"Gotcha boss. Anything else?"

"Yeah. I need bodyguards on all four corners and one directly in front."

"Of your crib?"

"Yeah and I need three soldiers that won't be turned by a dollar. Your most loyal soldiers."

"I gotcha boss. I'll see you at six."

"Glancing his watch he realized that Mr. Rosenberg was meeting with Mattie and called to see how all was going.

"Great!" Mattie responded. "What about you?"

"Good. Is Rosenberg there?"

"OMG! Is he? He's brilliant. He's given me so much insight and already has the grant in play. He says we should have results within the next two weeks. It would have taken me six months. He says I'm on the right track though. His wife is doing something similar and has her own foundation to help wayward girls so I'm going to meet with her later this week. Thans so much baby."

"Anything for you sweetheart. Did the lady meet with Naomi?"

"Yeah. She's here. Naomi's still in class though."

"How is she?"

"Marvelous. She's helping me get organized. Black woman. Your type. Bright and beautiful. Gotta keep her away from you though."

"I'm glad you approve. She works for a temp agency. When she gets finished training Naomi consider keeping her on as your administrative assistant."

"Alrighty sweetheart. Oh, and since Rosenberg's there let me speak to him."

"Sure. Hold on."

"Yes, Mr. Close."

"Now that we'll be working together rather closely don't you think we should drop all the formalities? Call me Kane."

"Okay Mr. Kane. You have a wonderful wife and daughter Mr. Kane."

"What is it I can do for you?"

"I need to meet with you as soon as possible."

"Not a problem. Your wife are wrapping it up now. Why don't you meet me here in a half an hour?"

"I like to keep my wife and my business completely separate if at all possible."

"I understand then let's meet at my office in say an hour."

"I'll see you there."

Kane prided himself on being on time. Checking his watch he was fifteen minutes early but was leery of everything now. So, instead of waiting in the car and listening to satellite radio he walked up the steps to the attorneys office and stepped in to the lobby where he was greeted by the receptionist who was striking. Kane who had spent his life with some of the most beautiful women in Manhattan was blinded by the woman's beauty.

"May I help you?"

"The name is Close. Kane Close and I have an appointment with Mr. Rosenberg at one. I just spoke with him. Actually he just left my wife and is in route here."

"Oh yes, Mr. Close he phoned and told me that you would be arriving. Told me to make you comfortable. Can I get you anything? Water, soda, champagne, perhaps something stronger. Mr. Rosenberg likes to keep his clients happy. Actually I should say his client. Mr. Grayson had an affinity for Johnny Walker Red."

"Water will be fine," Kane said staring at the woman's face which reminded him of a Spanish goddess.

"Are you sure? We have a whole host of beverages."

"No. Water's fine for now. I have a long day ahead of me. Gotta stay sharp."

"From what Mr. Rosenberg tells me you're very sharp. He tells me that you were the real brains and the heart and soul behind Mr. Grayson's enterprise. By the way I'm sorry about Mr. Grayson. I hear you two were very close."

"You hear a lot," Kane laughed. "By the way I don't think I got your name?"

"I'm sorry. It's Victoria but most of my friends just call me Vicky. And yes I do hear a lot but mostly I just listen. I think and if I'm right he's been working for Mr. Grayson

143

for twenty years and he was always referring to his partner and friend when he had a new idea. But Mr. Rosenberg said that though he always wanted to attach the name to the face. And when he did he said he understood everything then. He referred to you as the calm behind the storm. You were the conservative one, the idea man, you the brains behind the outfit. He said you were the future of the franchise. Is that true?"

"I wouldn't say that was entirely true. It's certainly quite flattering to be held in such high regard but like I said I don't think it's entirely true. I think we had different roles and we complimented each other. I don't think I would have made it this far without Mike or he without me. Kind of a symbiotic relationship…"

"I think you're being modest."

Kane smiled.

"Mr. Close would I be too forward if I asked you out to lunch to simply pick your brain and ask you the keys to your success?"

"No, I don't think you would be too forward but I would have to ask myself what my wife would think of me taking out a woman as beautiful as yourself. I'm inclined to think she would have a problem with it," Kane said. "But once again you've flattered me."

"That wasn't my intention."

"Now if you don't mind my being too forward please tell me what are really your intentions?" Kane said peeping the receptions hole card. "No worries, we'll keep this as our little secret. No need for it to go any further."

"Thank you Mr. Close. I really do need this job."

"Like I said before; no worries and be patient and take in everything you can from Mr. Rosenberg and you'll be fine."

"Thank you again Mr. Close," she said lowering her eyes and shuffling the papers cluttering her desk.

"Mr. Kane."

Kane turned quickly and saw Mr. Rosenberg, hand extended. Kane grabbed it and shook it.

"How are you? Victoria did you have Mr. Kane sign all the necessary paperwork and make him a copy?"

Victoria looked up and began to speak when Kane cut her off.

"I'm sorry I just walked in the door and I guess I didn't give her an opportunity to do much of anything."

"Okay well we'll be in my office. Please bring them in when you have them in order so he can sign them."

"Yes sir."

Kane winked as he passed her desk. Once inside he laid his cards on the table and the short, little man leaned back. It was clear he'd never expected anything like this and the notion that he'd been involved in laundering money was like an epiphany but he was game.

"We could leak a little something to the press that would raise some eyebrows but nothing so incriminating that it would cause a grand jury investigation or scandal. It would be just enough to raise some eyebrows and let Mr. Chase know that there is still wriggle room if he wants to free himself from this entanglement. And that would be the smart move on his part. He could always have a knee jerk reaction and come out guns blazing. You and I both know that this wouldn't be the wisest move but there's no counting for human emotion and ego."

"You're right. But if we leak this information chances are the police will take Chase down and possibly eliminate him so they're not implicated. They'll basically be doing the dirty work."

"True but they're main concern after Chase will be finding the books and eliminating the evidence. You don't want that."

"So, what do we do?"

"Hold on. Let me give that some thought."

Kane was thinking as well. But his thoughts centered on the girl in the outer office. There was no doubt she was attractive. No she was fine and would have made a suitable partner on those nights there was no Mattie. And for twenty years there had been no Mattie. And women had come and gone. Some were mere bed warmers on those cold winter nights when a man's needs got the best of him. Others he had real relationships but there had always been women. A multitude ever since he could remember and none had ever lasted for more than a few months. So, what made Mattie different when this girl had turned his head if only for a minute and he was still a newlywed?

"Mr. Kane."

Kane's head jumped.

"Sorry. I must have been daydreaming."

"Well, Mr. Kane the only plausible thing I see possible at this stage is that you leak something to the press. Nothing major but something to let Mr. Chase know that you're a formidable opponent not opposed to going public with his ventures and exposing him for the thug he really is. That in itself should be enough to get his attention and let him know that you're not about to soil yourself or let yourself or your young people engage in guerilla warfare. If that doesn't work then the only other alternative is to take to the streets. What I wouldn't do however is unveil the contents of these documents. There are so many people in positions of authority; judges, politicians, different precincts that you'd have half of the New York City hierarchy out for your head. Mr. Chase is a choir boy in comparison to some of the names in these books. Anyway, those are my recommendations. If you want me to go with a leak to draw his attention then let me know."

"My wife said the same thing."

"She's a shrewd cookie. They said behind every good man there's a good woman. She's certainly a testament to that."

"Yes she is," Kane replied appreciatively. "So we're going with the leak?"

"If that's what you want to do."

147

"Let me know when you post it."

"Will do Mr. Kane."

Kane stood up and shook the lawyer's hand. It was four thirty and he had enough time to stop by and see how the girls were doing but he thought better against it. Mattie, he was sure was immersed in getting the center up and running and to hear her spew about the progress she'd made on day one would relax him and ease the stress after a long and trying day and he certainly needed that.

As he approached Juniors he saw a large contingent of young men outside. He recognized T.J and spoke.

"What's up fam?"

"Waitin' on you Kane. We ready to do the damn thing and get home. Is you ready?"

"I was born ready but slow your roll. If you wanna insure success you have to have a plan. So let's grab a booth and go over the plan."

The men filed in looking better than the average Black man roaming the streets of the city in their black and blue leathers with the words Uptown on the back and butter Tims.

"How many?"

"Eight," Born Ready replied.

"Where's Marcus and the white boy?" Kane asked.

"Marcus didn't like where he parked the car so he had him move it like three blocks over."

"Okay, well go ahead and order if you like. We need to wait for Marcus and the white boy. But I will tell you this so you'll understand what we're doing tonight. The cartel has three crack houses within five minutes of each other. We're robbing all three. The white boy is going to get us in the door. We go in with guns drawn but I want no shots fired unless you're fired at. We need it to be as quiet as possible and we want to be in and out with the quickness and no casualties. And I mean no casualties on either side. Remember we want the stash and anything else they may have. Customers, dope boys, everyone… I want everyone in there robbed. And if anybody makes a move touch 'em."

"And then we bail?"

"Just as quickly as we made the scene I want us out of there."

Marcus walked in shortly thereafter and Kane went over the same thing again for him and the white boy who didn't seem to be listening. Kane pulled T.J. towards him so he was blocking Kane from the view of the rest of the restaurants patrons and backhanded him as hard as he could. Blood spurted everywhere.

"Listen up you junkie motherfucker, I don't like crackers anyway but a whole lot of motherfucker's lives are depending on you getting this shit straight so you'd better listen up," Kane had the young man's attention as well as everyone elses. Everyone at the table now seemed fully aware of the gravity of the situation. "You look suspicious and three or four of us are going out in body bags. So you better pay attention."

Kane went through the plan again, checked his watch again and leaned back in his chair. You could hear a pin drop. He then turned to Marcus.

"What are peak hours?"

"For business? I guess between eight and nine. After people get off work, eat dinner and put their kids to bed."

"So we should get in and get out before rush hour if we want to catch them with a full load huh?" Ali the youngest and brightest of the crew remarked. Kane had already made note of the kid. He was not only the brightest but most mature. And if Kane had his way and could hang in there just a little longer he was going to have this kid off the street. He had too much going for him to be languishing on the street. All he needed was some direction.

"Kane, if we hit 'em now there's little or no collateral damage and that's a positive but all we get is their stash and we have plenty of that. The work comes from changing that stash into dollars and if we hit 'em at the end of the night they've done our work for us and even though the risks go up so do the profits."

"That's true but we're not really interested in their stash or their papers. This run tonight is a statement run. All we're interested in doing tonight is sending them a message and that message is we won't lie down while you come into our neighborhood and take what's ours. This ain't about the money. Ain't shit they have that we need?"

150

"Tell my woman that," Ali whispered loud enough for everyone to hear. "After the past three weeks she talkin' 'bout going to war herself."

Everyone laughed.

"But Ali's right. There is more to be made if we hit 'em when the night is over. But we gonna make it. And my concern is my family. That's you. And them fellas workin'. They just like you. They tryna eat and feed their families. They ain't responsible for this war. And ain't no need to take them out for tryna to live. I'm working on alleviating the man in charge. If the head falls the body will follow. But we have to let them know that they can't run over the Uptown Crew."

The short soliloquy came with a chorus of affirmations and Kane knew it was the right time to make their move.

"I want the team of Marcus, Ali and Born on this first one. Ali you have the duct tape?"

"Yeah, boss."

"Let's do this."

Marcus, Ali, Kane and the white boy got out of the royal blue sedan at two minute intervals so as not to arouse suspicion and entered the old brick tenement building. Once inside they took the stairs up to the third floor with the white boy leading the way. When the hall was clear he motioned for them and they joined him. Marcus and Ali stood on one side of the door while Kane stood on the other. Knocking gently the white boy waited.

"Who?"

"I need two dubs."

As soon as the door opened. Kane shoved the white boy in. Marcus and Ali followed. Shotgun held high Kane surveyed the room quickly. Caught totally off guard and by surprise the young brother behind the table with the forty five in front of him had little time to react. On the side, stood a rather large man, who was obviously the man's bodyguard. Instinctively he went for the gun in his waistband."

"Try it and I'll be sending your mama a wreath," Kane said lowering the sawed off shotgun and pointing it squarely at the young man's mid-section. By this time, Marcus and Ali had herded the six or seven other people in the small apartment into the living room and Ali was hard at work duct taping their arms, legs and mouth. In the next five minutes he'd duct taped everyone present and when finished began to repeat the process.

"Can't be too safe," He said to Kane who was marveling at the efficiency of the young man. Meanwhile, Marcus checked the house thoroughly and not long afterwards entered the living room with a small kitchen garbage bag.

"We're paid baby," he said winking at Kane.

Kane checked his watched and just as quickly as they entered they left. Not a shot had been fired. No one had been hurt. And they left the building in the same two minute intervals they'd entered in. Once in the car the adrenaline was high and Kane who usually showed little or no emotion had to admit he was impressed.

"Now that's what I'm talking about. Beautiful job fellas! Bautiful! What's the take?"

"I got a little less than four keys and I don't know how many loose vials. They were breaking it up when I walked in on 'em."

"How 'bout you Ali?"

"Little over eight g's in cash, two Roleys and a Movado."

"Not bad for eight minutes work."

"That should make up for the three weeks off."

"Not if we can't turn that hard white into cold green," Ali remarked.

"You're right. But being off the streets you can't spend it anyway."

"You right Kane but my baby and my baby mama gotta eat too."

"Okay at the end of the night you split up what you have and if she's still trying to eat with two grand then maybe you need another baby mama."

Ali and the others laughed. The other two jobs went smoothly and with the night moving on the cash take grew larger. Went it was all over and the crew was safely back at their own headquarters back uptown they counted a little over forty-three thousand in cash, nine keys and jewelry and other valuables in the neighbor of ten or twelve thousand dollars.

Marcus and Kane split up the take with the cocaine being held in reserve until the streets were open for business again.

"The way you put money in a niggas pocket I might have to get my baby's mama to give you some," Ali laughed as he hugged Kane.

"Alright my brothers, I need for you to sit tight. Sit back, chill watch some television and relax. Remember there is to be no contact with anybody. These motherfuckers will be looking for you. Marcus is going to use the other team to hit 'em again tomorrow night. They won't be expecting so bold a move and hopefully we'll get the same results. This is guerilla warfare baby. After that we'll change up and hit their couriers. But in the meantime, you are to stay locked and loaded and on lock down. If any of you need to get word or money to your families let Marcus know and we'll take care of that. Any questions?"

"Long as you putting money in my pocket I ain't got nothin' to say," Ali remarked. "I'll stay in until my pension kicks in as long as I'm pulling in cheddar like this. At this rate I'm thinkin' early retirement and it sho' beats workin' them streets day in and day out."

"Good," Kane smiled. "I'll check back in a day or so."

Kane knew that it was only a matter of time before word got back to Chase about the crack house raids and prepared himself for the worse. It was time to move his own safe houses but that could wait until morning. Right now he had more important things on his mind.

"Hello."

154

"Black here."

"What's up Black?"

"Nothing Kane. We've been watching the house for two days now. We know he's there but there has been no movement. He's had a few people go in and out but he hasn't shown his face. I've got two snipers on the roof but he's pulled the curtains and hasn't opened them in two days. He's got two guards watching the entrance and security but it's not impenetrable. You say the word and we'll go in and get him."

"No. Let's hold off on that for now. From what I understand he has a wife and two small children. I don't wan8t to do anything in front of the kids. But I want all communication cut off. He won't use a landmine or his cell and if he doesn't have a courier or any contact with visitors he has no way to keep abreast of what's going on out here. And right now he's too paranoid to come out. So, we're in good shape. Let's just keep tightening the screws. Stop anyone trying to go in, question them and find out what you can and get back to me.

"I'll do that. I don't think old boy's used to anything like this Kane. He ain't never been in a war of attrition," Black laughed. "He don't know what it's like to go the mattresses like we do does he Kane? Thought he could just ride roughshod over us."

"And I'm hoping he continues to underestimate us," Kane replied. "Pride and arrogance has been the demise for many a leader."

"I know that's right."

"Keep me abreast."

"Will do."

Kane was stopped at the entrance to his block and was glad to see that the soldiers were checking every car that tried to pass through.

"Sorry boss. I didn't know it was you."

"Don't be sorry if you hadn't stopped me I would have been upset. Are the girl's home?"

"Yeah. Miss Mattie tried to go out a little while ago but I wouldn't let her. No disrespect boss."

"None taken. You did the right thing. Thanks for taking care of business Born."

"Oh and boss… Marcus called. Said he's been trying to reach you."

"Alright. I'll give him a call. Be safe."

"Later boss."

Kane entered the house and breathed a sigh of relief. He was exhausted. Mattie greeted him at the door.

"Hey baby. I missed you so much. "

"I missed you too."

"Should I ask how you're your day was?"

"I'd much rather you tell me how yours was."

"That bad huh?"

"Not really. I'd just rather not talk about it. Tell me about yours," Kane said smiling.

"Well, aside from the fact that I'm under lockdown it was great. Do you know that Born wouldn't let me go to the store to get Naomi some Tampons and a few other items we need?"

"He's just looking out for my best interest and you are certainly my best interest. What else is new?"

"Not much. I met with Mrs. Rosenberg. She's a beautiful person. She agreed to actually walk me through the first couple of months until I'm situated and gave me some great tips. And her husband seems as excited as I am with the possibilities. He reminds me of you though."

"How's that?"

"All he sees is the financial possibilities."

Kane laughed.

"Oh, and you should see Naomi. She's a natural. She moved in like she was born to it. Just as friendly and cordial. Honestly you'd think she'd been a receptionist for years. And that's in light of her condition. I am so proud of her."

"Well, I'm glad things are working out for you love."

"You made it all possible," she said bending over and kissing him on his forehead. "You hungry?"

"I could stand a bite."

"Good. I didn't cook though. I thought you might be in the mood for something a little different so I ordered you the jerked chicken from that little Jamaican restaurant on 135th. Thought it would be a welcome change."

"Sounds good Mattie. Where's Naomi?"

"Upstairs in her room doing her homework. She's not doing too well. That woman thing is on her."

"Well, let me go say hello anyway," Kane said making his way up the stairs. Finding the door open Kane still knocked before entering and had a seat opposite the young woman.

"Hey Kane," Naomi said her face lighting up upon seeing him.

"Hey sweetheart. Heard your first day was fantastic."

Naomi's smile grew larger.

"That's nobody but Mattie talking."

"Still, that's a lot coming from Mattie. She's not one to easily give away compliments. Keep up the good work," Kane said getting up and kissing the young girl on her forehead.

"And look," she said handing Kane a paper to look at. "It's my first test." There was an 'A' on top and Kane pulled Naomi to him and hugged her deeply.

As happy as Naomi seemed most of the time here was no doubt that there was still something missing. How often had he caught her sitting staring, despondent and though she tried to mask her sorrow it still shown through far too often. Mattie noticed it too and would swoop the girl off on to some new venture whenever she noticed.

"Could be she's still trying to overcome the traumatization at the hands of her uncle or could be the ordeal she went through in her village."

"Or both. The girl's had a rough life. I'm surprised she's doing as well as she is."

"I know that's right. It took me year's to overcome my stepfather's abuse. I just hope I never run into him. I hear he's out you know. But in Naomi's case the more she has on her plate the less time she has to sit back and reflect."

"That's true."

"That's why I try to keep her busyconstantly."

The rest of the evening went on without a hitch with Mattie fussing about the shape of the house and what it needed to be a true home. The rest of the time she spent poring over papers and researching progressive educational programs for young women. Obsessed with the women's center and its possibilities for making a change there were simply not enough hours in the day for Mattie Close.

Kane had other things on his mind and when it became excessive he did what he always did. He took the tiny pad from his jacket pocket and jotted down a few reminders before closing his eyes and falling asleep.

At six a.m. Kane Close was up with a lurch. It wasn't that he had anything against Beyonce. He would be the last one to say that she wasn't talented but her talent was more visually inspired than vocally transmitted and though he would never say so he hated waking up to her pleading for someone to put a ring on it.

Dragging himself out of bed, he picked up the pack of Marlboros. After ten years and he'd gone back to smoking. Mattie had already brought his coffee and after sipping it

and lighting a cigarette Kane glanced his watch. It was six thirty. He then checked his notepad and reached for his phone.

"Charlie? This is Kane Close. Did I wake you?"

"No sir," the lawyer lied sitting up in his bed and grabbing his pencil and paper. "What can I do for you Mr. Kane."

Kane had to chuckle.

"Listen I need for you to find out everything you can about the family of a Mr. Anwar Allewende. I need to know his occupation and if he can obtain a visa for he and his family. I need to know how many school age children they have. Who is currently alive and who is deceased due to the civil war in the Sudan and if possible how soon we can obtain work visas, etc. I'm attempting to get them out of that war torn country and havethem reunited with family members currently stateside. Then I need you to concentrate your efforts on you surrounding my wife with as many programs and persons possible to get some of these teenage girls off the streets back into school and achieving. I want the very real possibility of college to be an avenue to every one of them. And the third thing I need you to do is to plan on partnering with me to do the same with our teenage boys up in Harlem. I don't care how many grants and fellowship you acquire or where from but I want this dream to become a reality within a year and at the latest two. Put Victoria on it. I want her to do as much of the research as possible. I want a meeting scheduled for this time next Monday morning to see where we are? You understand. Have a good day Charlie."

And with that said Kane hung up and proceeded to call Marcus.

"Marcus. How the fellas doin'?"

"They're good. A couple of them are homesick. But overall they're in pretty good spirits. A little antsy but they're good.

"Good. Listen I want six teams in action tonight. Run it the same exact way including a meeting at each of the safe houses and then I want three teams at a time to meet at Juniors for the final dress rehearsal befor you hit 'em. Find another white boy and I want you to raid the three crack houses in Queens. I want Ali to run the Brooklyn raids 'cause he's familiar with it so tell him to meet me at the Dunbar at eight a.m.

"No problem. On another tip, do you remember that fool that started this whole shit?"

"Hell yeah. I still see him from time-to-time. Nigga walkin' round like he special. Like he got a pass or some shit although I ain't seen him since this shit kicked off. Probably runnin' scared now."

"Check with ol' lady Murphy. See if he's still got his place up in Esplanarde Gardens."

"Won't guess who else I saw switchin' her pretty ass up and down the avenue?"

Kane ignored the man speaking and continued.

"Do you know Antonio Cruz?"

"You mean crazy ass Tony Cruz from up on 148th—ol' would be gangsta from back in the day? The nigga that just got outta Elmira about two weeks ago?"

"Yeah that's the one."

"Yeah, I just seen him yesterday. He lookin' good. Don't look a day older than when he went in and he did somethin' like an eighteen year bid for rapin' some thirteen year old girl. He's still crazy as hell though. Told me that they said I was holdin' it down when he was upstate and he told me he gonna run alla Harlem by the end of the year. Nigga was serious as hell too. I just laughed. Why?"

"Call those Jersey boys; the ones from Newark and have both of those fools laid to rest."

"Damn Kane. Cruz ain't a bad guy. He's just crazy as hell. But the other fool is the reason for all this shit. He's the one that started all this shit and fucking with my livelihood. Plus he fucked up my girl Eva. Why don't you let me rock that motherfucker to sleep personally Kane? Those Jersey boys are gonna cost you a grip. Let me do that motherfucker free of charge on the house?"

"I need you for other things Marcus. Call them as soon as you get off the phone with me and like I said; have them laid to rest. Call me when it's done."

"Damn Kane. Cruz and me is cool. He the one that first put me on to the game when I was just a hopper." Marcus thought to himself then just as easily dismissed the thought. Must be something personal that went down between him and Kane.

Marcus moved to make the phone call then thought about the conversation he'd just had with Kane. Should he call him back? He'd forgotten to tell him about Eva and her fine ass. He then thought better of making the call. Yesterday was the first time he'd seen Eva in months and Lord knows she was no worse for the wear with her pretty ass. He remembered when he and his old crew were just teens and they'd stand around selling nickel bags of weed and betting who would be the first to crack on Eva for some pussy. But Eva had always been strictly about the loot and if you didn't have a Benjamin youdidn't even approach Eva. Most of the fellas from back in the day were gone now. They were either upstate, strung out on the very same product they were hustlin' or dead. But for Marcus the craving remained. It had been no different when he saw her yesterday looking just as fine as she always had. She was looking for a taste and though he didn't have any on him at the time he promised her that he'd hook up with her today. The fellas always joked but Marcus knew it was no joke. As long as you had product you had pussy. Today he would find out. There was no getting hooked or turned out by some bitch. It was no more than a transaction like any other. Only this was crack for pussy. And how many times had he done this? But first he had to contact them niggas in Jersey. It was nine now. But first he needed to contact Ali.

"Yo nigga is you sleep?"

Ali answered his boss with no particular respect.

"How a nigga gonna sleep with forty two niggas at the rest and all they wanna do is drink and smoke and party twenty four seven?"

"You got paper and pencil?"

"Hold on."

Marcus knew Eva was bad news and was having second thoughts about giving her a call back but Eva's ass was like visions of sugar plums dancin' in his head.

"Go ahead Shakespeare what you got for me?"

"Take this number down bro. It looks like you on the come up. Kane wants you to call him."

"No shit?"

"Give him a call and be careful of what you wish for."

"I gotcha."

Marcus called Jersey before making his rounds of the safe houses. It was eleven and all appeared well when he called Eva.

"What's up baby?"

"Hey Marcus. How you doing?"

"I'm good. Got that thang you asked me for."

"Oh, baby you must have known I needed my morning wake up."

"Somethin' like that but listen as you know I just got home yesterday and haven't been workin' so I'm a little strapped for cash right now."

"I know that Eva. It doesn't necessarily have to be in cash baby."

"Oh it doesn't? Things have changed. I've seen other girls come to you offering themselves and promising to pay you later and they were out there working and could have paid you before the night was out and I watched you tell them no."

"Those were the other girls and credit is a bad thing to start. I've seen friends become enemies way too often where this shit is concerned."

"I hear you. So, what is it that makes me different?"

"I wanted you when I was just a lookout but I could never afford you."

"Think you can afford me now or just this morning?"

"Don't know. Depends on what you have to offer and how good it is on whether I want to afford you or not."

"Oh really? Well, come up and you show me yours and I'll show you mine."

"Give me a few I need to make a run, Will you be there say in an hour?"

"Where can I go with Kane having the block on lock?"

Marcus laughed.

More on more people were having the same thoughts and Marcus who was still out there was hearing it. If only Kane would listen but he wasn't out there on the streets so there was no way he would know. Kane was becoming more and more like one of those old slumlords sitting back on the fruits of someone else's labor merely collecting the rent while the building was crumbling with him and others in it.

An hour later Marcus rang the bell and was surprised to find Eva looking even better than he'd imagined her. Stepping in he found the place tastefully decorated. The walls were painted in earth tones and Sade could be heard crooning throughout the apartment.

"I don't usually invite men into my inner sanctum but then you're not the usual man. Have a seat Marcus."

Marcus had a seat on the brown living sofa.

"I never did get a chance to thank you and your boys for looking after me that night."

"You were in pretty bad shape but you look as though you've recovered completely," Marcus said looking the woman up and down with a smile on his face.

"Thank God. The whole experience was like an epiphany for me. It really made me take a look at things. I don't mean to sound corny but it really changed my life."

"Don't tell me you're born again?"

"Would you be here if I was born again silly? But it did make me see things from a completely different perspective."

"Tell me about it."

"I will but let me get situated first. Would you like something to drink?"

"Some water would be fine."

Eva was back in a minute with a bottled water and her pocketbook. From it she took a stem and waited for Marcus who dug into his pocket and pulled out an eight ball and chipped off a twenty.

"C'mon baby you're not got going to feed me kibbles and bits all day."

"Ain't got time for that. Ain't got no time for no games Eva. Hit that and then we go into the bedroom and get to some serious work and I'll leave that," Marcus said pointing to the chunk of crack on the living room table.

"You promise Marcus?"

"Word is bond Eva. When have I ever lied to you?"

"You're right. I'm sorry Marcus. It's just that so many motherfuckers are sheisty nowadays."

"Ain't no future in that."

"You right," Eva said breaking off a piece of the rock and putting it on the stem then lighting it. Pulling slow and steady Marcus watched as her breasts heaved exposing the forty double D's rising above her camisole.

"Damn this shit is good. It's been awhile," Eva said smiling and looking for some tissue to put the stem on to cool. "Let me ask you something Marcus?"

"I'm listening."

"Why me? I mean I'm an old lady. There are a bunch of cute young girls that would gladly give you some ass and I've seen you turn them down for a twenty. I mean they would have sucked your dick, given you some pussy and some ass if you wanted that."

Marcus laughed.

"When I was growing up there were ho's out there and then there was you and Mattie. You were the queens and we would stand around and fantasize about who would have you first. Mattie was quiet and used to keep to herself like she was unapproachable but you were approachable accept you were meaner than a pit bull in heat and were all about the papers. The fellas all went away but the fantasy never did. At least for me it never did."

Eva smiled.

"I wasn't that mean. You should have told me. I would have hooked your little ass up. I've got another proposition for you Marcus but let's go see if this old lady can still fulfill some of those young boy's fantasies."

Eva filled the stem once more and pulled slowly before grabbing Marcus' hand and leading him into the bedroom.

An hour later Marcus watched Eva repeat the procedure over and over until there was little less than half the rock left.

"Better save some for later. I don't know when I'll get a chance to get around here again."

"Make it sooner than later," Eva smiled. "But tell before you go tell me something. Was it as good as your fantasy?"

"To be honest Eva. It was better than even I imagined."

"Thanks Marcus. I think you're just being a gentleman but thanks nonetheless. And thanks for blessing me. Oh, and before I forget I was asked to throw something out to you. A certain gentleman approached me and set forth a proposition that I'm supposed to present to you."

"I'm listening."

"Don't get angry Marcus. Just entertain it for a minute. They asked me to give you this number and asked that you call them either way."

"What's the proposition?"

"Well, the gentleman that approached me said that he knew you and a whole lot of other people were unhappy because of this whole moratorium on drugs and prostitution and being that you're the number two man out here you were probably suffering more than anyone from the loss of revenues while Kane ain't suffering at all. So what he's proposing is that you eliminate Kane. The contract is worth a hundred grand and then you take over the top spot and truth be told you're already running the show."

Marcus' eyes flushed a crimson red and he wanted to stomp Eva but he knew he'd be wasting his time.

"And what do you get out of me killing Kane."

"No more than being your first lady and maybe some more of what you showed me in the bedroom."

Marcus had to do everything to control his temper. Standing he could do no more than stare at her.

"And to think I really thought you'd changed. I guess there's no changing you. You'll always be a bottom feeding no good ho bitch."

"Marcus. Marcus please take the number. If you feel anything for me you have to take the number. They said they'd kill me if they didn't hear from you one way or another in the next twenty four hours."

"I can't believe you'd do some shit like that. Mattie's your best friend and Kane has saved your life on more than one occasion. What do you think would happen to you if I let Kane know what you asked me to do?"

"Oh Marcus! Please don't baby! Just think about it baby. We could rule Harlem. With your connects and my street smarts we could be the royal family baby. We could live like royalty.

"You're sick bitch. You're really sick. If I were you I'd get out of town on the first thing smoking."

As soon as he reached his car Marcus was on the phone.

"Kane meet me at Small's now!"

Marcus waited in front of Small's for all of ten minutes before he noticed the white two door Sonata pull up. He quickly got, crossed the street and joined Kane.

"I was trying to tell you that Eva was back in town when you cut me off."

"Okay. My bad Marcus. No disrespect intended it's just that I have so much on my mind that I can't take in everything and Eva isn't someone I want to talk about on a good day. She's bad news, always has been bad news, always will be bad news. But anyway what has she done this time?"

Marcus recounted the story.

"So what would you propose I do Marcus?"

"Lay her head right next to those other two. When those boys come from Jersey I'll tell them to add one more. Shit! Ol' man Cruz is crazy as hell but he ain't never done no shit like Eva. She tried to set you up Kane. How many times have you bailed her out of some shit she got herself into? She's Mattie's best friend. You going to have Cruz whacked and he ain't never done shit compared to what this bitch is trying to do."

"You're a good man Marcus and I'm glad to have you as a partner but there's some things you don't know. Mattie is my wife."

"That's exactly what I'm saying Kane."

"Hold on young blood. Mattie is my wife. What was her maiden name before we got married?"

"You know I never thought to ask."

"Her name was Cruz and what I'm about to tell you I don't ever want to hear again. Her step daddy is Antonio or as you know him Tony Cruz and that man you know as Crazy Tony would come home roaring drunk every day and rape his nine year old step daughter. When she turned thirteen and couldn't take it anymore Eva convinced her that since she was fucking for free she might as well get paid for it and that's how Mattie ended

up on the street. She was trying to get a place of her own to get away from this man that was raping her every day. Didn't know that did you?"

Marcus was dumbfounded.

"As far as Eva goes believe it or not I knew you'd be approached. I've known this for two or three days. I'm not surprised. It's a smart move. What is surprising to me is that you stuck your dick in that microwave." Kane laughed. "But anyway Eva's not worth the trouble. What you're going to do is play right along with her."

"What?!?"

"Yep. I want you to keep on feeding her. Women are vain you know. And there's no more vain a woman and a whore that's fighting middle age. I mean think about it. What does a whore have left when her looks are gone? But you my friend are going to keep Miss Eva so high and so drunk that she's going to start believing the hype. I want you to make her a kept woman. Buy her what she wants. Treat her to the nicest restaurants. Take her to plays. I want you to win her over. Nothing is too good for Eva. In turn she'll keep you informed of all their plans. And stay loyal. I don't want your dick anywhere but where Eva asks you to put it. To Eva you'll be no more than a puppy dog in heat. And to the Cartel you'll be their puppet with Eva doing her best to report back on your every move through her rose colored lens which you will keep cloudy with drugs, alcohol and money. And when they let their guard down we'll draw this cowardly motherfucker out of hiding and assassinate the motherfucker and take over all of his real estate."

"Do you really think we can pull it off Kane?"

"I think you can with me pulling the strings. Remember you're about to kill me."

"Don't even play."

"I'm not playing. The only people that will know I'm still alive will be you and Mattie."

"Are you sure this is what you want to do Kane?"

"Positive. I already talked to Jersey. I'm going with you when they take Cruz and that other fool and when they care of them you'll do me and with a few dollars more we'll get them to go along with the story and fake my death. I'll fly out of Newark to whereabouts unknown. Mattie will give you my number and you'll call using disposables until things are settled. I have friends that have Chase under surveillance and when he's sure he's in the clear and relaxes enough he'll get careless and it's a wrap."

173

"Sounds foolproof in theory anyway but what's to say that they won't whack me and put their own people in place?"

"Because we have a system that works and is profitable and to knock off two neighborhood icons would not only draw attention but it would make the natives restless and Chase knows that's not good business."

"You really think it'll work boss?"

"Don't know and can't really be sure but we'll see. Right now the mere thought of war has shut us down and is killing us financially and you can best believe they know that. I have a couple of other things in the works to bring this to a close but we'll have to see what happens. In the meantime I want you to go ahead with tonight as planned. Did you tell Ali to call me?"

"Yeah boss."

"I want you to take him under your wing and make him your lieutenant. The kid has potential."

"I'll do that. It won't make Born or TJ happy though."

"Fuck Born and TJ. Surround yourself with those that are going to be loyal and make you look good. And given the right motivation Ali will work his ass off for you and make you shine as well. I'm telling you the kid is bright, hungry and has potential. You and he are the future of the outfit. Born and TJ are thugs. They make good soldiers but outside of that they bring nothing. If you want to keep them on the payroll do that but they're just taking money out of your pocket. If you really want to know if Born is ready to be your second and to lead should something

174

happen to you then give him three or four blocks and see how long he can lead and make it profitable. I'm telling you he can't. But then that's your decision to make. Call me when you get in tonight and let me know how it goes. Oh, and be nice to Eva," Kane said smiling as he made his way to the white Sonata.

Charlie Rosenberg stood as Kane made his way into the inner office.

"How are you doing Charlie?"

"I'm good Mr. Kane. How are you doing today?"

"Stressed but then that comes with the territory."

"Do you work out Mr. Kane?"

"When I get a chance to. Why?"

"It helps me when I'm truly having a stressful day. Just thought it my help some. As far as the information you requested the family is still pretty much intact despite the unrest. The two younger boys have been recruited by the Sudanese Liberation Army but are fine. They come home from time-to-time and are required to do a mandatory stay of two years in the military. The daughters are fine except for one who somehow managed to come here to stay in the states with an uncle but neither he nor anyone else seems to know her whereabouts. I believe she's the oldest. She just turned eighteen a few months ago."

"Well, we can't worry about her she's basically an adult. What are the chances the rest of the family here?"

"I'm working on that. It could be somewhat expensive. Bribery is running rampant and everyone has their hand out."

"Don't worry about the money. Just do what you have to do Charlie. And see if you can't smuggle the boys out while they're home on furlough. Set up something comfortable, yet affordable in Queens or Jersey."

"I'm on it."

"Were you able to find out what the parents do? Anything that translates into employment here?"

"Not unless you know someone her in need of a sheep herder?"

"Okay work on that. See if you can't find some work so they can gain financial independence. I don't care if it's janitorial or washing cars."

"I'll see what we can do."

"How's Mattie doing?"

"She's extremely independent and has basically taken the bull by the horns. She really doesn't need my help."

Kane smiled knowing that the lawyer was right on. If Mattie put her mind to something she needed little except for you to move aside.

"And our little project?"

"Sir?"

"The boys center."

"Oh, Victoria's started researching it. I'm going to join her as soon as I can free myself up from rounding up and moving a family of Sudanese refugees to America, get the women's center and leaking tid bits to the Times."

"Are you being cynical Charlie?"

"Not at all Mr. Kane. But I may need to hit the gym at lunch. I heard it relieves stress."

"You are being cynical aren't you Charlie," Kane said smiling. He liked the little Jewish lawyer and now understood why Mike kept him on for all these years.

"Not at all sir," Charlie said smiling.

"Alright then. Call me if you need me for anything Kane said before exiting the office. Passing Victoria's desk, he smiled cordially. "You're looking even more ravishing than the last time I saw you."

"Thank you Mr. Kane. You're not doing too bad yourself," Victoria said licking her lips suggestively.

'Damn.' Kane thought to himself. His thoughts were still on Victoria when the phone rang.

"Kane."

"Yeah this is Ali. Marcus told me to give you a call."

"Yeah Ali. You mobile?"

"I can be. Whatcha need?"

"I need you to meet me on 1-2-5 at the bank. Just come in and have a seat."

"I like the way this sounds already. But Kane my boss said I shouldn't leave the safe house."

"I'm super ceding that directive smartass. Be there in fifteen."

"Just making sure boss. Didn't want to get caught in a Catch-22 or nothin' like that."

"Be there in twenty."

Kane hung up the phone and smiled. The kid was a thinker. Moments later when Kane walked in the bank he saw Ali who was deep into some magazine. Kane tapped him on his shoulder and then walked over to the bank teller who after several words ran over to one of the bank managers. Ali watched. He admired this man who commanded so much respect and whose mere presence made people change speeds. One day he thought...

"Ali," Kane said sitting down and relaxing while bank personnel scurried this way and that. "What do you know about Catch 22."

"Ah man I love Vonnegurt."

"You read a lot?"

"All the time. Most of them niggas you got on lockdown is just sittin' around smokin' and drinkin' and shit. And while they be doin' that I be readin'; you know buildin'. Got to improve my mind so I'm ready for the next stage."

"And what's the next stage if you don't mind me askin'?"

"Nah I don't mind you askin' cause I'm not rightly sure what the next stage is but you might be able to tell me. I know you ain't call me down here for nothin' so maybe you have plans for me?"

"You still in school?"

"I should be. I was doing really good but my girl came up pregnant and so I had to take care of her and my seed. It's the right thing to do. I didn't want to fit the stereotype of a deadbeat dad so I'm out here like the rest of these simple niggas tryna eat."

"What year were you in when you dropped out?"

"I just dropped out. I was a second semester senior. Honor roll student too. I didn't want to. I mean it's hard enough with a college degree but without high school you ain't shit."

"I know that's right," Kane said smiling. "So, what are your plans now?"

"I don't know. That's up to you boss. I ain't really tryin' to stay in the game or make a career of it. That ain't really where my head's at. But like I said I fucked up and so I gotta stack some papers to take care of the fam and maybe I'll put enough away to go back to school and finish up. Depends on how much I can stash in the next year."

"So, you only plan to stay in the game a year?"

"Ain't no future in selling poison. Just jail and death. Ain't no longevity. They tell me that you were only in it for a minute and went back to school."

"I did."

"And what is you now? A millionaire? That's what I want to do. I want to make all I can make and then bail, invest and sit back and watch my money work for me."

"Sounds like a plan."

"It has to be. I don't want my son growing up no orphan. I want to be there for him and I want him to be proud. These streets is dangerous and the sooner I get off them the better. I ain't tryna be no kingpin like Marcus."

Kane said nothing. He just sat there staring at the young man in front of him. Here was a young man with a good head on his shoulders and no options. Charlie Rosenberg couldn't build the center quick enough. How many boys were there, bright boys just like Ali that needed a mentor and some direction? These boys needed options, alternatives other than the streets.

"You alright Kane?"

"I'm fine. Let me ask you something Ali."

"Ask away."

"Okay hypothetically let's just say you make a 'g' or a 'g' and a half a week and you shower your woman and your kid with that type of lifestyle. How easy or how hard do you think it'll be to just walk away from that? And even if you see something out there better for yourself how's your woman gonna react when she can't have all the shit she's grown accustomed to?"

"I never thought about it like that."

"Foresight son… You have to acquire foresight and wisdom to accompany the knowledge you're acquiring."

"You're on the right track though which is why I called you here today."

"Was wondering when you were going to get around to that," Ali said smiling.

"You're going to stop being a smartass," Kane said smiling.

"Here you are Mr. Kane," the thirtyish looking Black bank manager stated matter-of-factly. "May I take the liberty of speaking freely?"

"By all means. This is my youngest son Ali. Ali I'd like to introduce you to Mr. Jones." Ali stood to shake the young banker's hand.

"Nice to meet you Ali. Didn't know you had children Mr. Close."

"You were saying," Kane said.

"Oh yes. There's a hundred and twenty five thousand in one hundred dollar denominations. All I need is your signature and I'll have the security guards escort you to your vehicle."

"We'll be fine," Kane said ignoring the man.

"Have a good day Mr. Close."

"In any case, every now and then I see certain qualities in my workers and I realize that their particular talents aren't being utilized correctly and should be used in some other capacity."

"And you see that?"

"I most certainly do! I wanted you to head the raid in Brooklyn tonight at the same spots we hit two days ago. Marcus is gonna take another crew and hit the spots in Queens. Should bring four or five times the loot we did on the first haul because we're going to run with a strategy from one of our bright young lieutenants on the come up. This particular young man said to hit the spots at the end of the night instead of early when the product has already been turned into cash which would give us a higher yield. Let them do the work of cutting, packaging and selling the product and we just go in and pick up the cash at the end of the night after all the work is done."

Ali beamed with pride.

"Gotta use yo' head. That's what I keep tellin' the fellas. Ya gotta think things out fully and in their entirety. I keep tryna tell them."

"So, if that's the upside then there naturally…"

"Has to be a downside," Ali chimed in. "And the downside is that if the reward is much greater the risk is gonna be far greater as well. And being that we just robbed the place two days ago security's gonna be heightened and the chances for casualties is gonna double."

"So, is the risk worth the gain?"

Ali laughed.

"That all depends on who you're asking. If my name was Kane and I was sitting on top of the world and making withdrawals from the bank for a hundred g's then I'd say hell to the no. On the other hand, if I'm a young 'g' living in a rat and roach infested tenement with a newborn and a woman that always got her hand out I might cut the rest of the niggas out altogether and go up in there cowboy style and just start blastin' away and hoping I come out alive and with some start up money. You feel me? Just depends on where your mind set is."

"You know there's no even split when you're a lieutenant? The team leader sets the split."

"It's gotta be the same split all around Kane if you want these niggas to be loyal and watch you back on the next job. You always have to be straight up and the funny thing is even if you are some of these fools are still going to come off funny. Just because…"

"Just because?"

"Man I just finished reading Machiavelli and it really helped me to see things clearer. A whole lot of factors come into play when money and power are involved. A lot of times it leads to jealousy and deceit for no apparent reason other than that's what money and power breed."

Kane smiled.

"So, you want to do this?"

"No I don't want to do this. I need to do this. This is for my kid."

"And after this you're out Ali."

"What are you saying Kane?"

"I'm saying that if you were in this for the long haul I'd go along with you on the thing about divvying up shares equally and the loyalty bullshit but your future ain't on the streets. And all you need to do is take down the scores and deliver the take to me. You work for me just like they work for me. Kane decides what goes where. Think of your son and know that you were the mastermind behind this and make sure you and your seed are taken care of. Don't worry about the rest of your crew. Understand? It seems ugly now but in the long run it's the right thing to do. Trust me on this one. The worst thing in life is wasted potential and missed opportunities. Remember that."

"I gotcha. And thanks for the opportunity Kane."

"Don't thank me until it's over Ali. This might be the most dangerous thing you've ever done in your life. You'll be the first in and the last out and like you said chances are they've beefed up security so they'll be waiting on you. This is more or less a suicide mission so don't thank me."

"What kind of cash do I have a chance to make tonight?"

"I'm no Nostradamus Ali but there's a good chance you could make your son an orphan. Think about that."

"Thought about that when I first hit the street. I'm down baby."

"Okay. You be safe young brother."

"No doubt. Can I ask you for a favor man?"

"Name it."

"I want your word that you'll take care of my son if anything should happen to me."

Kane stood and stared deep into the young man's eyes. No words were needed.

"Call me when it's done."

Ali's words struck home. It was one thing to put himself on the front line but quite another to send a seventeen year old to fight a war he hadn't even chosen. But that's what he'd done and he was having difficulty coming to terms with that.

Kane walked in the door at well after eight o'clock and was greeted by the warm smell of greens, ham hocks, candied yams and pork roast.

"Hope you're hungry baby," Mattie said kissing him quickly before preparing his plate.

"Hey Kane," Naomi said popping her head in the kitchen.

"Naomi's becoming quite a cook. She fixed the greens and candied yams."

"And I'm starved."

Kane's phone rang.

"Kane here."

"Kane, it's me Marcus. Is this a secure line?"

"Yeah. Go ahead. What's up?"

"Boy's in Jersey don't want the contract. It seems they don't want to be in the middle of a war and don't want to go up against Chase and it seems that the young man you want to take out is Mr. Chase's nephew."

"Didn't know that. But if they won't do it someone else will. Don't worry about it. I'll take care of it. Anything else I should know about?"

"No. I made the call and spoke to one of Chase's flunkies and told him I'd take the contract. Eva was ecstatic. They're giving me a hundred grand to take you out and they want it done within the week."

"Damn is that all. Thought I was worth more than that."

Marcus laughed.

"Anyway, when this is over promise me one thing Kane. Promise I can personally take care of Eva."

"You got it. Call me when you get in tonight and be safe Marcus."

"No worries."

Ali and Marcus met at the safe house later that night.

"They gonna be waitin' for us. Ain't gonna be no more walk in the park and I'm gonna be the first one in so I'm gonna need for y'all to have my back. Is that understood? I've got a two month son at home and I would like to see him when this is all over and it's up to you if I do so take this shit seriously and if any one looks like they wanna do somethin' besides layin' down then lay them down permanently. You feel me?"

"We got you Ali," Born said among the chorus of affirmations.

"I ain't got no seeds but I wanna come home too," Marcus chimed in.

Everyone laughed as they filed out of the tiny apartment and headed for the cars. "

"Kane wants us to hit the houses simultaneously in Brooklyn and Queens. That way they know it's no random act and it's the same people and when he gets the call he's hoping that it'll draw him out in the open so give me a call when you're in position," Marcus said to Ali. "And good luck my brother."

An hour later Ali got the call.

"It's a quarter after twelve. Are you in position?"

"Sittin' here chillin' just waitin' for your call."

"Let's do the damn thang then. Call me when it's all over."

Ali signaled the fellas and they staggered the flow into the building. Traffic was extremely high for a Friday night and Ali knew that if all went right it would be a great score to take down. Ali's four man crew was disciplined and ready only there was no white boy this time, Ali tilted the hat to his side and knocked.

"What you need?"

"A gram," the door opened slightly and Ali was escorted to the living room where the dope boy took out a small knife and began to chip off the equivalent of a gram and placed it

187

on the small scale while several other buyers lined up behind Ali.

When the young man seemed to be finished weighing it and began wrapping it Ali started complaining.

"Ah man you can do better than that. I thought we was cool and you was gonna bless me."

"Nigga I ain't never seen you before in my life. The scale

don't lie. You asked for a gram. That's a gram. Take it or leave it I've got other customers to serve."

Born who was next in line suddenly moved up.

"Move out of the way nigga and let somebody who's spendin' step up. I ain't got time for all this bullshit."

Born moved from behind Ali with both pistols drawn while Ali grabbed the duct tape and began securing the dope boys to the chairs. TJ and Dre scoured the other rooms which were packed with crack smoking fiends who hardly noticed them with guns drawn.

Ali grabbed the keys and unlocked the stash and put it as well as watches chains and any other valuables into a large kitchen garbage bag while dispersing twenties of crack to all in attendance. There was no need to tie them down now and Ali and Born and the crew made it out just as smoothly as they'd entered. The other two crack houses went down in much the same manner and Ali joked on the way home that he'd found a new career that demanded far less work and the hours were better but after the joking was finished and the job over Ali was sure of one thing, He didn't want to do that again.

Marcus only wished his night had gone so smoothly. With the last house secured and them backing out of the house a door had been open as if someone was trying to retaliate when Marcus shot killing the intruder instantly only to find it was a four year old boy who died on the spot

"Man he came out of nowhere," was all he kept repeating.

"It happens Marcus and it's sad but why was a four year old there in the first place? Why would anyone have a toddler in the house with guns and drugs? That's the question you have to ask yourself. But don't get down on yourself. War's an ugly business and sometimes there are innocents among the casualties and that's why this was your last job," Kane said turning to Ali as Ali smiled dumping the cash and other loot from the raids on the kitchen table.

"Whoa! Whoa! Whoa! Let me deal with Marcus first. He's had a particularly trying night so let's get him squared away and home so he can rest. Where you staying Marcus?"

"Following your orders boss. I'm at Eva's crib although I ain't really feelin' her. All she does is walk around with that damn stem in her mouth or a spoon up her nose. At the rate she's going she gonna snort up Columbia."

Kane smiled.

"So, she's staying home?"

"Why the hell would she go anywhere? She's got her own personal supplier right there in the crib. And being that that's all she cares about she's pretty much in heaven.

She's constantly trying to show her appreciation though and who am I to stop her."

"I sure wouldn't. Eva's fine as hell," Ali commented.

"Eva's a snake," Marcus spewed.

"With some good damn pussy."

"How would you know?"

"Who doesn't know? My whole crew done had that. She's a monster. You dangle that nose candy in front of her and she'll do anything you ask her to do. Eva's a U.S.D.A grade A certified freak. Gave her an eight ball and spent the night with her a couple of years ago. Bitch had me where I didn't know my name and didn't wanna go home when I left her," Ali laughed. "That's some of the best pussy I ever had. Half of them old bitches on the strip be hustling and tryna get you to front 'em a little something something but I ain't frontin' no crack head bitch nothin' cause I don't want to have to hurt 'em when they come up short or with some lame ass excuse when they can't pay me so I just get 'em to give me head. But you know I really like the older bitches cause they experienced and know all the tricks but half of them just lie there and just let you get your shit off. But Eva's different. Eva can make you come in a minute. Damn! I'm getting a woody just thinkin' bout it. Eva's shit be like kryptonite. You walk in there feeling like Superman and walk out like what the fuck just hit me," Ali said laughing now. "If you ain't up to it Marcus you just let me know. I can step in there as the second team."

Let me tell you two things you may not be aware of young blood. First of all, everything that seems good is not good

190

for you. And the second thing is you don't step in every hole you see," Marcus said.

"That's sound advice he's giving you Ali."

"Eva's a snake and has spent her whole life using her pussy to get what she wants. She'll just as soon as soon shoot you as to rob you. If I were you I'd stay away from her and those like her. She's the reason where at war now."

Marcus got up, a weary look on his face and walked away.

"Kane, I'm leaving the bag here. I'm beat man. I'll talk to you in the morning."

"Alright Marcus. You be safe and don't be so hard on yourself. It's gonna get better."

"I hear you boss," Marcus said closing the door behind him.

The cold air felt good and Marcus left the car there and decided to walk the four blocks to Eva's. Being in charge of the dope boys on the strip was one thing. Someone out there always had game. If it wasn't one of the crew trying to rip him off for a couple of dollars on a package then it was some dope fiend trying to run game. And until Kane came along it was the police too. It seemed it was always something. In the beginning it had been fun but he was thirty four now and the things that had seemed fun at eighteen or nineteen just didn't have the same allure. Sure he was making money but he didn't have the kind of money where he could just call it a day and sit back and chill.

And yet he managed. But with Kane pairing him up with Eva's looney ass he no longer had the comfort of going back to the rest when the day was over and just kick back and let everything melt away. No, he had to be even more careful and aware than when he was on the street with Eva's crazy ass. Marcus took a deep breath and walked the last block to her building. As if that weren't enough the recurring thought of the boy's eyes staring at him in amazement as the bullet smacked him flush and sent him sprawling across the room in a heap of blood and flesh only made him want to scream out. He could fail the nauseousness in his belly and held on to a nearby fence where he threw up over and over until there was nothing left. Marcus made his way over to the curb where he sat holding his head between his legs.

He'd been doing this ever since he could remember and was tired. He was just tired.

Meanwhile back in the Dunbar apartment, Ali watched as Kane counted the money for the third time.

"Half a key. You can give that to your boys. They could make close to sixty five, seventy on the street or you can offer them these ten g's to split giving them about thirty five hundred apiece. What do you think they're gonna do?"

"Ain't no doubt. They gonna take the thirty five hundred ready cash. Me, myself I'd take the half a cake and sit on it. That's seventy grand or more dependin' on the cut you put on it."

Kane smiled again.

"And that my friend is what separates you from the crowd. You have insight and as long as you can see the big picture you won't stand for small things. But tonight you got to see the other side of things."

"What?!? I ain't seeing nothin' but love Kane. How much we do?"

"A little over ninety g's, a half a brick and those trinkets whatever they're worth. If I were you I'd take some time while your boys are sitting around partying to think about tonight and your future."

"What's to think about Kane? We brought in ninety something g's and half a brick to boot. It's all good baby."

Kane paused to let the boy reflect.

"One of the worst things about youth is the impulsiveness." Kane said pulling out a cigarette.

"I don't get you man."

"Marcus brought in over a hundred and twenty grand and two bricks and walked out of here looking like his best friend just passed away."

"Yeah, I know. Shooting that kid really fucked him up but he'll be alright. Marcus ain't no punk. He'll rebound. In a couple of days he'll be back to his old self."

"Maybe but I doubt it. You see Ali, it's not just that it was a kid. It's the fact that he took a life. Most people go through life never pulling down a score like you did night and never killing a kid or anyone for that matter and I'd be willing to bet you that Marcus would give up all the cash

193

and dope if he could have that kid back. That's something that changes your life forever and I only pray that you'll never have to experience that but that's where you're headed."

Ali dropped his head.

"You brought in ninety grand. Ten goes to your crew and I'm giving you ten for you being crew leader."

"That's love Kane," Ali said jumping up and hugging the older man.

"Sit down boy."

Ali still grinning from ear-to-ear did as he was told. "Ali as I told you earlier today you're different. These streets ain't for everybody and from what I've seen over the last month or so it ain't for you. No disrespect son. I think you could probably do it and do it well for a couple of years 'til someone found you dead in some alley. But I think you could make a real impact if you gave this shit up. So, I've got a proposal for you Ali. What I have to propose ain't no quick loot. In all seriousness you might not see loot like this for another five or ten years but it'll be worth it over the long run."

"I'm listening."

"Ali, I want you to do is get your G.E.D. Don't worry about your rent and bills. I want you to live off this ten g's over the next few months. Then once you get your G.E.D. I want you to come see me and we'll go from there. One thing I don't want you to do is be on those streets. You catch a charge or anything like that the deals off. And don't sweat if you hear talk or don't see me for a while. I'll be outta sight and outta mind but trust I'll still be around."

"All sounds like a riddle to me but I'll ride it out."

"Good man," Kane said hugging the young man. "And remember no matter what people say out here in these streets I'm okay. I'll be watching you Ali."

"I hear ya boss. You sure you gonna be alright?"

"I'll be fine Ali as long as you do what I ask you to do."

"You ain't gotta worry about me boss. I'm gonna hold it down just like you asked me to."

Kane headed towards the door.

"You be safe."

"Always."

Kane headed home. Born and the boys were standing guard at the entrance of his block and nodded as he passed. His thoughts were jumbled but he was in control. Chase hadn't made a move since spraying the pool hall and Kane had to wonder if Chase had simply given up or was he simply biding his time and waiting for Marcus to play out his hand and end it all. He had to have gotten the threat of the leak by now but still he hadn't made any clearly defined offensive and this bothered Kane. Picking up his phone he called Black. "It's the strangest thing Kane. This cat hasn't set foot outside the crib in over a week. We've basically cut off all communication between him and the outside and from the one person we let in and out he's as cool as a cucumber. From what we understand his people in the streets are clamoring for him to do something. They're yelling for revenge after you hit their spots. He's their main distributor and from what we're getting three of the six spots are bone drop and the other three are running on fume. Couple of the dope fiends on the streets are saying that they're cutting the shit so much trying to stretch it that they're not even shopping with 'em anymore. But this cat is cool as a cucumber. He doesn't seem flustered or anything. They say he's just layin low, enjoying his kids and is content to just sit and wait it out. He's either scared to death or he has something up his sleeve."

"I'm pretty sure he's up to something but I've got something for him."

"You be careful Kane."

"Always," Kane said letting the dial tone go dead before calling Marcus.

"Just calling to check on you man. How you doing?"

"Better man. What's up?"

"I was just thinkin' with Chase thinkin' he's got you why don't you give him a call and tell him I'm on the run. Tell him you haven't seen me in days and see if you can't get permission to put your people back to work. See if you can't get us back out there tonight."

"Sounds like a plan."

"Give him a call and then call me back and let me know."

"I'll do that."

Kane took the pad from his pocket and drew a line through the things he'd accomplished. Everything was going according to plan. But what was the saying? Man plans and God laughs. There was still something amiss, something he'd forgotten to tie up. But what was it?

"Charlie. This is Kane speaking. Just wanted to know if you had any news, any updates."

"No sir. I'll give you a call as soon as I hear something."

"Alright Charlie. You have a good evening."

No sooner had he hung than Marcus called.

"We're back on boss. He says we can go back to work. Asked me what kind of split we were getting before. I told him there was no split that I was an independent contractor and I paid a small tax for protection and from police harassment. And that was it."

"And?"

"He said we didn't know what money was. Said he'd supply this high grade shit on commission and we'd sell it for the same price and sell more and it would be a seventy thirty split and we'd still make twice as much as we do now. Now you and I both know that shit ain't happenin' Kane."

"Just play along until this motherfucker gets lax and then we take him out."

"Greedy motherfucker."

"What we give you Kane? Ten percent?"

"Yeah. I might have to raise my rates," Kane laughed. "Does he supply protection?"

"Hell no. Police lock your ass and to him it's just an occupational hazard but his ass ain't spending one day in Rikers or the Tombs."

"I may have to extend my vacation a week or two. For the first time in I don't know how long I'm starting to feel appreciated," Kane laughed.

"Let's just hurry and take this motherfucker out Kane. Between Chase and Eva I may just go ham."

Kane laughed.

"Be easy Marcus. It's the nature of the game these things come up every few years."

"Alright Kane. Do what you have to do. You know you only have six days to live so handle your business. He says he's gonna let us exhaust our supply and then

we're supposed to call him to re-up. What he doesn't know is that he's already supplied us. We can go a good month just off the shit we confiscated from the crack houses we raided."

"Keep that shit on the low low or you won't even be lookin' at thirty percent."

"I hear you."

"And do me a favor Marcus."

"Yeah boss."

"Keep Ali off the streets. I don't want him near the streets. He's retired."

"Ali? He's a good kid Kane. What did he do?"

"That's just it. He's a good kid. He doesn't need to be out there. He needs to be in school. Did you know that he was an honor roll student before he dropped out? He and I made a deal that he's going to finish school and I don't want him out there on them streets. So if you see him chase his ass home."

"Will do boss."

"Alright Marcus. I'm heading in. Watch out for the fam."

"Okay Kane."

Chapter 7

"Hey sweetheart," Mattie smiled hugging Kane tightly. "How was your day?"

"Surprisingly busy but uneventful."

"You tired?"

"I've got too much to do to be tired baby. How was your day?"

Mattie followed Kane upstairs and was surprised when he pulled out two suitcases and an overnight bag.

"Going somewhere love?"

"I have to leave town for a few weeks."

"What's that supposed to mean? When were you going to tell me or weren't you? What if I hadn't been home? What were you going to do then? Just leave a note on the fridge?"

Kane turned and grabbed Mattie by the shoulders. Pulling her towards him he bent down and whispered softly in her ear.

"I have to go Mattie. But it won't be for long. I'm the only thing stopping Chase from going on a killing spree. My being here is what's stopping people from working and eating. How many of your friends have called you asking you to speak to me so they can get back to work."

"I ain't thinking about those greedy bitches. They shouldn't be calling me at all. What they should have been doing is putting away money for a rainy day. They have the

nerve to call and put pressure on you and you're the reason half of 'em ain't in the psyche ward, jail or dead. I don't give a fuck what them looney bitches think. You see that's the fuckin' problem with you Kane. You always worried about some fuckin' body when you should be worryin' about yourself."

There was more truth in Mattie's words than Kane wanted to admit. How long had he worked and protected those very same people that were now blaming him for taking money out of their pocket?

Still, Kane was not new to any of this and knew that on the streets the very same person that claimed they'd lay down their very life for you one day was the same person that would pull the trigger the next for the right kind of money. Mattie was right but these were his people and no matter what he had to protect them. It was as if this were his birthright.

"Charlie Rosenberg is setting up two accounts for you. One is a business account for the women's center and the other is a personal account for you, the house and Naomi."

"I don't need Charlie Rosenberg to do shit for me. Only thing I need is my fuckin' husband."

Kane smiled. He loved Mattie more than life itself and knew there was nothing he could do or say to make her understand.

Kane continued.

"I shouldn't be gone any more than a month. If you need me contact Charlie. He'll know how to get in touch."

"I'm not calling Charlie to get in touch with my husband. How the fuck does that sound?" And then Mattie opened the door to her own closet and pulled a suitcase out.

"What are you doing Mattie?"

"I'm going with you Kane."

"You can't sweetheart. I need you here. Naomi needs you. The women's center needs you. You have to appear as the broken widow. I need you here if we're going to make this thing work. We have to play this out until the very end if we're going to pull this off."

"But it's not fair," Mattie said sitting on the edge of the bed crying. "You asked me to leave the streets and I did. What about you Kane? You said you were getting out as well and you've never been deeper."

"Life has a way of changing a man's plans Mattie. I'm responsible for more than just you and I and they look to me to get them out of this mess and if staying away for a few weeks so they can have a better quality of life and not let them get slaughtered in the street like they used to then it's the least I can do."

"You're right and I know I'm being selfish but I don't have to like it."

"No, you don't and if you did I know I'd married the wrong woman. This is the last hurrah baby. Once this is over I'm leaving the whole she-bang in Marcus' hands. I have other plans on ways to improve the community."

"I've heard that before. What can I say Kane," Mattie said rather disgustedly throwing the suitcase back in the closet.

"I have to leave Mattie." Kane grabbed Mattie and brought him to her. "I love you Mattie Close," he said before grabbing the bag from the bed and heading towards the door.

That first night back was a good night and Marcus like the rest of his crew was glad to be on the streets and earning once more but for Marcus his motivation was of a different nature. In truth he despised drugs and those that used them. Eva had only heightened his distaste and he like Kane had come to the firm conclusion that when this was finished and Kane's return he too would leave the streets to those that would have it.

His days numbered Marcus had already begun to consolidate his funds. No more did he own the plush downtown condominium. Eva's little apartment wasn't much and wasn't only economical but was convenient being only a couple of blocks from the spot. And with the hundred g's from he'd get assassinating Kane he'd have enough for a modest little home down South somewhere.

Now all he had to do in the month's to come was to handle his business. He had nine keys from the raids worth close to two hundred and fifty thousand. Seventy five thousand would go to pay his crew. The rest would be his startup money to invest and establish himself elsewhere.

The first week back was sensational. Everybody seemed happy. The dope boy's under the impression they'd won the war couldn't supply their customer's fast enough. Making money hand over fist there was little or no concern. Well that was for everyone except Marcus who dreaded going home to Eva each morning. No matter what time of morning there she was always there with her hand out. And she had long since stopped asking for money. The clothes and other things Marcus would grace her with had suddenly lost their appeal. Diamonds and other jewelry which not so long ago she craved for were no longer a passion with Eva now and little seemed to exist aside from the crack rock which Marcus kept locked up in the wall safe he'd had installed in the bedroom.

Kane left him with instructions to give her whatever it was that she wanted and it had seemed a fair demand in lieu of the fact that Eva served as the only pipeline between Kane and what Chase had on his mind. And it hadn't been such a bad trade off at the time but in the short time since he'd begun residing there she'd gone from eight balls to half ounces to ounces in only a matter of a few days. Eva had gotten so bad that Marcus had to break her off chunks at regular intervals during the day. If he left her a day's supply she'd smoke it all by noon and call him all day begging him for more. It was all more than Marcus could take. But tonight took the cake. After blowing up his phone for several hours Marcus turned it off and vowed to hit Boost Mobile first thing in the morning to have his number changed. Eva however, who couldn't wait until Marcus finished his shift ade her way down the three blocks in her stocking feet and the same house robe she'd had on since Marcus had first gone to see her. She was filthy and quite mad.

"Marcus Cousins I'm tired of you treating me like a kid, like some kind of pet. I'm your woman motherfucker. I've been calling you all night. Now give me some shit. If you want any more of this pussy you better feed me bitch."

For a moment it was as if gunshots had been fired. All eyes turned towards the woman with pin curlers in her head and then to Marcus who had a knack for snatching up those who were loud and obnoxious. But not tonight. Marcus just signaled to Born who grabbed Eva by the arm, slid something into her hand that seemed to satisfy her and turned her back in the direction she'd come from.

Moments later he stood by his boss' side.

"What you gonna do about that boss? Shit like that scares customers. They hear all that cussin' and screamin' and think somethin's gonna pop off."

"I'll handle that when I get home. Right now let's just concentrate on getting this cheddar."

"Tell me something boss and no disrespect intended but is she that good in the sack? No disrespect but I ain't never seen you let no ho disrespect you in public."

"This goes way deeper than that. I'll tell you about it in time but for right now just let it go. How much did you give her?"

"Only a twenty. I told her you'd be home in an hour and you'd take care of her then."

"Good. How are sales?"

"Off the hook. Even better than when Kane was here."

"Good. Stay on them boys and keep pumpin'."

Born moved to the other side of the street and was soon immersed in the group of men. 'Even better than when Kane was here'. The words reverberated in Marcus' head. Kane was right. Born was stupid. Couldn't he see that Kane was responsible for all of this? The coke they were now selling was one hundred per cent profit because of the raids that Kane had arranged and business was so good because everyone knew that they could come here and buy with no hassle, no chance of getting beat or ripped off and there was no drama. And that was all the result of the law that Kane had laid down.

On this night curb service was especially busy. Marcus fingered the glock in his waistband. At six foot two and two hundred and twenty pounds he had assumed Kane's role as enforcer and now had little time for menial conversation. But Born was right about one thing. Never before would he have taken some ho bad-mouthing him on the street and in his new role as enforcer he really couldn't allow someone challenging his authority as Eva had just done but now with her gone there was little to be done. And he like Born was now questioning his response to her screaming at him on the streets. Street mentality, like Borns' either figured he was pussy whipped or soft. And on these mean streets there could be little doubt about either.

Marcus knew that a twenty would only quiet Eva for a minute and so he turned his phone back on to await her call. No sooner had he when it rang.

"Baby I need a little something."

"I'm workin' Eva. You'll just have to wait 'til I get home."

"Baby, I'm hurtin'."

"I'll tell you what. Wash your funky ass. You've had that nasty ass robe on since I first came to the crib. Then get dressed. You embarrassed me comin' down here lookin' a hot mess with curlers in your hair like you just got out of bed. Put some clothes on. Don't you ever come down here telling people you're my woman lookin' like that again. Do you hear me? Have some respect for yourself."

"I'm sorry daddy. I'm going to get myself together and make you proud of me. I'll see you in a little while."

Marcus had little or no feeling for the woman but only entertained her because Kane had asked him to. He knew Eva only tolerated him because he supplied her with the drugs she needed in larger and larger doses now. The way her habit had grown there was no way she could sustain it from prostituting herself.

Business was still booming when Eva showed up in a white sweat suit and white Tims. Still a good looking woman Eva had always had the ability to turn heads and she did so on this night but Eva saw no one but Marcus who held the key to all of her woes.

"Hey baby. Is this better?"

"Much," Marcus said ignoring the woman standing beside him.

"Can you take care of a sista daddy?"

"You just standing there Marcus looking just as good as you want to," Eva said standing on her tippy toes in an attempt to kiss Marcus now.

"Eva stand to the side now. Can't you see I'm working?"

"Damn you acting like Kane more and more everyday Marcus. But Kane ain't never said no to his woman. From what I hear he give Mattie anything she want."

"And Mattie ain't no crackhead. She don't spend her whole day suckin' on a glass pipe and beggin' for more. You know what Mattie's doing? She's set up a women's center up on 8th to try and stop these young girls from putting themselves out there prostitutin' themselves and sucking on glass dicks. She's trying to stop young girls from turning out like you. You didn't know that did you?"

Eva stood there stunned. Marcus had never talked to her like this before. Stunned by the onslaught it took her a few to regain her composure.

"Why you bastard, I opened up my home and my life to you. I gave you the opportunity to make a hundred g's and all I asked was for you to show you a little compassion and you treat me like this. You know I could have easily thrown you under the bus with Kane but I always thought you were a stand-up guy Marcus. I've offered you everything I have."

"You don't have shit I want Eva? Face it! Who wants to say my woman's a pipe head, a crack head, a dope fiend that'll suck your dick for a hit. Who wants that? Hey Born, Marcus yelled, "Ask my woman here if she'll suck your dick for a twenty?"

"Oh shit," was Born's reply as he and the rest of the crew burst out in raucous laughter.

"You motherfucker!" Eva screamed.

With all attention now on the fighting couple Marcus grabbed the butt of the glock and in one easy motion backhanded Eva who fell to the ground her nose bloody. Born was at Marcus' side before he could bring the butt of the gun down again.

"Chill Marcus! This is bad for business baby."

Marcus held back. "I should shoot this bitch," he yelled cocking the glock and shoving it in Eva's mouth. "You want something to suck on? Suck on this bitch!"

"C'mon boss. She ain't worth it."

Marcus removed the gun from Eva's mouth. Speechless she stood up and took the bandana from Born's outstretched hand and wiped her nose.

"I ain't your daddy and I ain't your man bitch," Marcus shouted at her. "You better take that tired worn out ol' pussy and get to trickin' bitch. That's the only way you gonna get a thimble full of crack outta me bitch. Now pay me!"

Eva was clearly stunned.

"Marcus."

"Start walkin' you skank bitch," Marcus said sliding the gun back in his waistband.

The whole thing had become a spectacle and any concern with Marcus being pussy whipped quickly became a thing of the past.

"I told you that bitch was going to pay," Born said to the crew. "Boss ain't no fool. M-O-B baby. It's always been money over bitches. I'm thinkin' that sheisty bitch got the message. She layin' up getting puffed but like I said Marcus ain't no fool. He put her ass right back out on the street. She back where she's supposed to be. I don't know why he put up with her ass that long."

Used to the drama, the fellas went right back to plying their trade as if nothing had happened. Eva however, had other thoughts. And by five o'clock in the morning she was done and walked the three blocks back to the apartment. She picked up a twenty from Born on her way in and was saving most of the six hundred she'd made to buy from Marcus who she figured would be feeling some kind of way about hitting her. Both her lip and nose were swollen and she knew if this man felt anything he would feel remorse and her money would be best spent with him.

Little was she to know that the beat down had had just the opposite effect on Marcus who had weeks ago grown tired of pandering to her.

Walking in the house, Marcus took the blue and black leather Avirex jacket off and threw it over the arm of the recliner before grabbing a cold one from the fridge. He was exhausted. Sitting down he couldn't believe how tired he was. He only hoped that Eva was sleep or still out when he heard the bedroom door closed. Marcus quickly gathered the stacks of money from the living room table. He was at thirteen five and still counting.

The extra money from Kane's protection certainly added to his nightly haul and that was after taking care of his boys.

"Hey sweetie," Eva said holding the ice pack to her lip and nose. "I apologize for all the trouble I caused tonight."

Marcus looked at the woman.

"It's a substance abuse problem. I'm going to get help the first of the month just as soon as my health benefits kick in. I didn't mean to embarrass you in front of everyone baby," she said leaning over and grabbing his free hand.

"You didn't embarrass me Eva. The only person you embarrassed is yourself. You was a fucked up individual before. Now you a fucked individual with a habit that makes you beg and grovel. You at least had some pride before."

"I can't argue with you Marcus but please just give me a little time to get myself together. I swear I'll make it up to you. I'm going to admit myself into rehab just as soon as I get my benefits but in the meantime can you bless me sweetheart."

"Did you pay me?"

"Oh c'mon Marcus. You're not really gonna tax me are you? I mean I haven't been working in over three months and the first day back you're going to charge me?"

"Everybody pays dear. Somebody's gotta pay the overhead. If I have to stop slinging to make sure you're protected then somebody's gotta pay. And ten percent is a whole lot less than you'd have to give a pimp. Then I'm providing security at the trap houses. Tell me who's supposed to pay the rent? C'mon Eva. You were out there for half a night and what did you pull in?"

"A little over six hundred."

"And you don't see any reason to pay the house?"

"I'm not going to argue with you Marcus. What do I owe you Marcus?"

"You know what you owe me Eva. I don't even know why you're trying it. You haven't paid rent in two months and haven't had to pay for a motherfuckin' thing since I've been here."

Eva pouted before going into her bra and peeling off five twenties.

"I guess I have to pay for everything now, huh?" she said before counting off another two hundred and twenty five dollars.

213

"What's that for Eva?"

"I need an eight ball, Marcus."

"I thought you were going to stop this shit and going into rehab?"

"I have to wait 'til my benefits kick in. I told you that Marcus."

"Yeah, okay Eva but this is the last time. So pull slowly. You're killin' yourself girl. I'm going to bless you this one last time but don't you come asking me for shit again. Do you hear me? Now put your money away. If this is how you want to kill yourself then fine but I'm not going to help you do it. Your money ain't gonna make me or break me but this shit is gonna kill you and like I said I ain't gonna be responsible for nothing but telling you to stop. From now on when you wanna get high you get it from somewhere else and I don't wanna know."

"Okay daddy and I am sorry for the way I acted tonight. It won't happen again," she said doing her best to act contrite as Marcus broke her off more than the eight ball she had asked for.

"If you were smart you'd put some up for tomorrow but you won't. I'm serious Eva. Don't come begging me when this shit is gone. I don't care how much money you have don't ask me for shit."

"I heard you Marcus."

"Good night Eva."

"Good night and thank you Marcus. By the way can I ask you something?"

"When are you going to do the hit on Kane?"

Marcus felt something akin to what he'd felt the night he'd mistakenly shot the little boy as he vomit rose to his mouth. He was truly beginning to loathe Eva and if it wasn't for Kane's instruction he would have made short work of her long ago. But for now he simply locked the bedroom door and put both the money and drugs in the safe and locked it before crawling into bed.

When he awoke the next morning there was Eva lying next to him sleeping soundly. Getting up to use the bathroom he was surpirised to find most if not all he'd given her was still on the living room table. He smiled. Perhaps she was serious about quitting. He'd seen people do it. One day they were smoking like there was no tomorrow and then just like that they stopped and turned their lives around. Maybe just maybe. But then this was Eva. Nah...

She was still asleep when he hit the streets. Five days had passed since he'd spoken to Chase and time was running out. He'd gotten a phone call from Kane as he was leaving town hooking him up with some cat named Black who was supposed to be handling the Cruz hit and Naomi's uncle. He had a hundred thousand for this nigga Black for some surveillance work they were doing as well as the hits and he was supposed to meet them today in South Jamaica Queens. Ali was going to meet him and the two of them were supposed to do the meet. That was all Marcus knew and that was all he wanted to know. The less the better.

Marcus and Ali met and it was as if the two hadn't parted company at all.

"So Kane is gone."

"I haven't seen Kane in a minute."

"C'mon Marcus you know more than you're telling me."

"I can't talk about it Ali. Just keep the faith baby and follow his instructions. He loves you boy and only wants to see the best for you so don't ask questions just do what you're supposed to be doing."

After the meet Ali seemed impressed.

"Those were some pretty together brothers to be from Queens. The nigga they called Black—you know the one that pulled me in the back room…"

"Yeah," Marcus laughed. "You should have seen your face. Yo. You was scareder than a bitch."

"You fuckin' right. I ain't know those niggas and you said we ain't need no freezes and you gotta admit those niggas was spooky. I ain't seen 'em smile yet. Them motherfuckers was serious as hell. Matter-of-fact they all acted like Kane with that no nonsense I'll fuck you up then kill you shit. So, hell yeah I was scared. Who was they anyway?"

"That was Kane's crew when he was coming up. Now they all got they own districts but ain't a one of 'em to be fucked with. You right. They some cold niggas. All a dem go hard. So, what he call you in the back for?"

"Don't really know. Told me to take this envelope to some attorney's office and introduce myself and give it to him. Then he gave me five one hundred dollar bills and told me to just keep doing what I'm doing and there'd be more where those came from. I ain't say shit but yessir."

"Do what they tell you Ali."

"Hell, I'd be afraid not to. Them niggas is real gangstas."

Marcus laughed.

"They used to be. They've all gone legit a long time ago. They just stepped in to help Kane in his time of need. Most of them own their own businesses. I think Black owns four or five McDonalds franchises on Long Island. That's the man that took you in the back and gave you the loot. From what I hear he made most of his paper in investment banking down on Wall Street. These ain't no common everyday street thugs. I'm telling you son. You're in high cotton now. I don't know why Kane chose you as his stepson but if I were you I'd do exactly as he said whether you see him ever again or not."

"I hear you," Ali muttered.

The two men rode the rest of the way in silence. Ali's thoughts revolved around Marcus' last comment and he too wondered what Kane had in store for him. Whatever it was he was on board having just passed his G.E.D. he was still puzzled as to what to do next.

Chapter 8

"Mrs. Close this is Charlie Rosenberg. How are things coming along at the women's center? I've been meaning to get down there but I've been so busy trying to get things in order with your husband's accounts that I haven't really had a chance to breathe."

"Charlie have you heard anything from my husband?"

"No, Mrs. Close I haven't and if I did it would be an admission of guilt and admissible in court that I knew of his whereabouts and I honestly don't. Let's just hope that he's fine. That's all we can do."

Mattie hung her head. She'd been despondent the last week or so. It wasn't like Kane not to stay in touch. It was now going on three weeks and she hadn't received as much as a text. It just wasn't Kane. Oh, how she wished she'd persisted about his getting out but no he and his damn loyalty to Mike. And where was Mike now? He was headed down the same road but you couldn't tell him anything. That damn code of the streets. Hell, half of those that he gave his life protecting would have given him up for a few hits and a couple of dollars.

"Mrs. Close are you there?"

"Yes. I'm here Charlie? What can I do for you?"

"There's a young man here who has a letter of introduction from some of your husband's business partners. I am to send him to you and you are to use him in any way

you deem necessary. His name is Ali Mohammed. He'll be reporting to work tomorrow at eight a.m."

"And he is to receive a salary?"

"That's all been taken care of. Just put him to work. Good day Mrs. Close."

Ali stood in front of the lawyer.

"Don't know if you know it or not son but someone has really taken a fondness to you. You have an endowment here for a pretty sizeable chunk of change if you agree to it. Would you like me to read it verbatim or simply summarize it for you?"

"I suppose a summarization would be okay."

"Okay. Ali you'll be granted all your living expenses and a small stipend which comes to a little over forty thousand a year which I must say is more than adequate since your basic necessities have all been taken care of. But the real perk is that your college education is paid in full. All you have to do is pick a college out of the five that have been selected. I only wish I had had this when I was starting out. Anyway, if you agree you will be expected to volunteer your services at the new women's center on 8th for one year before switching over to the young men's center as a youth counselor on Adam Clayton Powell Blvd."

Ali sat in the lawyer's office in deep thought. He'd try to follow Kane's instructions and be frugal but bills had been steadily mounting. Now after a month he was

finally caught up but his funds were nearly exhausted. Ali thought of his son and the young mother who tried so feverishly to create a good home and show her support for her man. Accepting the offer was a no brainer. He needed the money but what occupied his thoughts more than anything was the fact that he was blessed and someone really believed in him.

"So, and if you're in accordance I need your signature on the dotted line and I can give you your itinerary."

Ali was still in shock as he leaned over and signed the forms. His own daddy hadn't thought to do anything close to this. When he'd

finished the little white attorney handed him a manila envelope.

"In it you'll find a short list of colleges. I think there are five or six. Pick one. Fill out the application. Send it in and send me a copy and do it quickly. The fall semester starts in a couple of weeks.

Tomorrow morning at eight a.m. you will report to the women's center and meet with Mrs. Close. She will assign you with your duties. You will work there from eight 'til four every day until you start school when you will adapt your work schedule around your classes. And please don't ask Mrs. Close anything about your salary. She has nothing at all to do with your being paid. In the manila envelope you'll find a debit card. It's active and every two weeks from this date you'll find your pay for the past two weeks. If you have any questions or concerns or are sick you'll find Mrs. Close and my card in there. Give us a call. And if there are no further questions then I wish you the best of luck."

"No sir and thank you sir."

Getting up from the leather and oak chair Ali was dizzy with excitement. His girl would be ecstatic. First his G.E.D. and now just the mere idea that he was enrolling in college and had obtained a full time job all in the same day was almost too much.

"Thank you again sir," Ali said shaking the attorney's hand vigorously. "I can't believe I'm going to college. This is almost like a dream come true."

"Make the best of it. Not a lot of kids from uptown get this opportunity."

"I will sir. You best believe I will," Ali said grabbing the man's hand and shaking it again.

The next morning Ali woke to the sun beaming in diagonally through the torn shade. The floor was cold underfoot but on this morning he hardly noticed as he ran into the kitchen to check the time on the stove. A cockroach stunned by the kitchen light tried to find refuge between the stove and the sink but Ali was on him like a hired killer and with one swat from the fly swatter he had him stunned and with the next the cockroach rolled on his back kicking and screaming in desperation in his cockroach voice as he met with his unenviable fate. It was seven o'clock and the last thing Ali wanted was to be late on his first day. He was tired beyond belief between the idea of his attending college, filling out all five applications and getting up to feed the baby. Still he dressed quickly kissed the baby and his girl and headed down the four flights of stairs and out on the street. Carrying the manila envelope in his back pack Ali darted both the people and cars on the busy avenue until he reached the subway steps which he promptly took two at a time.

As was his luck the train came screaming into the station. It was a cold, gray morning but Ali never felt better. The three stops seemed a blur. Ali checked his watch. It was seven forty five when he came to the street. If the women's center was within a block or two he might still make it. Taking out the business card Ali searched for the address 2645 8th Avenue. Looking up at the building in front of him he saw the sign 8th Avenue Women's Center. God was definitely smiling on him and had been for some time now. Ali adjusted his clothes and backpack and ran his hand through the short kinky afro. Taking a deep breath he was a bit nervous.

Glancing at the dark skinned girl at the front desk Ali had to admit that she was quite attractive but there was something else about her. He was sure he knew her from

somewhere and someone as fine as she was Ali wasn't prone to forget. No he'd seen her somewhere and taken notice then too.

"May I help you sir?"

"Uh yes. My name is Ali Mohammed and I have an eight o'clock appointment with a Mrs. Close."

"Okay. Do me a favor and just sign in and I'll let Mrs. Close know you're here."

"Thank you," Ali said staring all the more deeper now. Yes there was something very familiar about all of this and even the name Close seemed to ring a bell. Was it déjà vu? Ali didn't know. What he did know that this was his first real job, his first day and whatever these crackers asked him to do he'd do it and do it well.

Ali glanced around at the clients who were all Black except for a couple of Puerto Rican mommies. Why was it that even in Harlem where Black people were in the majority there always was some cracker running some institution and deciding their fate? Whatever the reason there was a new day coming and he was gonna use whatever power he had to change things. Moments later a door shut and a stunning figure emerged from the conference room. Dressed in a grey wool suit and black heels she glided

224

down the hall. Ali was mesmerized. And the sense of having been here before was cast over him once again.

"Ali?"

"Mattie?" Ali said in amazement. "You're Mrs. Close? "

"Have been for two month's now. I married Kane—let me see—in July."

"Oh my God! It all makes sense now. So Kane is the one behind all this," Ali said falling back onto the plush brown sofa. "You know I never knew his last name. I'd heardit a couple of times but ain't never put two-and-two together. I was sitting here feeling a certain kind of way but I couldn't piece it together. Like I knew I knew ol' girl at the front desk but I just couldn't piece it together. But anyway it's good to see you Mattie," Ali said smiling broadly. "How are you doing? The fellas and I were wondering what happened to you. It was like you and Eva just upped and disappeared."

"I'm good and you?"

"Better than I've been in a long time thanks to Kane."

"I think a lot us have Kane to thank."

"He's a beautiful brother."

"That he is. He'd been trying to get me off the streets for years but you know how Kane is. He never comes out and says things directly. He puts things out there and you have to be smart enough to pick up on 'em. I guess I wasn't."

"Obviously you did. You're here."

"Well, after all those years getting' grimy on the strip I guess he figured I wasn't going to ever wake up so one day he just snatched me up and took me to the Bahamas and slid this ring on it and said that from now on you'll be known as Mattie Close. End of story. Well, that was the end of the story aside from asking me what I wanted to do now that I didn't have to be out there. I told him that if there was any way I could help the young girls so they wouldn't have to go through the same thing that I had to go through then that's what I wanted to do. So, I came up with the idea of a women's center and one day he came home and dropped a set of keys in my hands. And wala... You have the 8th Avenue Women's Center."

"And what all do you do here?"

"We help young women in every way we can. We try to give them the education and job training skills so they won't have to hit the streets and prostitute themselves and get caught up in the whole street culture."

"You can start with your girl Eva. She's out there."

"What are you saying Ali?"

"When's the last time you've seen Eva, Mattie?"

"It's been a few months."

"She's bad Mattie. She's on the pipe and worse than any dope fiend out there. You know a year ago I rented her an apartment when she was down and out. Checked on her every day when that white boy from Yonkers stomped her and broke four ribs after she tried to rob him."

"I remember."

226

"I would feed her soup every day when she stopped eating. Last week I saw her on the block and spoke to her. Mattie she didn't even recognize me. She had no shoes on and was out there barefoot with a robe on and curlers in her hair. She's bad Mattie. She really is."

"Do you know where she's staying?"

"No doubt. Marcus has her at her crib. He feeds her and keeps her in. She doesn't work no more. I don't know that she can. I think if she were to try and go back out there somebody would dead her with a week. I think Marcus takes care of her because he feels sorry for her but from what I hear she came out on the strip and started acting crazy and Marcus beat her ass. Now you know you have to really be acting crazy to get Marcus to raise his hands."

"That's so sad and that's why we're so needed. We've got to give these girls some options, some alternatives so they don't end up like Eva."

Mattie went on to introduce Ali to the rest of the program's ever-growing staff and the facility. Kane's sudden disappearance however did not come up. In the weeks that followed, Mattie was surprised at how fast Ali picked up the little nuances of the center. He quickly became an integral part of the center and was cognizant and cordial to the clients knowing the plight of most of the young ladies who frequented the now growing center. His easy demeanor made him easy to talk to and despite his age both young and old sought him out for help and advice. When Mattie felt overwhelmed it was Ali who she called first. And in a crisis it was Ali whom she trusted most to deescalate a situation. And for the first time in his life Ali felt he was a part of something, something good, and he

227

couldn't do enough to help Mattie. After all, it was Mattie and Kane who'd made it all possible. Mattie and he were soon inseparable. And it wasn't long before she approached Ali.

"Yes mam, I'm working now on Ms. Cromartie's file. I'm checking now to see if her insurance won't get her in the rehab downtown.   She's only been using for a couple of weeks and seems really sincere about getting off so if I can just get her in somewhere I thinks she stands a good chance of kicking."

"That's good but this isn't about Ms. Cromartie. I think she'll be fine. What I need is something of a more personal nature."

"You already know."

"Good. Grab your coat and things and meet me at the car in five."

Ali was a little suspicious but Mattie had never done anything but look out for him so and although he was a little wary he trusted her. Getting in the car she unlocked the passenger's side door and got in.

"Do you have your license?"

"No, ma'am but you remember when I used to drive Gypsy cabs."

"I know you can drive that's why I asked you if you had your license."

"No ma'am."

"Okay. I'm going to need for you to get that taken care of in the next month. I want to get a small mini-van and see if we can't start transporting some of these ladies to their appointments. Just the cost of bus and train tickets alone is costing the center a small fortune and a lot of it is coming out of pocket because we haven't received full funding yet. It's all bureaucracy you know. If Kane were here he'd have all this bullshit pushed through months ago." As soon as Mattie's words were out she wished she could have taken them back. Up until now she'd made it a point not to mention Kane. This was as much for her benefit as it was for those who wanted to know where he was or if he was still alive.

"Have you heard from him Mattie?"

She knew Ali was one of the few that she could truly trust and was as worried as she was but the truth of the matter was that she hadn't heard anything since he'd left.

"Not a peep."

"Are you worried?"

"To death but I do my best not to think about it."

They were riding through the strip now and Ali stared out the window at his boys posted up plying their trade as the girls walked up and down soliciting onlookers. It was only weeks ago that he was right out there with them but it seemed so long ago. Now he was studying for mid-terms at Baruch and had a full time gig. He wondered how life could get any better and thought of ex-Celtic Hall of Famer Bill Russell's comment on ESPN when asked what his life looked like in retrospect. He recounted Russell saying that

229

he feared heaven would be a letdown after the life he'd led. Ali smiled nodding his head in agreement. So, would his.

A few minutes later Mattie pulled up in front of Esplanarde Gardens. Little was said as they exited the elevator and they were soon knocking at one of the countless doors on the long hall. A man's voice answered. Ali recognized it at once.

"Mattie. Ali. What's up?" Marcus said grinning broadly and grabbing each of them and hugging them tightly. "Boy it's good to see some of the old crowd."

The three reminisced and exchanged pleasantries until Mattie broke the easy banter.

"Marcus is Eva here?"

Marcus' demeanor changed just as soon as the words left Mattie's mouth.

"Yeah, she's here. Probably in the bedroom."

"How's she doing Marcus?"

Marcus stared at the floor without responding. Mattie grabbed his hand in an attempt to get his attention. Marcus looked up into Mattie's questioning eyes then shook his head.

"See for yourself," Marcus replied. "Brace yourself though Mattie. She's not the Eva that you used to know."

Mattie approached the bedroom tentatively. She knocked twice and when there was no answer pushed the door open slowly.

"Eva?"

The woman who had been her friend since grade school was balled up in a fetal position. She was forty pounds thinner her cheekbones protruding through her skin made her resemble a skeleton in a Wes Craven horror flick. Her eyes were vacant and devoid of life as if someone had robbed her very soul.

"Is that you Marcus? Did you bring me a taste? Oh, Marcus I knew you'd bring me a taste. You're such a good man. Here let me hit it daddy and then I'll suck our dick for as long as you want me to. Marcus. Marcus. Please don't tease me. Don't make me beg daddy."

"It's not Marcus Eva. It's me, Mattie."

Eva's head jerked around as she stared at the figure in the doorway.

"Is it really you Mattie?" Eva said as the tears rolled down her gaunt cheeks. "Where have you been Mattie? You were all I had and you just left me. How could you just leave me? You know I needed you and you just left me. You used to always take care of me and you just left me."

"I'm here Eva."

"Yeah! Now you're here. It's too late now," Eva screamed. "Look at me Mattie. Look at what I've become."

"It's never too late," Mattie said taking Eva in her arms and holding her as the woman wept openly squeezing Mattie as if she would find salvation in her grip.

"Can you help me Mattie?"

"Only if you want help Eva."

"I do Mattie. I really do but I'm sick Mattie and that bastard Marcus won't help me get well. I just need a little taste Mattie and then I can get myself together enough to go and get help. My benefits should be in affect by now. I just haven't had the chance to check them but I'm pretty sure they've kicked in by now."

"Okay Eva. I'm going to get you a taste and only a taste but I want you to get up and take a shower and throw some clean clothes on. Once you do that I'll let you have a taste and then Marcus and Ali are going to take you and have you admitted in a program. Do you understand?"

"I knew you'd help me Mattie. I knew if there was anybody on God's green earth that cared about me it was you Mattie."

"You're right. Now hurry up Eva. These gentlemen don't have all day to be messin' around with you."

"You gonna get me a taste Mattie?"

"I'll work on that. You work on getting in the shower."

"Okay Mattie," Eva said sitting up and hugging Mattie tightly. "Do you ever see Jose with the green eyes around Mattie?"

"Not since the sixth grade. Now get in the shower while I go work my magic for your trifling ass."

Eva smiled and for the first time in months there was a sign that there still existed some life in there. Mattie made her way back into the living room where Marcus and Ali were still catching up on news from around the way. Mattie's face told it all.

"I tried to tell you," was all Marcus could say.

"She's a lot worse than I thought," Mattie muttered to no one in particular.

"Worse off than you thought?" Marcus repeated. "No, that bitch is crazy!"

Mattie ignored the comment.

"Listen Marcus. I need your help. I promised her a taste and after she does that she promised me she'd allow me to admit her into rehab."

"She's scammin' you Mattie. The bitch just wants to smoke."

"That's cool because I don't give a fuck how you have to get her in there she's going. But what I need for you to do is to sell me a twenty and check and see if you have any downers o knock her ass out."

"A twenty won't do shit but make her angry. You don't know what you got there Mattie. That's a monster and all you're about to do is wake up them demons," Marcus said all humor gone from him now.

"Let me handle this Marcus. Just get me what I need please."

Marcus broke off a nice chunk and slid it and the twenty back across the table.

"You should know your money's no good here Mattie. I think I have some Ambien in my drawer if the bitch didn't steal 'em."

Within minutes Marcus was back.

"One usually puts me out but she's not normal so it may take two."

"Do you have any liquor, brown preferably?"

Marcus handed Mattie a bottle of Jack Daniels and two glasses. Mattie promptly dropped an Ambien into the glass furthest from her and just enough Jack to dissolve the pill. Hearing the bedroom door open and seeing Eva Mattie lifted the bottle once more.

"Mattie it's really good to see you."

"It's good to see you too. I've really been meaning to come by sooner but I've been so busy."

"Too busy or just afraid the rumors were true and you were afraid of what you might find?"

"Remember I grew up with you. I've seen you in a lot worse situations and you always pulled through. I wasn't worried about you in that sense. I really have been busy."

"Okay Mattie. By the way were you able to get that for me?"

"Yeah but you know you don't need that shit."

"Wish I could say that."

"C'mon let's have a taste for old times' sake before I lose you?"

Mattie poured a little better than a shot in both glasses before toasting to better days. Eva threw hers down and then looked to Mattie, eyes eagerly awaiting. Mattie slid the rock to Eva.

"Bastard won't sell me any. Makes me go chase down niggas who take my money and crumb me to death when he be sitting on pounds. Acts like I can't pay my way," Eva said reaching into her pocketbook and pulling out four or five singles and throwing them on the table. "I have money. Tell him Mattie. Eva keeps money. And look at the size of this. What did he charge you? I know he ain't charge you no more than forty for all of this. Nigga gonna bless you and here I am sucking his dick and he won't give me shit."

"That's cause you're a fuckin' monster. A fuckin' crack monster," Marcus yelled.

"Calm down Eva. I didn't get this from Marcus. I got this from Ali," she said lying to avoid any confrontation.

"Ali. Where's Ali?"

"Right here Eva."

"Is that you Ali?" Eva said not looking up from the table where she was arranging the rocks into different piles. "Damn I wouldn't have recognized you if Mattie hadn't pointed you out to me. Boy you done got big," Eva pronounced as she put the rock on top of the stem.

"You still haven't recognized me," Ali said smiling. The remarked went right over Eva's head as she dropped the stem and slumped over.

"I think we're good to go," Mattie said scooping the rocks up and handing them back to Marcus. "The place downtown is a lockdown facility isn't it?"

"Yep. It's a mandatory sixty day stay. That's the minimum."

"Good can you run her down there and admit her. Here's a letter that should get her in. If she protests in any way beat her ass but make sure she's admitted."

"Damn Mattie, you don't know how long I've wanted to do that," Marcus grinned. "That's all she really needs is someone to put a firm foot in her ass."

"Now now Marcus."

"Any word from Kane Mattie?"

"None. You?"

"Not a word."

And not another word was said on the subject. Eva who was in an out of consciousness, seemed completely subdued except for the occasional drunken accusation.

"I know y'all niggas is tryin' to steal my shit."

Everyone smiled.

"Go ahead and get her admitted Marcus."

Marcus threw the drugged Eva over his shoulder and carried her to the elevator.

"Call me if you hear anything from Kane." Mattie said hugging Marcus.

"You do the same."

Mattie and Ali drove in silence until Mattie reached the dilapidated tenement Ali called home.

"Come up for a minute Mattie and meet my fiancée and my son."

Mattie walked into the tiny one bedroom flat. A small but shapely young girl met them. She was a pretty little girl with some Oriental blood from the shape of her face and eyes. The way she stared and hung on Ali's every word it was obvious she was deeply in love with Ali but then who wasn't. Naomi had done everything to turn his head and half the client's; old and young had inquired about his availability at one time or another. Now she understood why their efforts were in vain. Mia was beautiful and complimented Ali well. Quiet, she was subservient up to a point yet warm and hospitable and kept an immaculate house.

"You are even more beautiful than Ali described," Mia said hugging Mattie. "And I truly want to thank you and your husband for getting Ali off the streets before something happened to him. He has always had all the potential in the world but as you know this is a hard place to grow up and if you hadn't done what you did these streets would have swallowed my baby up. Now we at least have a chance."

"Whoa! Whoa! Whoa! Believe me Mia Ali has done as much for my family if not more than anyone has done for him. All we did was give him the key. Ali took it unlocked the door and is basically running the house now. Seriously. I have professional women working with me, women with master's degrees that your husband is training."

Ali and Mia both beamed with pride upon hearing this.

"Honestly, I'd be lost without him. I don't have anyone there with the charisma, the smarts or the common sense that he has. And when I leave do you know who I put in charge? And there is never a problem when I get back. That's a testament to him. But anyway let me get out of here."

"Oh no. C'mon Mattie. You have to stay for dinner. It would be awfully nice. We don't have a lot of people drop by and since Ali started school it's almost nobody."

"I really wish I could. Maybe some other time. It's been a pleasure meeting you Mia."

Mattie smiled as she got into the 2014 BMW. There was nothing like young love she mused and had to admit that old love wasn't too bad either. The young couple in their one bedroom flat gave Mattie a reprieve from an otherwise horrid day surrounded by young women in so much turmoil. Coupled with her half crazed best friend in and out of a drug induced madness it was good to see a couple on an upward spiral. Mattie only wished she could do something about the filth and squalor they were forced to live in. She didn't know what was worse the rats peeking their twitching noses around corners like some sort of welcoming committee when they entered the building or the countless roaches that scurried to and fro across the living room furniture. It was certainly no way to live and certainly no place to raise a child. It was then that Mattie thought of the vacant apartments over the women's center and picked up her tiny cell phone. Before the week was over Ali and Mia were situated above the 8th Avenue Women's Center.

Now every morning Ali could be heard whistling as he headed to school. In the afternoon, he'd run upstairs after classes and help Mia fix lunch for Mattie and Naomi.

Mia was so appreciative that when Mattie fired the daycare sitter she just stepped in and monitored the children without saying anything to Mattie or anyone else.

With Eva safely tucked away in rehab and Ali and Naomi both doing well in school Mattie had little to worry about. The center was flourishing and had more clients than she'd ever dreamed. It kept her busy and for the first time in her life she really felt she was contributing to the common good. There was only one thing missing. Kane Close.

The weeks went on and autumn turned to winter and Harlem took on a different tint. As the skies became dark and gray so did the streets. No longer did one hear the children laughing and playing their city games. No longer did the reggae music come from the open door of the corner Jamaican restaurant and it wasn't soon before there was a new wave of street corner hustlers making claim to the strip. The keys Marcus and Kane had stolen from Chase were now gone and Chase was now pushing his own poison at below market prices and there was little Marcus could do but accept it. He was making far less on the dope end of the action. His primary revenues were made up of the protection he provided for the streetwalkers.

There was little he could do and had neither Kane's prowess or strength to go up against the likes of Chase and the cartel. He did his best to bide his time and put away all he could. After all, he had no army, no soldiers nor the know how to go up against Chase.

Knowing this Marcus gave himself 'til the end of the month and then he too would follow his workers and bail.

At five a.m. Marcus headed home after another grueling night. It had been a particular trying night with some loser from Jersey deciding he was going to rob one of the girls right there on the street. When Marcus tried to intervene the man had pulled a gun on him and in all likelihood would have shot him if Born hadn't come up from behind him and wrestled the gun away from him but only after being shot in the leg.

If that wasn't enough one of his oldest regular customers tried to switch some crack for some soap. This was always cause for a beat down but whereas normally he would have chastised him severely and sent him packing the cartel chose to beat him to a bloody

pulp and leave him with a broken arm and one eyeball hanging from his socket. It had all been a bit too much.

Marcus walked slowly. He'd always been loyal to Kane but it was going on five months and he hadn't heard a thing. A couple of months ago he would have laid his life on the line for Kane and there was no doubt Kane would have done the same for him but now Kane was gone and after five months he wondered if he'd found his own peace and paradise and forgotten about him. But Kane would never do that. And if Mattie and Ali believed and held fast to the thought of his eventual return then why was it so hard for him? Perhaps it was because Kane had given them safe havens from the maddening crowd whereas he was still in the trenches where the fighting was intense and the spoils of war few and far between. Yeah, he'd finish out the month and then he was throwing the towel in. Chase could have it. And then everything went red and Marcus lay flat on the sidewalk the blood gushing from his head.

He didn't know how long it'd been when he heard, "Marcus? Marcus Roberts? Can you hear me?"

Marcus felt the throbbing in his head and went to touch it but it hurt too badly. Squinting slighting he could barely make out the white uniform and the heavyset nurse wearing it.

"Well, it's good to have you back with us Mr. Roberts. I really didn't know if you were going to rejoin us or not. How are you feeling this morning?"

Marcus wanted to ask her where he was but the effort was too much and he hurt too badly to even try to form the words.

"Well, at least you're looking a lot better," she said. "Now just open a little so I can take your temp."

Even opening his mouth to let the nurse take his temp hurt.

"It's either you open your mouth or I take it rectally and I know you don't want me to see your goodies."

Marcus didn't care what the woman saw at this point as long as she just left him alone.

"I suspect from the size of that lump on your head that you're in a great deal of pain so I'm going to give you a little something for the pain and we'll come back in a few hours and see if you're doing any better. How's that sound," she said as she tapped his arm in attempts to find a vein before inserting the I.V. back into his arm.

Moments later Marcus was dead to the world.

Chapter 9

Ali stared out of his window. He held his young son in his arms rocking him as Mia made the bed and put on the coffee. Gray and overcast the day still loomed bright for Ali. Midterm tests were in and from every indication he'd made dean's list. Life had certainly taken a turn for the better. Turning to Mia he handed her his first born before pulling out his prayer rug and kneeling down. He really had so much to be thankful for.

Standing he grabbed Mia and kissed her then threw his book bag on and headed for the door. Passing the living room he saw Naomi and Mattie getting out of the car. That was his cue. It was seven forty-five and he should be on his way. Out the door and bounding down the stairs two at a time he was soon out the door and on the streets in front of the women's center. Ali immediately sensed something was askew and from the corner of his eye saw the two men approaching the car in haste. Sensing something wrong Ali raced across the street dodging traffic screaming.

"Run Mattie. Run," Mattie seemed frozen. She knew danger was approaching when she saw the terrified look in Ali's eyes as he reached her just in time to grab her before the two men reached her. As the men reached her and went to grab her Ali hit the man with a vicious shot to the kidney which doubled him over in pain but couldn't reach Naomi before his partner had a chance to scoop her up and throw her in the passing van.

"Oh my God Ali. They've got Naomi," Mattie shouted hysterically.

"Get inside," Ali said before grabbing the man and coming down with another hard right that lay the man flat. A crowd was now forming and Ali saw Mia standing there looking horrified, frozen.

"Mia!"

The tiny woman crossed the busy street and was at his side within seconds.

"Take Mattie upstairs and make sure the door is locked. Tell Ms. Farley that Mrs. Close won't be until later and to handle things until then. I want you to take Naomi's place and man the phones until I can arrange a temp."

"And where are you going?"

"Don't worry about me. I'll be back within the hour. Now please do what I ask?" Ali said kissing his wife on the forehead before turning to Mattie.

"Everything's going to be okay Mattie. I promise you. But for now I don't want you to do anything but go upstairs and lie down until I can find out what's going on. Do you understand?"

Mattie shook her head.

Ali crossed the street and disappeared into the subway. Minutes later he was with Charlie Rosenberg.

"Ali. I suppose you're here for your check," he said handing him his check.

"Charlie, I need you to get a message to Kane for me."

"If I said I could do that it would be tantamount to me saying that I know where Mr. Close is?"

"Listen motherfucker! You can kill all that legalese bullshit. Kane said if I needed to get in touch with him to come to you. So, I'm coming to you. I don't need to hear this shit. Either you're going to handle his business or you're not in which case I'm sure Kane will let your ass go if you can't. Now I'm thinking if you plan on keeping Kane as a client you'll let him know that a kidnap attempt was made on his wife but I intervened but that they got Naomi. "

The man known as Charles Rosenberg stood there speechless. Ali turned and walked out. He had to find

Marcus. After several attempts at calling him with no answer he called Born.

"Born, you seen or heard form Marcus?"

"Nah bro. I been tryna reach him all morning. These niggas from the cartel is tellin' us we been banned and can't post up. They got wall-to-wall niggas out here slingin' but we can't put no work in whatsoever. Why? What up?"

"They just tried to kidnap Mattie in front of the women's center. I got to Mattie before they did but they got Naomi."

"Stop playing? Get the fuck outta here. Who's with her now?"

"No one. I'm out here lookin' for Marcus."

"Where she at?"

"At my crib. Over top of the center."

"Okay I'll send some of the fellows over there."

"Tell them to keep everything on the down low. The center's still open for business but make sure they check everybody going in and out. If anyone looks suspicious check 'em out and Born that doesn't mean them hittin' on every female that looks good. Seriously, make sure they keep it professional."

"Will do and have Marcus call you as soon as he checks in."

"Good lookin' dude. Listen I got another call let me get back."

"Handle yours baby boy."

"Hello."

"Yes make I speak to Ali please?"

"Go ahead Charlie."

"Kane says for you to sit tight. Said don't make a move until you receive a ransom note with demands. He should be home by then."

"Gotcha."

Ali hung the phone up and then dialed Born up.

"Listen Born. Put the blocks on lock and beat down any motherfucker who tries to cop from the cartel. Then call an emergency meeting with the neighborhood association and let 'em know we got roaches but we gonna exterminate them once and for all. I'll get

back. Make sure all the fellas are packing. Have them in the safe houses and ready for my call. Where are you?"

"On my way to the women's center," Born said smiling. "I love your boy Kane but this is what you should have been doing from jump. Exterminating these motherfuckers!"

Ali hung up and jumped back on the subway where he promptly starting calling the local hospitals.

"Yes ma'am I'm trying to locate my brother Marcus Roberts. Yes ma'am. He didn't come home last night and

247

my parents are worried that something may have happened to him. Okay thank you ma'am."

On the third call he located Marcus at Harlem Hospital. Ali changed trains and found himself there in less than fifteen minutes.

"Ma'am I'm looking for room three fifteen."

"Down the hall and to the left," the nurse said never looking up from her clipboard.

Ali found his friend lying in bed asleep, a bandage wrapped around his head and heavily sedated.

"Marcus. Marcus." Marcus grunted and opened his eyes enough to peer through the slits.

"What's up Ali?" he said reaching for his head.

"What happened?"

"What happened is that someone used a bat to mug your brother and he's suffered a severe concussion," the heavyset nursed responded before checking Marcus' vitals and the intravenous drip. "How's the pain on a scale of one to ten with ten being the most severe?"

"A twelve," Marcus managed to mutter.

"Okay, Mr. Roberts. Then let me get a doctor to sign off so I can administer you something a little stronger for the pain. I'll be right back."

Ali waited for the woman to leave before speaking.

"I think the cartel's making their move Marcus. I don't think you were mugged. I think that was a botched attempt on your life. That blow was supposed to kill you. Probably gave the hit to some crack head. Did you have any run ins with anyone from around the way lately?"

"Nah but I let ol' man Saleem take a beat down a couple of days ago."

"Get the fuck outta here. I thought Saleem was your boy?"

"Yeah, but all kind of crazy shit has started happening the last couple of weeks. Things were really getting lax and it was time to lock shit down and let these motherfuckers know that's not the way we do things around here so I used Saleem as an example. And Saleem used your head as baseball. They probably gave that fool an eight ball to follow you and take you out. How much were you carrying?"

"I don't know. Not much. Maybe eight or nine thousand," Marcus said sitting up.

"May have saved your life. Probably saw the cash and bailed instead of finishing the job. But trust me someone put him up to it and with them trying to kidnap Mattie and Naomi and knock you off it can't be anybody but that punk ass Chase trying to get back from us hitting his spots."

"Stop playing Ali!"

"That's why I'm here. I called everybody. Yeah, they tried to get Mattie and Naomi this morning going into the women's center. I grabbed Mattie but they got Naomi."

"That's the African bitch that's hooked up with them right? You think she's working for them?"

"Doesn't make sense. She's still affiliated with them and who do they think is going to pay ransom for kidnapping one of their own?"

"I don't get it either but I had Born pull all of our people off the streets so no one else gets hurt."

"Smart move but I don't know how we're going to hold them off. They've already taken control of the trade and must of our soldiers broke camp weeks ago and either went to the Bronx or Queens and are shacked up and doing their own thing since the cartel

pushed them out. I can give them a call but I doubt that they're going to come back just to get their wigs pushed back. Right now we're looking at forty soldiers at best."

"Give them a call. I got a feeling after being away for a couple of weeks on someone else's turf without police protection they'll be dying to get back to the old ways."

"You may have a point there after all."

"So, you ready to do the damn thing?"

"Never been more ready."

"Help me up Ali."

Marcus grimaced as Kane helped him sit up.

"It hurt bad?"

"Like a motherfucker," Marcus said. "Wait 'til I get my hands on that bitch ass nigga."

"We've got more important fish to fry my brother. We need to take back our neighborhood and keep it a demilitarized zone. This time we'll set up a perimeter and provide enough security so that we check out every car coming in and out. Soon as we take these cartel motherfuckers out."

"And how we gonna do that?"

"Very quietly and very efficiently... I got the fellas on standby in the safe houses. Lotta young boys that wanna be down are gnna make their bones tonight. The way I see it we're gonna post a few old heads in there. You know like you and Born and a couple of

other cats to act as back up. How many does the cartel usually send in? Like ten or twelve?"

"Maybe ten at the most and a couple of big boys that are strapped in case anything pops off."

"Okay. Good. Soon as you get posted up at your usual spots then me and these young dudes are going to come in as buyers. We comin' in strapped with silencers. I got the girls movin' up the strip to 150th so they don't get caught up in the crossfire. They don't know me so I'll be with the young boys and once we engage all of them in transactions at the same time then we let 'em have it. If you and Born see anything go astray then you walk up from behind and let them have it with both barrels. I got two vans, one at each end of the street and I want the bodies in them before they hit the ground."

"Have you thought of the collateral damage?"

"Always. When I couldn't reach you I hit Born up and told him to move the girls up to 150th Street. Then I made sure he let the tenant's associations know that we were on lockdown until further notice. Word on the street is if you're lookin' for shit go up to 150th and see the girls. I gave them the half a key I'd been sitting on from the raid and told them to bless everyone so when this shit is over the dope fiends will come running back to us. And gonna stack a little paper too."

"You handlin' shit ain'tcha boy?"

"I was taught by one of the best."

Both men smiled then hugged each other in brotherhood

"C'mon man. You know I don't do hospitals. You ready?"

"Yeah man. Throw me my pants."

No sooner than he said that the busty nurse with the big ass walked in. Marcus turned and saw her for what seemed like the first time.

"Damn. I must have really been out of it if I let your pretty ass go unnoticed."

Ignoring him the nurse spoke up.

"And where do you think you're going Mr. Roberts? Looking at your charts it looks like the doctor is still awaiting tests to see how bad the head trauma is and if you have any internal bleeding. Right now all we are able to ascertain from the preliminary tests is that you do have some head trauma and a severe concussion but we aren't really able to see the severity at this point."

Marcus and Ali ignored the petite nurse with the shapely body.

"Damn baby, have you been my nurse since I've been here?"

"Yes Mr. Roberts."

"They must have really hit me hard if I didn't notice you."

The nurse smiled.

"Turn your head baby," Marcus said pulling his pants on.

"Mr. Roberts I am trying to inform you that if you leave the hospital it is against all medical advice and not recommended. If you insist I'll need you to sign a waiver saying that you've been advised by medical staff that the hospital is not responsible if something should happen to you."

"Come here sweetheart. Come closer so I can see your name tag. Thank you. Okay Beverly, let me inform you of something that you are not fully aware of. I'm responsible for a whole lot of people's lives and I can't be responsible sitting here in the hospital but I'll tell you what. I'll be here tomorrow to sign these papers if you promise to have lunch with me Beverly."

She smiled and gathered her paperwork.

"Can I ask you something?"

"Anything?"

"Well, I was just noticing your jackets…"

"They look expensive."

"About twelve hundred. And?"

"And I noticed the 'Uptown' on the back and wanted to know if that had some type of affiliation with a bike club, gang, social organization or what?"

"Not at all. We are actually the founders and architects of the new Harlem Renaissance. It's actually a progressive movement to take back the streets and provide a pride in our community that has too long been overlooked. We hope to bring back the true

Harlem culture that spawned the Harlem Renaissance but I'll tell you more about it over lunch tomorrow," he said winking at her and squeezing her hand. "Do we have a date?"

"We'll see," she said hoping not to sound too anxious.

Marcus and Ali walked out of the hospital and grabbed a cab. It wasn't that Ali felt a need for power or that he felt he had a better strategy. It was just emotion, pure emotion and all that need for planning and strategizing was good but the fact that they had tried to seize two women so close to him and under his watch was out of the question. Call it unbridled anger. But the Chase Cartel would pay tonight despite what Kane or anyone else had to say.

At eight that night Ali met the fellas at the safe house.

"We silencin' these motherfuckers once and for all and takin' back our shit. I want it done quickly and quietly. I want you to rock these motherfuckers to sleep then take their shit and continue where they left off. These are our fuckin' blocks. We run this shit. Tonight we let 'em know."

A large cheer went up.

"At eight o'clock we step to these punks and peel their wigs back. I have seven thirty by my watch. Make sure everybody has the same time. Stay in groups of twos so as not to draw too much attention. Alright, Uptown let's do this."

Born, Marcus and Ali walked together in silence.

"You really think this is a good move Ali?" Born asked. "You for one know I'll lay my life down for my fam but ahm just saying. You know this is an all-out call for war and we just ain't got the soldiers."

"You right. I'm not sure this is a good move but I do know it's a necessary one. Let me ask you something Born. Why do we only have forty soldiers? When I was on the block two months ago we was up to around a yard. How did we go from a hundred down to forty and most of these are pee wees and hoppers. What's up with that?"

"I guess it has something to do with the fact that the Cartel has moved in."

"And taken over the best landscape in the city. Our landscape. The shit that we built. And you're asking me if this is a good move. Would you let Amtrak run through your living room?"

"I feel ya. I just know that a lot of young kids are going to die tonight."

"And I hate to agree with you but you're probably right."

"Damn shame."

Marcus was still deliberating over Beverly the fine young nurse at the hospital. The first day she'd seemed obese and grotesque but as the swelling in his head subsided so had she. Her interest in him peaked his curiosity along with her cute little shape and he felt a smile creep to his face.

"What you smilin' about Marcus? This nigga gettin' ready to go to war and smilin' his ass off. That's a motherfucker you gotta watch," Born said.

"Marcus thinkin' about that cute little shorty with the rotund ass from the hospital. That bitch turn the corner of 8th and 149th and still got ass on 8th tryna to catch up."

The three laughed. The mood was much more somber as they hit the strip. Ali checked his watch. Seven fifty five. The vans were in place and began warming their engines when they saw Ali. The street was empty aside from a few stragglers and a wino who obviously hadn't gotten the memo. The crews were split but moving in quickly. In teams of twos they aroused little suspicion and at eight o'clock they were all conducting business and checking the dope boys stashes which would be soon be theirs.

Ali fired the first shot at point blank range and most of the others accept for the few that were awaiting this knew and then in unison there was a cacophony of small weapons fire and seven or eight bodies hit the street in unison. The two vans drove slowly to where groups of men stood huddled around fallen bodies. Small circles surrounded the bodies who were now writhing and beginning to shout out in agonizing pain. But this too ended quickly as a few more mercy shots were fired and within minutes it was over. Ali watched as the bodies were loaded in the vans before crossing the street where Born held the remaining survivor. The cartel's enforcer had been caught totally off guard and Born had the nine millimeter in his ribs by the time the young man had a chance to react. Born still held the nine on him when Marcus and Ali joined him.

"Whatcha want to do with him?" Born asked.

"Llulaby his ass," Marcus said looking disdainfully at the trembling man before him.

"Ahh come on man. If you let me go I promise I'll leave and you'll never see me again."

"You're right I don't expect we will see you again. You ain't never lied about that," Born said holding the nine millimeter to the young man's face and squeezing the trigger twice. Ali seemingly unfazed by the whole incident summoned the remaining van who promptly came and picked up the body.

"Marcus set up a perimeter like we talked about and bring everybody back. It's back to business as usual." All three men appeared unfazed by the killings. Ali had witnessed more than his share of killings and had never grown accustomed to it. No matter the circumstances he grieved. He doubted that Marcus and Born gave it a second thought.

Ali remained strong and composed but the uneasiness and nauseous that accompanied his first killing was mounting. No one was smiling but neither did they exhibit any remorse.

"Born, let's go see if we can get anything from that nigga that tried to kidnap Mattie this morning. If we can get him to talk we may be able to grab Naomi and   end this shit tonight. I'm going to check on Mia and Mattie. I'll meet you at the safe house in forty five."

Ali called Mattie as he approached the brownstone then circled the block twice to make sure security was in place and everything was normal. Seeing nothing out of place he rang the doorbell. "Mattie how are you doing," Kane said before stepping in and following her down the long hallway.

"I'm okay. I guess," she replied half-heartedly leading Ali into the parlor. "I'm just so worried about Naomi. You don't think they'll hurt her do you?"

"No. I think they were out to get you to find out where Kane is and if he's still alive so they could cement the takeover with little or no opposition. I'm pretty sure that Naomi was a mistake and when they find out who her uncle is they'll simply let her go."

Ali grabbed Mattie's hands and held them in his own reassuringly. No sooner had he done this than Mattie grabbed the nineteen year old placed her head on his shoulder and began to cry in shuddering gasps. "C'mon Mattie. If Kane were here he would you need for you to be strong. I need you to be strong."

"You're right."

"Okay then. What I would like for you to do is pack up enough clothes for work for the rest of the week and either come and stay with us or take the empty apartment next door. I'll be back in an hour or so to pick you up. And don't worry about anything. I have a real good crew providing security outside. So, rest easy."

"Thanks Ali," she said hugging him again. "Thanks for everything."

"No problem and no worries you understand? By the way did you check out Ms. Cromartie's insurance coverage?"

"Yes Ali she's fully covered and was admitted today."

"Did the guy bring the van by today?"

"Yeah, he left it and the mechanics supposed to come by and check it out and make sure it's in good working order tomorrow. Now let me ask you a question."

"Shoot."

"Have you been by to check on Mia and my little guy since you left home this morning?"

"I'm on my way now," he said smiling.

Mattie knew that Mia and his baby meant the world to him. Yet in the last few months Ali's life had taken on a whole new dynamics. He was now not only confronted with the responsibilities of loving and providing for his family but had the added responsibility of having a part time job that had turned into a full time position, college and providing security for the residents of Manhattan from Spanish Harlem to the Bronx. Mattie knewthis was quite a load for a nineteen year old but Mattie knew that Ali was no ordinary young man. He seemed to be handling it with ease.

"See you in an hour."

"Be safe Ali."

Mattie knew better than to ask what actions he'd taken in the Naomi kidnapping or what was going on in the streets. The Uptown clique was like some sort of secret society like the Mason's and so she let it go. But she could sense that changes were being made and this young man was commanding it.

Ali pulled up across the street from the safe house where Born was interrogating the young man who participated in the attempted kidnapping.

"We find out anything?"

"Yeah. It didn't take much. Nigga ain't no gangster. Slapped him around a couple of times and he spilt everything. Told me all kinds of shit. From what I got from him Chase is the pipeline from the Sudan to the U.S. Heroin, manpower, you name it. He's bringing these motherfuckers in and working them for damn near nothing. Says Chase took him from one war to another. I actually felt kind of sorry for the motherfucker but says Chase has all intentions of expanding and is gonna take over Harlem and then is going to the Bronx and Jersey afterward. From what he's telling me Chase believes he's got a God given right; like he's been chosen and that God is on his side and he's going to eventually go national and bullets and nothing else can touch him. Some ol' crazy African voodoo shit…"

"Well we're gonna test his theory tonight. Gonna see if we can touch him…"

"And what about this poor soul?"

"Soon as I talk to him dead him."

"You getting' ruthless Ali."

"Just coverin' our tracks. Uptown leaves no witnesses."

Ali walked into the back bedroom where he found the young man he'd accosted earlier that morning bound and gagged. Ali took the gag from the man's mouth and stared at the young man in front of him who appeared no older than he was.

"What's up bro? Remember me?"

The young man who appeared petrified shook his head.

"Do you smoke?"

Again he shook his head.

"Born you have a smoke?"

Within seconds Born handed the pack of Newports to Ali who shook one out. Untying the man's hand he handed him the cigarette and lit it.

"My man was just telling me that you should be spared because you were a good dude. I think that any man that puts his hand on a female or brings a woman into a man's world should be fucked up and that goes for you and your boss."

"I was just following orders brother. I am a soldier. I do what I am told."

"I'm a soldier too but if I receive an order that involves women and children then I am a man first with both a mother and a child and those orders could and would not be followed out. It all comes down to your own personal constitution. Now any other time I would simply have my boy lullaby your ass to sleep but because he says you're a pretty good dude that's just a little confused I'm thinking about giving you a pass."

"Oh, thank you brother. Thank you so much. Alah will bless you."

"I said I was thinking about it. I didn't say it was going to happen. Let's see how you answer these questions I have for you. How well you do know Chase and where are you in the organization." An hour later Ali had all the answers he needed and all but formatted the plan for Chase's assassination just from all the information Hasem had given him. When the questioning was over the two had formed a relationship, a common bond.

"How did I do?" Hasem asked confident now that he would be let loose.

"Even better than I expected," Ali smiled. "Dead him," he said turning to Born.

"Sorry holmes," Born said screwing the silencer on before placing the gun to the man's forehead and squeezing off a round.

"Get a cleaner in here and get a couple of fellas to dump the body out by Kennedy."

"I gotcha. Where you going?"

"To follow up on what ol' boy told me then home."

"You going alone?"

"Yeah."

"I don't think that's a good move Ali. Why don't you give me a couple of minutes and I'll run shotgun."

"No Born. I appreciate the love but this is one I need to do alone. I owe Kane and Mattie this much."

"I feel you my brother but they didn't take you off the streets to get killed on 'em."

"I best not get killed then huh?" Ali said smiling as he headed out the door.

Heading to Brooklyn Ali knew Born was right but after all that Kane and Mattie had done for him it was the least he could do. Ali left the car some blocks from his destination. Taking the AK-47 with the scope and held it to his side as he found his way to the little private social club. Sizing it up he entered the building across the street. The first floor hallway was narrow and dimly lit. Littered with debris it smelled of urine. It was vacant except for an old wino huddled in the corner attempting to hide from the cold. Ali stepped over him and made his way up the stairs which were badly in need of repair.

Reaching the landing Ali cracked the window and then using the butt of the nine millimeter busted a hole big enough to fit the tip of the rifle barrel through before kneeling down to wait. It was nine thirty when Ali finally heard laughter from across the street. So, the now deceased Hasem's intel was good. Ali could barely make out the faces from this distance though and wasn't sure that he could hit them all before they would recover and start returning fire. And in all his haste he hadn't given himself a way out. He knew if he didn't take at least two of the four men out he would be easily trapped and now was no time to check the roof. Still, Ali knew that this was his last best chance to end the war and get Naomi back. What was it that Kane used to say? Kill the head and the body will follow. Ali watched the fat man surrounded by the other three and knew that that was Chase. Damn! They were good Ali thought to himself as the men walked in unison never once exposing Chase for a clear shot and Ali only wished he'd taken Born up on his offer now. A distraction would have been perfect now. A well-ordered shot gun blast would have scattered the men leaving Chase open for a clean shot. And then as if someone had heard Ali shots rang out and for a split second Chase's henchmen turned and Ali had his shot and placed one in the fat man's shoulder spinning him half way around. Whoever the other shooter was was a crack shot and all three men lay around their fallen leader. Ali raised the AK-47 again and aimed squarely at the man's head when he heard a familiar voice.

"Don't shoot him Ali. He knows where Naomi is."

Ali smiled as he watched the shooter approach the fat man who was clutching his shoulder and groaning in pain. Grabbing him by his good arm he yanked the fat man to his feet.

"You're going to take me to find the girl or you're a dead man. Do you understand me Chase?" You started this war you bastard and I'm going to finish it. Ali bring the car around and hurry."

Two minutes later Ali pulled up and the fat man was thrown in the backseat.

"Thought I was dead didn't you boy?"

Ali couldn't speak and just stared at the man known as Kane.

The war was over. Or was it?

"Thought I told you to sit tight 'til I got here," Kane said to Ali.

"I tried boss but someone had to pay for these motherfuckers trying to kidnap Mattie and Naomi this morning."

"I understand but you can't be irrational or impulsive. If I hadn't shown up you would have been dead. You left yourself no way out. All you were intent on doing was seeking revenge. Even if it cost you your own life and that's not a fair trade off especially after all I've got invested in you."

"And I'm glad to see you too, Kane," Ali said sarcastically.

Kane laughed.

"Man you don't know how much I missed you but this ain't the way I wanted to come oack and see you. Make a right at the corner. But we'll talk later. Let's finish this business and then we can get caught up."

"No doubt. It's good to have you back though Kane."

"It's good to be back," Kane said before turning to Chase. "If that girl's harmed you're done fat man. Now where the fuck is she?"

"She's fine but you're finished Kane. Do you understand me? Finished! When this is over you're a dead man. Turn left at the next block."

"Hardly think you're in a position to be making that call," Kane smiled before bringing the forty five caliber up and crushing the fat man's nose. "Your ego will be your demise," he said handing him a handkerchief to wipe his bleeding nose.

Speaking more softly and in obvious pain Chase looked incredulously at Kane.

"It's the last warehouse at the end of the block."

"And how many are there guarding her?"

"There's only one."

"Armed?"

Chase simply stared at Kane.

"Ali keep your freeze on this cat's head. If he even looks like he wants to sneeze drop him right where he is. Chase if you want to take another breath of God's good air you'd better say the right things to whoever's in there. Now knock."

Chase knocked loudly and waited listening for the footsteps to come closer.

"Who is it?" came a voice from the other side of the heavy metal door.

"It's me Chase. Just stopping by to check on the girl and see what she knows."

The heavy metal bar slid from the door and the sound of two or three bolt locks could be heard turning. Ali tensed up but Kane remained relaxed and when the door finally opened and the young man saw Chase and smiled until he saw the freeze pointed at his boss' head. The smile turned into a frown and knowing that he was outnumbered he still showed the heart of a lion and before Chase could warn him he tried to get a shot off and Kane dropped him where he stood.

"You son of a bitch. You murderin' bastard. He was just a kid. He was my nephew. Oh my God! How am I going to explain this to my sister? He was her baby."

"Perhaps you should have thought of that before you put a gun in his hand," Kane said with little remorse. "Now where's the girl?"

Chase pointed to a room to the right.

"Bring that fat rat bastard Ali. I don't want any more surpises."

Ali pushed chased out in front of him.

"Lead the way and if there's anyone in there besides the girl it's two to the dome fat man," Ali threatened.

The man walked quickly to the room and opened the door. Naomi laid on the cold concrete floor her dress up past her waist, her panties ripped and soiled lay across the room. Hands bound behind her she was gagged and her eyes were squeezed tightly together as if this would help her assailants next atrocity.

"Naomi. It's me Ali," he said tears running down in his face now. "Damn! What have they done to you? Oh my God! Naomi! What have they done to you?"

"C'mon Ali. Untie her. We need to get the fuck out of here. There's a corpse in the next room and we don't know who's comin' up in here next."

Naomi was despondent but after hearing the soothing sound of Ali's voice she opened her eyes and screamed when she saw the two men who now loomed over her broken body.

"Kane. Ali. Help me!" she said reaching for them.

"Can you walk sweetheart?" Kane said shoving the forty five in his waistband and reaching for the girl.

"I think so."

Moving towards the door Ali still holding the freeze to the fat man's head turned to Kane.

"What do you want me to do with this fat motherfucker that kidnaps and rapes women boss?" Ali asked before knocking Chase to the ground with two quick blows to the head. "Let me do him boss?"

"Not yet son. He's still got some things he's going to do for us."

"Did he put his hands on you Naomi?" Ali screamed.

The girl shook her head no.

"Who was it then?" Ali screamed again.

"My uncle," she whispered.

"Where is he?" Kane shouted at the man still down before kicking him in the ribs.

"I don't know," Chase screamed. "I don't know where that bastard is and I did not tell him to touch the girl. I specifically gave orders that the girl was to be unharmed."

"Well, that didn't go over to well did it fat man?" Ali said kicking him again.

The little Black fat man curled up in obvious pain. There was blood oozing from his parched lips.

"Please," he pleaded holding his ribs. "Please don't hit me anymore."

Ali kicked him again.

"You bastard," was all Chase could manage.

"Pick him up and bring him," Kane ordered. "We'll take care of the uncle later."

Ali drove with Naomi's head on his shoulder whispering as an older brother would to a younger sister that had fallen and scraped her knee. Inside he burned with anger.

"Where are we going?"

"To Mr. Chase's residence."

"No, no please. My wife and children are home. They have nothing to do with any of this."

"And neither did my wife who you tried to kidnap this morning."

"Please Kane forgive me. What is it that you want? Is it money? Tell me how much. Listen it's not too late for us to be partners. Fifty fifty? Okay Kane? That's fair isn't it? Just tell me what you want but please don't hurt my family."

"Like you hurt mine. I adopted this girl after her uncle raped and abused her. Then this morning you tried to kidnap my wife. My wife!" Kane shouted. "Why I ought to blow your brains all over Brooklyn you piece of shit."

The little fat Black man's head drooped and the blood continued to ooze but there were no more words.

"Stay with Naomi. I'll be right down." Ali saw the two men waiting in front of the high rise and was about to get out when he was approached from his blind side.

"Relax young blood. We got this."

270

Ali immediately recognized Black from the ride to Queens.

"Damn. You had me going there for a minute."

"It's all good. We just came in to aid our boy and add a little insurance. That's all. I guess you could say we're Kane's welcoming committee."

"You're not going up?"

"To be honest with you Ali. Kane doesn't need Prince or Nasem with him except to keep an eye on the fat man's family," Black said flicking the cigarette across the car. "Trust me. He's one of the best that's ever done it."

Chapter 10

Black and Ali traded chit chat for the better part of an hour before. With Naomi moaning in pain Ali became worried and restless.

"You think they're okay?" Ali queried.

"They're fine," Black laughed. "I used to worry too when I was a young dude like you standing lookout. The hardest thing is being on the outside looking in but I can assure you everything's okay. Those are veterans and one of the best crews you'll ever come across. The reason it seems like its taking so long is that Kane is thorough. He's going to make sure that he dots every 'i' and crosses every 't'.

Unless this fool Chase is crazy he'll never come uptown again and may just head back to wherever he's from by the time Kane puts the fear of God in him."

"I hope you're right."

"I know I'm right. See. Here they come now." Black looked one way and then the other before summoning them on. Chase was now blindfolded with a man on each arm and Kane held two large Wells Fargo money bags. The three men and Black got in the black S.U.V parked up the block.

"We're done here. How's Naomi?"

"Black said to tell you to admit her to St. Lukes so they can run some preliminary tests just to make sure there's no internal bleeding and just to be on the safe side."

"Then let's run her up there real quick. Get Marcus or Born and tell them to meet us there and provide security."

Marcus smiled and looked over at Kane who was sitting upfront.

"Glad to have you back Kane. It's like you never missed a beat. You're back running things like you never left."

"Did I have a choice? I leave for a hot minute and you fools lose the streets that we've held for twenty years. You let some fat 'lil man that watched too many reruns of Scarface try to kidnap my wife and you let revenues get cut in half. I had no choice but to come back and try to salvage something," Kane laughed. "It's a damn shame. If it weren't for Ali taking charge tonight, we'd have probably lost everything."

Ali beamed with pride hearing this but did not respond.

"I hear Mattie's tickled pink with you. Heard she has you damn near running the center."

"I do my best."

"Oh now you're being modest. How's school going? That's where you're supposed to be concentrating your efforts. I hope that hasn't taken a backseat to all the rest of this bullshit. That's what's going to take you the farthest when it comes to being a man a provider and keeping you alive. It ain't the money or the street rep. Trust me. After close to thirty years out there and a little savings what means most to me is my education and if I get a chance I'm going back the first chance I get."

"I'm doing okay. Made dean's list my first semester. This semester is a little easier so I'm thinking I should be able to do it again."

"Now that's what I'm talkin' about," he said reaching over and grabbing Ali's head. "How's Mia and the baby?"

"They're good. Mattie hooked us up and put us up in one of those fly apartments over the women's center. Mia loves it and it's got a mad view so she's happy. She volunteers at the women's center every afternoon. I think she's just trying to keep an eye on me with all those beautiful honeys up in there," Ali laughed. "But on the real, I have never seen her this happy."

"Well that's good. I'm glad everything is working out for you and I want you to know I'm proud of you. Every report I've gotten about you has been positive up until today. And again I have to insist that no matter how fucked up things get it is never as bad as those streets. Everything about them is poison. Don't let them lure you back in. I know you think you have to defend your code of honor but in all reality there is no code out there. For the right price your best boy will put two to the back of your head and not think twice. I've seen it. And the best way to avoid that from happening is to stay clear of them altogether."

"Ahh c'mon Kane the only reason I got involved today is because of what they did to Mattie and Naomi."

"And once you saved Mattie then you should have squashed it. There was nothing else you could have done. You gave an order that you'll have to live with the rest of your life. You took the lives of nine or ten Black men that given the right opportunity may have had the opportunity just like you to make the dean's list just like you? How many little boys did you make bastards of and now have to grow up without fathers? Did you think about that? Those young men that you had killed tonight were simply following orders and just trying to eat. The man responsible for sending those boys out there is soon to meet his own demise. C'mon Ali you've got to change your mindset if you want to truly be a man. Killing and dying is easy. Living and trying to live right is the real challenge."

"I hear you Kane." Ali knew the older man was right. Never had he felt worse than when the killing was done.

"Do you see Marcus?"

274

"No not yet but there's Born."

Kane got out and Born walked up to him and threw his arms around him in a warm embrace.

"Damn glad to see you man. What's good?"

Kane grinned.

"Same ol' same ol'. Heard you been holdin' it down."

"Just tryin' to do my best."

"Well, it's good to see you Born. We got Naomi back and I need you to look after her while they run some tests. I'm hoping they'll release her in a day or two. When they do give me a call and I'll meet you to settle up with you," Kane said before embracing his young lieutenant. "You seen Marcus?"

"He's either working or providing security for Mattie."

"Okay. I'll catch up with him later. Call me as soon as the doctor's give you an update on her condition."

"Will do," Born replied as he grabbed Naomi who was unconscious and carried her into the hospital.

"Where to Boss?"

"Call Marcus and tell him to drop whatever he's doing and meet me in front of ol' lady Murphy's building at Esplanarde Gardens."

Within minutes Ali pulled up in front of the Gardens where Marcus stood talking to some shorty's. The moment he saw Kane emerge from the car he broke into a wide grin.

"Boy you don't know how much I missed your ass. Man it's been mad crazy out here since you left. I was giving you a week then I was packing it in," Marcus said hugging Kane tightly.

"That bad huh?"

"And you were out here thirty years?!?! Man, I gots to give you your props. You can have this shit. I'm done with it. You can have this shit."

Kane laughed.

"I came back for my woman. You inherited this shit. It's all yours. The money, the fame, the glory… It's all yours Marcus."

"No, no, no. You're not understanding me Kane. It's not worth it my brother. Ain't that much money in Harlem. Do you know this lil crack head mother came close to killing me a couple of nights ago? I woke up in the hospital. I'd been out for two or three days. How long was it Ali?"

"Nurse said two days."

"Two days Kane. Nigga hit me in the head with a baseball bat. Tried to kill my ass. I'm telling you. You can have this shit. Then I got bitches like Eva verbally abusing me in the street and making me go ham and beat her ass just to save face. Gotta keep one eye open to make sure she don't rob me or slit my throat when I do get home all 'cause you think she's the pipeline to the cartel when all she was was a pipe head. It got so bad Mattie had to come by and drug her ass so we could admit her into rehab. Yeah, boy you can have all this shit back."

Kane laughed heartily as Marcus recounted the happenings of the last week

"I'm feeling like my lil vacation has caused my stock to go up."

"No doubt. I do appreciate you my brother and after the one or two days it takes for you to get acclimated to being home this shit is yours."

"Not so fast Marcus. Do you remember me asking you if this was something you wanted to do and you said yes?"

"But Kane I didn't know…"

"And now you do. Sorry, Marcus there ain't no turning back now."

"All jokes aside Kane, the kid handled himself well tonight. You might want to groom him for the position cause on the serious side I'm looking at early retirement."

"I left you specific instructions not to let Ali anywhere near the street and I come back to find that he's the one behind this bloodbath. If I were you Marcus I would seriously consider not making that recommendation."

"My bad. He was cool and doing everything just like you said until they touched those women and then you and nobody else could have told him nothing. You know how he is."

"Just be glad it all worked out."

"I'm glad it did but don't you see he's ready. And with you back and under your tutelage he'll be fine. I've got a little saved up and I'm seriously considering purchasing a couple of small convenience stores down South and calling it a day."

"That whack upside the head must have really done a number on you."

"That and crazy ass Eva," Ali laughed.

"Listen we have some work to put in. We can talk about you going to Disneyland later."

"What up boss?"

"Call the cleaner and tell him we're going to need him. Right now I need the roll of plastic, the electric saw, and some black contractor's bags."

"Anybody I know?"

"Naomi's uncle. The one that stomped Eva and raped Naomi."

"That motherfucker should have been done," Marcus said to everyone and no one in particular.

"Can I just have five minutes with before you do him?" Ali asked.

"What part of this aren't you getting?" Kane said stopping and staring at Ali. "I don't want you involved in any of this. I don't even want you standing look out. If the cops or anyone else comes I want you to bail. Do you understand me? I have other plans for you."

Marcus left and the two sat in the car and waited. No words were spoken. Kane's phone rang.

"It's done."

Kane recognized Black's voice immediately and did not reply but knew that the fat man known as Chase would no longer pose a problem uptown. There would be no more attempts at hostile takeovers and the cartel was for all intents and purposes defunct.

Marcus showed up moments later and nodded as he passed the car. Kane waited a minute or two before followin Marcus into the building and waited for the elevator without acknowledging each other. Stepping off the elevator on the fourth floor they approached the apartment slowly. Marcus knocked softly.

"Who is it?"

"Marcus. I got that information you wanted on Eva."

"Who's Eva?"

"Stop playin'. Eva's the chick that robbed you. C'mon man I ain't got time to play."

Kane crouched down behind Marcus burly frame and waited for the door to open. When it did open both Kane and Marcus barreled in bum rushing the man inside. They were on him before he knew what hit him each pinning an arm to his side before Kane cold cocked him leaving him unconscious in the middle of the living room floor. Marcus quickly tied his hands and feet then joined Kane in scouring the apartment for money and drugs.

"Bingo!!" Marcus yelled stepping back into the living room holding six keys. "Ol' boy must be one of Chase's couriers. There's a lot of yayo but I haven't found any cash yet. You think he has a safe?"

"Did you check the mattresses and the closets?

"Marcus returned to the bedroom. But no sooner than he was there Kane called him again.

"What's up?"

"I was just thinking of something Mattie told me right before I left. She said it's always better to work smarter not harder."

"That's true."

"So why are we looking when this motherfucker knows exactly where the stash is at?"

Marcus smiled.

"Good to have you back Kane," Marcus said smiling broadly.

"Grab the rope and help me get him in the chair."

Once he was propped up Kane went into the kitchen and took the jar of cold water from the fridge and poured over the man's head. The shock of the cold water brought him to sudden attention.

"When Chase finds out about this he will…"

"Relax that shit holmes. Chase is dead," Kane said. "What I want to know is where the cash is. And once you tell me that I'm going to give you just enough to get the fuck outta town."

"You're a liar. Chase is not dead. And if I told you that he would kill me anyway so what's the difference? Well, we already have the keys so you might as well say you're a dead man. Show him the keys Marcus." Marcus dug into the bag and held them out in plain view. "Now tell us where the cash is and I'll give you enough so you can get a running start or we can kill you and toss the place."

"Fuck you," the man said staring at Kane and grinning.

"This motherfucker really is crazy," Marcus said grinning at Kane.

"Well, we're going to see just how crazy he really is. Bring me the sharpest butcher knife you can find. Then bring me the dullest."When Marcus returned Kane took the one he deemed sharpest and placed it in back of him.

"Do me a favor Marcus and gag this fool so he doesn't wake up the whole neighborhood."

Gagged tightly, Kane slid the man's pants and boxers down to his ankles.

"Now you're absolutely sure there isn't anything you'd like to share with us before we begin?"

"Keep looking Marcus. I'll see if I can't convince our friend here that there might be a better way for this to end."

Marcus walked back into the bedroom but could still here the chilling screams from the living room despite the gag.

"You ready to talk now my friend?" Kane said. Tears rolled down the man's face. "Tell me where the money is so we don't have to go through this again." Blood dripped from the man's penis where Kane had drawn slits from the head of the man's to his scrotum."

"The money is in the back of the toilet and under the beneath the floor board."

"And if this was strictly about Chase and the cartel I would give you a pass right through here. But this isn't. Chase is dead and we Naomi—your own niece—who said it was you who raped and sodomized her. Then there's Eva and just so you don't get that opportunity again..."

Kane lifted the butcher knife up and brought it down swiftly and accurately chopping the man's penis off. A blood curdling scream came from deep down in the man's gut and Kane quickly tied the gag tightly around his mouth.

Marcus came rushing in the room to see what all the commotion was about. Looking at the blood spurting from the man's mid-section and then the penis which lay on the floor between the man's legs Marcus bent over and grabbed his stomach and began heaving. When he finally stood Marcus looked at Kane.

"Did he tell you where it was?"

"What do you think? But more importantly he won't be raping and beating any more helpless women. Grab your bag and leave the key under the mat for the cleaner."

Kane then walked to the bathroom and got the plastic bags full of money from out of the tank and then from under the sink. The man who was now unconscious and in shock was shaking now in uncontrollable spasms. Kane placed the garbage bag bulging with money by his feet took the nine millimeter from his pocket screwed the silencer on it, placed it in back of his ear and squeezed twice. The man's head slumped over. Kane calmly picked up the bag and made his way to the elevator and then to the car below.

"How did it go?" Ali asked.

"You ask too many damn questions Ali," Marcus snapped.

"Let's go," Kane said with ice in his tone.

A couple of blocks later Marcus got out. It was business as usual. Make sure you're seen tonight Marcus and then find a honey to spend the night with so you're alibis is skintight. And follow up. Make sure the cleaners do a thorough job. Put Born on it to inspect when they get through. And give me a call in the morning so we can talk about your retirement. For the first time since they left the dead man's apartment did Kane see a smile on Marcus' face.

"As for you sir… I'd appreciate it if you'd drop me off at the house. I can't wait to see Mattie's face."

"And I know she can't wait to see you either."

"What do you think about us having a kind of quick impromptu party tomorrow night to celebrate?"

"Celebrate what?"

"To celebrate life, to celebrate you making the dean's list, to celebrate your moving and getting a full time job, to celebrate the opening of the women's center, to celebrate us taking our streets back and can't be afraid to show Him the love that He bestows on us every day. C'mon Ali. You have to acknowledge your blessings."

"I thank Allah three times a day."

"Well let's let everyone that's been loyal and stuck by us take part tomorrow."

"I'm with it but you know how our people can get. That's almost like asking for trouble."

"Ahh Ali don't be such a pessimist."

"A realist is more like it but I understand. For you it's like you just getting out of lockdown. But okay I'll put the word out but only for those trusted lieutenants and their other haves. If not you'll have every dope fiend from here to Red Hook thinking you're having some sort of charity giveaway."

"Damn you're hard on your own people. But go ahead do it your way. Where are you going anyway?"

"Oh, my bad. I should have told you. I've had Mattie living next door to us over top of the women's center. That way it's cheaper and easier to arrange security not only for Mattie but for the women's center as well. Should anyone get by the downstairs security I hear anyone and everyone that comes up those steps. And ain't nobody getting past me."

"Maybe Marcus is right after all. You might be the right person for his position."

"Nope. I'm not the one. Today was enough to let me know that there ain't no amount of money worth me taking on that as a full time gig. And the occupational risks with people always wantin' to kill you somehow tells me there just ain't no future in it," Ali laughed.

"My boy," Kane laughed as they pulled up in front of the women's center.

"Here take the key. Let me park and I'll be right up."

Moments later Ali joined Kane. Kane followed Ali up the stairs and knocked lightly on the door. Mattie opened the door and was speechless. Tears ran down her cheeks as she stared at a meek and humbled Kane.

Kane took her in his arms and held her tightly. Oh, how he'd missed her. She suddenly pushed him away.

"Why haven't I heard from you Kane Close? I was so worried and you didn't even have the decency to call or leave word. Do you know what we've been through since you've been gone? Do you know they tried to abduct me and Naomi this morning? If it wasn't for Ali Lord knows where I'd be now. You know they got Naomi. Oh my God. They have Naomi," and then the skies opened and the tears flowed again.

"Now now Mattie," Kane said wrapping her in his arms again. "Relax all that. We have Naomi and she's going to be fine. She's up at St. Lukes but she's alright. Just wanted to have her tested to make sure there's nothing broken or any internal bleeding. It's just a precautionary measure. She should be home tomorrow or the day after."

"Well, that's a load off. And how are you?"

"I'm good Mattie aside from missing you."

"Well, let that be the last time that this occurs. I married you to be with you not apart from you. And if it happens again I'm leaving you. Do you understand me? Whatever you're involved in in that street you're going to let it go immediately. It took you close to thirty years to get me to come around but I'm not nearly so patient. You have one week to cut all your underworld ties. Do you understand me Kane? You have the nerve to give Ali and me ultimatums while you walk around like you're invincible. I want you out of the game and I mean now Kane Close. This is the last time I sit around wondering if you're coming home or not. I'm not going to do it? Do you understand? I'm not going to do it."

Kane smiled.

"I didn't know you cared."

"Oh I hate you," Mattie said hugging him tightly.

Despite her words they loved each other that night as though their very lives depended on it and when they awoke they both knew that what they had could never be threatened and that they would never part ways again.

In the morning there was a knock at the door. Kane turned to Mattie and embraced her.

"I love you Mattie Close."

"I love you more."

"Wake up lovebirds," came a voice from the hall.

"Oh my God. What time is it?" Mattie yelled looking at the clock radio. "Oh my goodness it's five to nine and I have a nine o'clock appointment."

"Yeah, and I have a nine thirty with Rosenberg."

"Let me go love. I need to get dressed."

"If you went down there just as you are most of those women would still envy you."

"You're silly but I love you for it."

An hour later Kane stepped into Charlie Rosenberg's offices and had a seat.

"Glad to have you back Mr. Close." Victoria said looking Kane up and down.

"It's good to be back. Charlie in?"

"I believe he's in his office waiting for you."

Kane walked back and found Charlie leafing through some files on his desk.

"My my my. You are a sight for sore eyes," he said rushing over and hugging Kane like he were the prodigal son finally returning home.

Kane grinned. He'd never seen Charlie show any type of emotion and knew it was genuine.

"I'm really thinking that I need to go away more often."

"No sir. You most certainly don't. There have been so many critical decisions to be made that required your expertise."

"That's why I gave you the power of attorney."

"That's true but I'm not you and whereas certain things were a no-brainer to me there were other matters that were just a little more questionable."

"Give me an example."

"Well, let's see I secured passage for Naomi's family. Got her parent's both jobs at a little janitorial firm over in Paterson."

"That's great Charlie."

"I set it up where they pay a hundred and fifty dollars a month since the father is proud and wouldn't accept the job and the home. Said he doesn't accept charity."

"And his alternative is to stay in a war torn Sudan and expose his family to rape and sodomy and his boys to soldiering."

"Looks that way but anyway I said a hundred and fifty would be fine. I have a friend that owes me a favor and has three or four houses in the area that he's

remodeled but being that it's Paterson he can't get the rent he wants so a couple of the houses have been vacant for a year or more. So, and because he owes me he gave me one for two years and I wash away his debt. So we're good to go there as far as employment and affordable living accommodations."

"Those are the major hurdles. So, what's the problem?"

"You're right those would seem to be the major hurdles but then this is where your tact and diplomacy was needed. The father claims that he's been trying to contact both his brother—Naomi's uncle—and Naomi to find out where his daughter is and if she's well. He says that the most he's getting is that she's living with an older man and the father wants to know why she's not living with her uncle. Now his initial reason for him sending her here was to get her out of a war torn nation where rape is all too common. He has already witnessed his wife and daughters falling victim to these atrocities so I couldn't very well tell him that his own brother who he sent her to as refuge was committing these same heinous crimes."

"Yeah, I could see where that could cause a dilemma," Kane chuckled. "But why do you think I would have had any more success than you would have had handling it?"

"You're much more people oriented than I am Mr. Kane. You deal with crisis situations every day. The very nature of your business is de-escalation and problem solving whereas mine is much more concrete. I simply read the law and make it applicable to a situation."

"So, how did you handle it?"

"I simply sold the father on this being a better situation for he and his family and assured him that his daughter was safe and she could fill him in on her whereabouts and why she chose not to live with her uncle. That's all I could do. Your directives were to bring her family here so they could be reunited so I concentrated on that and was simply waiting on you to do that."

"And that's exactly how I would have handled that. The family dynamics are up to the father and his brother. We have nothing to do with that. Good job Charlie. Let's get them on a plane. What's next on the agenda?"

"I would say that would be Ali. Aside from yesterday he has been beautiful. He's complied with the script and has far exceeded any and all expectations. All he needed was the opportunity. Dean's list his first semester while starting and leaning what was supposed to be a part time job. The young man has not only doubled the hours assigned to him but runs the internal workings of the center. He does everything and with ease. He's phenomenal."

"What happened yesterday?"

"He lost it when I told him contacting you would be tantamount to an admission of me knowing your whereabouts. Cursed me out in grand fashion and threatened me with having me fired."

Kane dropped his head and smiled.

"You're lucky that's all he threatened you with. I'll speak to him."

"Where are we as far as the young men's association?"

"Well, I had Victoria go down and meet Mattie at the women's center so she could a better grasp of what it is you're trying to do and accomplish. She came back glowing after talking to Mattie and has been researching similar centers ever since and together we have come up with a program that addresses most of the more pronounced needs of young Black males in Harlem. Just as a side note she asked me to speak to you about the possibilities of her acquiring a position with you at the center."

"The answer to that is no. What's time table for its opening?"

"Well, if it were anywhere else but at the location you requested I would say we could possibly see it opening in a little under two years but the armory is such an old building and has been shut down for so long that just to get it in compliance with today's building codes is a herculean task. You're looking at a good three years."

"Well let's do it and get it done. Anything else?"

"No. Not really. You asked me to draw up a will and I just need your signature. Can I ask you something Mr. Close?"

"Sure, Charlie."

"Why did you turn down Victoria's request. I think she'd be a valuable asset to the boy's center."

"Well, to be honest with you Charlie, the way I see Victoria is as a beautiful woman who won't hesitate to use those looks and whatever else she can muster to better Victoria and those type of people are the type of people that I want to avoid on this project. This is about the team, the entire group. I want the focus to be on inner city boys not on her or anyone elses individual achievements at the sake of the group. Those type of people I don't want around. But listen I'm having a little get together next Friday at the women's center. I'd like for you and the wife to make an appearance and tell Victoria she's also cordially invited and if there's nothing else I will see you tonight."

Kane returned home exhausted. It wasn't any one thing but the culmination of everything. Though not yet forty his life had been more than stressful and the day-to-day guerilla warfare on the streets of Harlem had him suffering from post-traumatic stress syndrome if he'd only been examined.

Mattie was still at the center when Kane arrived. The center was packed and Kane nodded to several of the women he knew from the neighborhood. Ali was all over the place, helping people check in, answering phones, playing receptionist and counseling people in need. Mattie was on the phone when Kane walked in. Her face lit up upon seeing him and he knew then that he was the luckiest man in the world.

"I'm headed upstairs to grab a quick nap. I'm tired as hell."

Mattie felt inside her pocketbook then handed him the key before covering the mouthpiece.

"I'll be up in about an hour. Are you hungry?"

"Starving. For you," he said smiling.

"Ahh, silly. Go ahead up. I'll get Ali to close up and be there shortly."

Kane waved at Ali who was still engaged with a young woman but was struggling to get away. Kane smiled before picking up a paper at the front desk. 'Obama Raises Minimum Wage' were the headlines. About time he did something for Black folks Kane thought. Sure he'd awarded Blacks cabinet positions but the masses were yet to feel the impact. Now they would. He was setting precedents. Glancing down the page another story caught Kane's attention. It dealt with an assistant to the ambassador of Sudan having been assassinated. He was suspected to have underworld ties and there was an ongoing investigation of bribery and other accusations by local authorities. That was an end in in itself and Kane knew it. The case was closed on Chase and the cartel. There would be no investigation. N.Y.P.D was not going to investigate itself for wrong doing.

Another chapter was closed and the streets of Harlem would return to normal.

"What's good Kane?"

"Just stopped by to see how things were going on here."

"It's all good. The center's beautiful baby. It offers alternatives. And if nothing else that's a positive. It lets them know that there are options. It's like what you and Mattie did for me and Mia. Now it gives me the opportunity to let them know. I just wish there were something out there for the brothers. They're the ones that really need it, The little hoppers twelve and thirteen with no hope that are already holding shoddys and ready t blast somebody for twenty or thirty dollars. Those are the ones that really need it."

Kane smiled.

"All things in time Ali. All things in time."

"When I got on my feet and put away enough that's what I intend on doing. I'm going to give some of these young cats and alternative to these drugs and violence. You know the worst thing in life is wasted potential."

"I feel you young brother. I hope your dream comes true."

"Ain't nothing to it but to do it."

"I hear you. Listen. If you need me I'll be up stairs."

"Alright man. It's good to have you home man."

Kane went upstairs kicked off his shoes and laid across the bed and grabbed the remote. No sooner than he found a program to his liking then he was asleep. Mattie arrived some time later and finding him asleep threw the comforter over him and kissed him lightly on his forehead.

Kane stirred slightly.

"Hey baby."

"Sorry sweetheart I didn't mean to wake you?"

"It's okay I need to get up anyway. When I woke up and saw you I thought I'd died and gone to heaven. You're one beautiful sight to see."

Mattie smiled broadly and was about to speak when Kane's phone rang.

"Damn that thing. I liked it better when you used to leave it in the car and left business outside when you came home," she said handing him the phone. "I hate having to share you after not seeing you for what? Three months…"

"Yeah, Kane here."

"Kane. Marcus. Yeah, I'm at the hospital. They're discharging her now."

"How is she?"

"She's in good spirits. She's a little disoriented. I think they had her on sedatives or something but her bill of health is good according to the doctor. They gave her

something to reduce the swelling and a mild anti-biotic to ward off any infection but otherwise she's good. Where are you?"

"At the women's center."

"Where do you want me to bring her?"

"You can bring her here."

"Are the fellas still there?"

"Yeah. I think Born's crew is outside. Why?"

"I was on my way to have dinner with a very lovely young lady I met when I was in the hospital the other night when I got the call about Naomi."

"And does this very lovely young lady have anything to do with your retirement?"

"I'm hoping to include her in those plans. Yeah."

"So you're really feeling her huh?"

"Yeah. I mean I've only been out with her once but I think that she's the one."

"After one date?"

"Yeah man. That's what I'm saying. She's not like the usual run of the mill chicks I'm used to. She's a nurse, comes from a good family and she's easy to talk to."

"Wonder what Eva's going to have to say about that," Kane laughed.

"Fuck Eva! Listen Kane. I gotta go. They're wheeling Naomi out now."

"Alright man. I'll send Ali down in about ten to grab her. We still need to sit down and talk about this retirement thing. I think I understand it a little better now. But yeah we'll get together before the weeks out. I'm having this little get together on Friday at the women's center. Maybe we can talk there."

"Sounds good. I gotta go man. I have this beautiful woman that's chomping at the bit and giving me the evil eye at the same time. I'm thinking she's ready to bounce."

"Okay Marcus. You handle that and good luck on your date."

"Thanks man. We'll talk."

Kane turned back to Mattie.

"Might want to head back downstairs and open the door. There's someone coming to see you."

"Oh, Kane why can't it be just you and I? I mean it's been three months since I've seen you and now you want me to

share time with Marcus and whoever else is coming by.
Can't we just share some quiet time together?"

"We've got the rest of our lives to do that," then patting her
on her backside he pushed a pouting Mattie towards the
door.

"Oh alright. Sometimes I don't think you have a
sentimental bone in your body, Kane Close."

"Tell me that when you come back up."

Mattie already in her bedroom gown had one objective that
night and that was to get her man to love her good. And
now this... She hadn't had company since they'd gotten
married and to be honest with you she didn't miss it. She
had her best friend there with her and what more could she
ask. The only thing her girlfriends wanted to talk about
was men and since she'd been married those conversations
hardly appealed to her anymore. Sometimes she thought
Kane was just a little too thoughtful. But now it was
coming at her expense. It wasn't like she could just throw
on a robe and go and answer the door. No. there were still
employees downstairs tying to tie up loose ends so she had
to get fully dressed. Oh, the things she did for this man.

When she reached the lobby she found a small contingent
of her workers had formed a small circle. Excited they
seemed to all be talking and laughing at the same time.
Mattie moved closer, excusing herself as she moved closer
to see who it was before screaming 'Naomi'.

Tears of joy filled her eyes and then a sense of melancholy
flooded her inner being. 'How could she have forgotten
Naomi? In the midst of her own happiness she'd been only

too selfish and completely forgotten the closest thing to a daughter. Not once did she think to go see her or even inquire about her welfare. Mattie stood before the young woman ashamed and found herself embarrassed even more when Naomi grabbed her and said, "Mattie I missed you so much."

When the celebration was over Mattie went to her office and just sat there. She was ashamed. And then she thought of Kane and was immediately grateful. Where she lacked he complimented her filling all her voids and oversights. She smiled, made peace with herself and rejoined the welcoming home committee eventually wrenching Naomi free and taking her upstairs where she and Kane sat and listened to the young woman's harrowing tale of rape, sodomy, and torture at the hands of her uncle.

Her tale brought the memories of Mattie's own abuse come rushing back and the tears ran down her face in rivers.

"Someone really needs to get that sick bastard," Mattie screamed.

Kane remained undaunted and said nothing. By the end of the evening it was agreed that Naomi would take the third apartment over the women's center and she was so elated by the news that she had Ali and Mia drive her to the old apartment and began her moving that night.

The rest of the week was quiet with everyone going about their regular routine and Ali making it his business to check on Kane and Naomi every night. Kane remained in bed remote in one hand hardly venturing to go out at all. If he did have a request it was usually Ali who would make the run.

Meanwhile Mattie and Naomi made arrangements for the party Kane wanted and when all was in place all there was to do was wait.

Friday night was on them before they knew it and Mattie, Kane, Ali and even the little Jewish lawyer were all running around like chickens with their heads cut off picking up this and that. When it was all in place and there was little or nothing left to do Kane went to the makeshift podium to rehearse the short speech he'd arranged when Mattie and Naomi came in with shopping bags from Lord & Taylors and Macys.

"Preach preacher preach you handsome devil you," Mattie said clapping loudly as Naomi smiled appreciatively. "I didn't know we had to give a speech."

"Get out of here Mattie." Kane laughed.

All was good an hour later. There was a line winding down the block and around the corner.

"Invites only," Born yelled. "Invites only… This is a private affair on behalf of the women's center."

When the doors opened flocks of people rushed in. The women dressed in their finery each trying to outdo their counterparts were a virtual fashion show. But Mattie in her black and silver Versace gown garnered the most attention as she greeted the guests at the door. The champagne flowed and after a few minutes of high spirited mingling Kane walked to the podium. The dj immediately turned down the smooth jazz and all attention turned to Kane. "Ladies and gentleman I would just like to thank you for coming out to support a contingent of Uptown's New

Harlem Renaissance; the 8th Avenue Women's Center run by my lovely wife and her talented staff most of whom are here in attendance tonight. I commend them on the wonderful job they've done thus far and will continue to do. I see several councilmen and other well-known local dignitaries are in attendance and I welcome you and all of your contributions.

I would like to also thank my attorney and a man who has been integral to the building and growth of the women's center Mr. Charles Rosenberg. Mr. Rosenberg has even gone so far as to help one of our first clients who most of you know as Naomi. At the time we found Naomi she was homeless and unemployed. The 8th Avenue Women's Center helped Naomi gain admission not just into college but into Columbia University where she has just completed her first semester with a 4.0 gpa. Perhaps the hardest thing

for a young person to do is leave the shelter of a home for college. Naomi has not simply left home she left her country. Naomi for those of you who don't know her is from the war torn country of the Sudan. Ladies and gentlemen can you imagine how hard it is not only to leave your parents, your family not knowing what will befall them, whether they will be raped or massacred at any time. To have the courage to leave them to come here to go to college with the hopes that in six years they will still be alive and you will be able to rescue them from their fate is not only heroic, but courageous. I applaud her conviction. Come here Naomi."

Naomi climbed the three steps to the podium. Tears streamed down her face.

"Naomi I want to thank and applaud you for staying focused. I want to thank you for the wonderful work you're providing the women's center and I'd also like to thank the women's center attorney Mr. Charles Rosenberg for arranging employment and housing for your family who have just arrived from the Sudan."

Everyone cheered and Naomi kissed everybody before running to meet her family.

Kane smiled. He was committed to bringing as much joy and life into the world as he'd taken from it.

"I have one last announcement and perhaps I'm stepping a little out of bounds when I say this. But there is a grimier side to all of this and a side that most people at functions such as these don't like to discuss so I'll make it as brief as possible. Marcus, would you join me please. Ladies and gentlemen I'd like to introduce you to Marcus and his lovely fiancée Beverly. Marcus is my successor and has been out in the streets for approximately twelve years handling the business at hand and keeping the streets safe."

"Marcus always been a good boy," Ol' lady Murphy chimed in.

"Thank you Mrs. Murphy," Kane smiled as everyone laughed. "He has always been loyal and he's well liked in the community. Well that is by most. There is always that element. Marcus received twenty eight stitches after someone hit him in the back of the head with a bat.

"I did that shit," a woman yelled from the middle of the crowd. "I should have killed your ass then."

The woman moved up parting the crowd. Kane and Marcus stood paralyzed. Brandishing a small caliber handgun she pointed the gun directly at Marcus.

"I don't know if I should shoot you or this bitch first. You told me I was your woman."

"Eva! Put the gun down," Mattie screamed but it was too late as Eva squeezed off round after round. When it was over all three people on the podium lay covered in blood.

CPSIA information can be obtained at www.ICGtesting.com
Printed in the USA
LVOW13s1003240714

PP8640300001B/3/P